THE KILYAIKIN FILE

Rich —

I hope you enjoy reading this as much as I did writing it.

T. Colley

P.D.

THE KILYAIKIN FILE

▼

Ted Colby

Writers Club Press
San Jose New York Lincoln Shanghai

The Kilyaikin File

Writers Club Press
an imprint of iUniverse.com, Inc.

For information address:
iUniverse.com, Inc.
5220 S 16th, Ste. 200
Lincoln, NE 68512
www.iuniverse.com

ISBN: 0-595-13538-2

Printed in the United States of America

CONTENTS

PROLOGUE

West 128th Street
New York City
Wednesday, October 22nd 1997

The scene wasn't all that unusual for the City. New York
has always had its violent side. At 3:28 AM, the darkness of the alley shrunk before the glare of spotlights
coming from the drivers' side of three patrol cars. Each
car's crown of rotating and flashing blue, white and red
lights produced a swirling aura of color adding a quality
of eeriness to the chill serenity of the early morning
stillness. Ed Harley thought to himself that October
could be damn cold at this time of the morning. He'd
been on the force only a few weeks, but this was the second time he'd answered a call on a dead body. He had
been standing at the entrance to the alley on West 128th
Street midway between 9th and 10th Avenue for about
ten minutes. Two other patrol cars had joined him soon
after he answered the first call.

"Who found it?" The hoarse voice came from a
stocky man in his late forties sitting in the driver's seat

of a brown Chevrolet Caprice that had just stopped in the middle of the street. The car looked older than it really was and showed its heavy usage in the NYPD. Harley walked across the street and bent down to reply to the older man through the car window.

"Hi, Sarg, the call sounded like a kid, according to 911," Harley said.

"What the hell was a kid doing here at this time of the morning?" questioned the figure in the car. "Don't parents ever keep their kids at home anymore?" he asked without expecting a reply. Homicide Detective Sergeant Kenneth Polk shoved the half-eaten pizza lying on the seat next to him under a newspaper and out of sight. "Do you think the kid did it?"

"Ask me again after you've seen the guy," returned Harley with a wry yet nervous chuckle in his voice. "If a kid was going to bust a drunk for a couple of bucks, he wouldn't have taken the time to mess him up so badly, he'd have grabbed what he could and gotten out'ta here; and he sure as hell wouldn't have called it in." Harley turned and walked back to the alley entrance.

"Oh, shit," exclaimed the detective, "What now? This is goin' to be another one of those weird-ass things; I can feel it. That's all I need."

Polk parked across the street from the alley, added his own blinking red roof light to the other lighting menagerie, and climbed out of the Chevy. He shoved his keys into his trench coat pocket and strolled over to where the three squad cars were lighting up the alley. "Where is it?" he asked quietly. The patrolman gestured to a pile of paper and garbage a few feet inside the left side of the alley. Polk followed the gesture and walked up to where a man's body slumped in a contorted shape, half-sitting up against the wall. The man's head drooped onto his chest and the detective could see that he appeared to be elderly, at least a long shock of white hair and general build gave that impression.

"Look at his face," urged the patrolman.

Polk squatted down. With his gloved hand, he reached under the man's chin and slowly raised the head. Hollow, fixed eyes stared from a pale shallow face at the detective. The staring quality unnerved him. He suddenly realized why the stare was so unnatural; the eyelids had been removed. A thin red line encircled the top half of the eye sockets. The face was crisscrossed with tiny cuts until it looked like a cross-stitched sampler. Polk could only imagine what the rest of the corpse might look like. The suit coat and shirt didn't give any immediate sign of blood, but Polk couldn't tell what might be underneath.

"Holy Jesus," he exclaimed, letting the head fall to the man's chest again. "I want the coroner to figure this one out; it looks like someone made mincemeat of his face,"

"Pretty, huh?" said Harley in a macho attempt at bravado. The detective let out a sigh and stood up.

"Yeah, you're right, this wasn't a kid getting money for a fix; this job must have taken a while to do," growled the detective. Polk re-crossed the street and opening the door to his car, slid in to the drivers seat and grabbed the radio mike from its hook. In about a minute, he had given instructions for a homicide team to be dispatched to the area and the City Coroner's office to be notified. Pulling himself from the car and shutting the door, he walked back to where the man lay slumped in the alley. Harley was sorting through some of the newspapers and garbage next to where the man was lying.

"Better not disturb things," warned the detective.

"I thought I saw something shining in the light," returned the patrolman. "Yeah, here it is," Harley reached down to pick up the object.

"Let me do that!" barked Polk. The patrolman stood up and backed away without a word. Polk bent down and brushed the leaves and papers off the object protruding from under the body. The brass handle of a cane sparkled in reflection of the flashing lights of the squad cars. Polk yanked a latex glove from his inside pocket, pulled his gloves off and wiggled his fingers into the latex glove on his right hand. The brass head of a cane with a falcon's head on the end of the handle showed about three inches from the left side of the body. The wooden length of the cane was lodged underneath the body and Polk braced his foot against the man's left hip, rolled the body slightly and slowly withdrew the cane with his newly gloved hand.

"Now that was thoughtful, they left him his cane," snorted Harley. "Must have been a real compassionate piece of shit that did this."

Polk walked back to one of the squad cars and examined the object in the harsh light of the side spotlight. As he turned the cane over in the light, the brass falcon-headed handle rotated loosely. Polk reached into his left coat pocket and removed a leather glove and worked it onto his left hand. Then holding the falcon-headed cane with the leather gloved hand, he rotated the handle with his right hand until it came loose from the shaft. The wooden portion had been hollowed out for about ten inches of its length and was empty. The detective re-screwed the handle onto the shaft and gave it a snug turn to secure it.

"I'll have the lab take a look at it," he exclaimed. Polk turned to the patrolman and asked, "Did you go through the guy's pockets yet?"

"He's been completely cleaned, Sarg…no ID, nothing," replied Harley.

"OK," said Polk. "When the team gets here, have them search the area and get this guy to the Coroner. I want every piece of clothing examined,"

"Sure, I'll handle it…. OK for the other two cars to go when the team gets here?"

"Yeah," muttered the detective. "They're not needed here anymore; I'm going back to the precinct."

Detective Polk crossed the street to his car, slid back into the driver's seat, and placed the cane beside him in the passenger's seat. At the turn of the key, the car roared into life; Polk shifted into drive and slid into traffic behind a large panel truck with "The Times" blazoned across the side. All he had wanted was one night without something weird. Maybe a mugging, or even a holdup or two would have been okay, but not this. A few more minutes and he would have been able to go home, but not now. He shuddered when he remembered the man's eyes. "What kind of a creep do we have out there now?" he said again to no one in particular.

New York City
Thursday, October 23rd 1997

It was 10:35 AM when Detective Polk walked into the Coroner's office. Deputy Coroner Willard Hastings was already in the morgue autopsy room. In the center of the room was a steel table with a human form under a green sheet. To one side was a table with an assortment of instruments that always made Polk shudder. A large overhead lamp bathed the table in a brilliant white light.

"We're ready to start," said Hastings in a dry New England voice. He placed a new cassette in the recording machine and switched it on. Reaching over the form on the table, he drew the sheet down exposing the naked body of a man and continued in a measured monotone voice, "Male, approximately 65 to 70 years of age, five foot, 10 inches, 185 pounds, white hair. Lacerations to the face inflicted by what was probably a small sharp instrument, possibility a razor or scalpel." The voice droned on describing a mass mutilation, which obviously occurred when the man was still alive and probably conscious. Whatever went on was an act of torture, pure and simple. Was it some weirdo looking for a thrill or was it an interrogation? With the body laid out before him, Polk could see that the mutilation was concentrated around the facial area. Parts of the man's ears were severed and the lips were lacerated. The upper lip had been severed and gums and teeth clearly showed through. He could not imagine the hatred it must have taken to inflict such pain on another human being. If it wasn't hatred, it was something worse and he put it out of his mind.

"Cause of death is not immediately apparent," continued Hastings. "It is probable, however, that shock brought on by the extended trauma and the man's age may have induced cardiac arrest. The pattern of cuts suggests that the torture may have occurred over some length of time, quite possibly several days. The reason could be to give the victim time to consider his situation between many episodes...a classic torture technique employed by the Soviets and Eastern European countries." He paused, "Chemical burns around the earlier lacerations would indicate the use of an astringent to possibly inflict more pain and to stop bleeding. Some of the cuts were also closed with what looks like acrylic glue."

"I didn't realize you were into the finer facets of torture, Doc," Polk interrupted.

"Only part of my considerable wealth of knowledge," shot back the Deputy Coroner impatiently. "Thank you Detective; now do you mind if I continue?"

"Sorry, Doc."

Polk's cell phone shattered the autopsy process once more and the look on Hastings face caused the Detective to make a hasty exit into the hallway. Polk thought, that it was just as well, he wasn't really enjoying it anyway. "Polk," he shot into the phone.

"I think we may have something really interesting for you, Sergeant." It was Joyce Higgins from the forensic lab. He had left the cane from the crime scene with her to see what, if anything, it might tell. "Also, I think I know where your guy was from."

"I'll be there in about 20 minutes," said Polk hitting the "end" button on the cell phone.

It took a lot less time for him to reach the lab and Joyce was waiting for him impatiently when he arrived. "What have you got?" demanded the Detective.

"Do I have to solve all of your cases for you?" she teased.

"No, just the weird ones," he answered.

"When you dropped off the cane, you said you had checked it and it was empty," she began, handing him a small two inch by three inch clear plastic box with six small black dots placed on a white paper. "Look what we found inside the top of the falcon head in the cane." Joyce walked over to the computer and typed a short command. On the monitor, a page of numbers appeared, neatly arranged in sets of six, five rows to a block and seven columns across the page. "Microdots!" Joyce exclaimed proudly. "Found them under a black sticky disk in the head,"

"What is it?" asked Polk.

"The first two look something like US Codes from the 60's. At least that's what I thought at first, but I'm no expert."

"Maybe that's only what they were meant to look like."

"As you see, both have some typing in what appears to be Russian or at least in Cyrillic characters on the top of the page; that wouldn't normally be on any US document; at least I don't think so," she continued.

"Sounds reasonable, what else?" asked the policeman.

"There's more," she added and punched at the RETURN key twice, scrolling past the second and third sheet of numbers. Finally, on the screen were two pages with numbered lists of characters in three columns on each page. The numbers went from 111 through 115, 121 through 125, 131 through 135, etc. "What do you make of it?" asked Polk.

"Don't really know," mused the technician. "I don't even know if they're related. The first two lists, providing they are the 'first two' lists, could be stolen US coded documents except for the Russian or Cyrillic characters at the top. The other could be a decoded translation; maybe it was being passed on, maybe its nothing at all...I just don't know; I really think we ought to inform someone from the Feds, though," she continued.

"Yeah, right," responded Polk. "I'd love to pass this one on."

The detective turned to go and then was stopped when Joyce said to his back, "More yet...I told you I could tell you where he came from,"

"OK, where?" questioned Polk.

"I get the opinion that you really don't want to know," returned Joyce.

The late night and weariness suddenly caught up with the detective. "Where and how in hell do you know?" he demanded and then added with a sigh, "I'm sorry, Joyce."

She ignored his outburst and calmly went on as though she were teaching a third grade class. "His clothes were sent over to us early this morning...we made some tentative discoveries."

"The shirt has a Hathaway label...US made, probably new; his sport coat was manufactured in the Soviet Union, and residue in the inside breast pocket are from a Havana cigar. His belt is artificial leather...obviously

Soviet made, but his shoes are Florsheim, a US make. His underwear and socks are also Soviet." Then she added, "There's more about the cane."

"What?" queried Polk.

"I wondered why it had been hollowed out," she continued. "If it was configured to carry only the microdots, all that was really needed was the small space behind the handle."

"Sometimes, a cane is hollowed out to hold a flask," offered the detective.

"I thought of that too, so I did a scraping of the interior. What I *didn't* find was any alcoholic residue. What I *did* find were fibers that are used in making paper...a paper of Soviet origin."

"So, it also hid papers as well as microdots," deduced the detective.

"That's how I make it," she concluded.

"I wonder if they were paper copies of what's on the dots?" he mused. "Would you print me a copy of those, Joyce?" Polk added, pointing to the monitor screen.

"Sure," she replied moving the cursor over to the PRINT icon and clicking twice.

"Did you get a translation of the Russian wording?" inquired the detective.

"Not yet, still working on it," she said with a shrug. "We don't have a wealth of Russian language people here."

"Keep trying; let me know if you come up with anything."

Polk picked up the sheets of paper from the printer, turned and walked out the doorway of the lab without hearing or expecting a reply.

It was a short ride to the precinct station, but Polk took his time. If there hadn't been a homicide, the whole affair would have seemed like an intellectual exercise in putting together the pieces to complete a puzzle. The Captain, to say nothing about his boss, would be looking for results. The codes bothered him. He knew Joyce was right; he needed to get the FBI involved as early as he could…with any luck, they'd take the heat off him. The thought pleased him; he never liked weird shit, and this certainly was weird.

CHAPTER ONE

▼

JACK DEITER

FBI Headquarters
J. Edgar Hoover Building
Thursday, October 23rd 1997

For a Federal Bureau of Investigation's Division Chief working out of the FBI Headquarters Building in Washington, it wasn't a very impressive office. But then again, that was not the kind of thing that had ever impressed Jack Deiter. Trappings of office always seemed to come off as artificial to him. Maybe that's why Bill Stewart, his boss, and he got along so well. Deiter leaned back half sitting on the edge of the secretary's desk while he watched Stewart through the glass window which surrounded the inner office. Stewart was on the phone, so Deiter waited. It was just past four o'clock in the afternoon and Deiter had been summoned to Stewart's office, but was not told the subject...he didn't like that because it kept him from preparing enough information to intelligently discuss whatever the topic might be. Deiter didn't like surprises.

Jack Deiter above all, was a dedicated Bureau man. The name outside his office read:

John Remington Deiter, III
Supervisor, Department of Investigations
Espionage and Counterintelligence

The Bureau had hired Deiter as an agent after he left the CIA and he had risen through the ranks to his present position because of outstanding reports and a reputation for being fearless and uncompromising when it came to the law or a sense of fairness. Respected and trusted by his superiors, he had also developed a strong sense of loyalty with his subordinates.

Deiter's life had not necessarily been easy and what success he had achieved was won by hard work and dedication. He never thought of his life as being difficult; that would have embarrassed and disgusted him just to think of it in those terms. Life was life; it wasn't supposed to be easy. Nobody owes you anything, would have been his motto...if he ever thought about it at all. Never the less, life had dealt harshly with him over the years. At eighteen, his parents John and Constance Deiter both died of strokes within two week of each other; his mother died immediately, his father held on for nearly ten days before he was declared brain dead and his life support removed. Jack suddenly became an adult and an orphan at the same time.

During the days immediately following his parents' funeral, however, something unexpected happened to him. A man he knew then only as a friend of his father had arranged for an immediate Vice Presidential appointment to the United States Naval Academy in Annapolis, Maryland. With nothing else to do and alone for the first time in his life, the young man accepted. Having graduated from St. Hillary's Roman Catholic High School in Boston, he enjoyed the benefit of a good academic background and the transition from a civilian and teenager to the regimens of military life was effortless for him. The rest of his life went pretty much according to his own predetermined plan; four years in the Navy, resigning to attend law school; on graduation, he joined the Central Intelligence Agency. In 1975 Deiter had left the Agency, joined the FBI and married Sally MacIntire...whom he had met while at the Academy. Eighteen years after the lost of his parents, Sally was killed in an automobile accident on her way back from visiting her parents in Ohio. Deiter had been devastated for over a year. Although their marriage had been short, it had been very happy. But that was a long time ago. Now, although he dated once in awhile, he hadn't developed any long-term relationships. At a strong and vital 55 years of age, Deiter had kept his athletic and catlike physique. He had a preference for wearing black. His bald and shaved head combined with his sharply arched black eyebrows gave Deiter a fierce impression to those who first met him or had sustained his pointed questioning. To women, however, he was immediately attractive in a "dangerous" and sexy way. His high cheekbones gave him a distinctly Eastern European, even Slavic look. A comparison to the actor,

Yul Brenner is the one most people drew upon to describe him.

Deiter could see that his boss was finishing up his conversation on the phone, so he moved towards the office door. Stewart looked up and motioned him in. "Thanks for the nod, Sergeant Polk," Stewart was saying into the mouthpiece. "I'm passing this on to my anti-spook guy, Jack Deiter; He'll be in touch with you...and oh yes, could you fax copies of what you found in that cane?" After a pause, he concluded with, "Thanks," and hung up the telephone.

"So, what's that all about?" Deiter asked, motioning to the telephone.

"You've got a slightly damaged corpse, some documents that appear to be old US code sheets and a list of what might be Ruskie names; I don't know what you're going to do with it," Stewart replied.

"Can I give it all back?" questioned Deiter.

"Wish you could," the other replied with a grin. "Your contact with New York's finest is a Detective Sergeant Polk in the 20th Precinct," Stewart said shoving a note with a number and name on it across the desk towards Deiter. "He says the corpse is an old guy who may come from Eastern Europe or Russia. Don't know if this is an internal squabble between operatives from the old Soviet Union or a Russian Mafia hit, but the guy had undergone some horrendous torture for some reason. Maybe he knew something someone else wanted to know."

"I'll wait for the fax from Polk before I touch base with him," returned Deiter. "I want to get a look at those documents first."

Stewart motioned his approval, which also sufficed as a dismissal, and Deiter left.

It was past five–thirty that afternoon when the fax finally arrived from the NYPD. Another half-hour passed before the clerk had dropped it on Deiter's desk. "Great timing to start a project," mumbled Deiter to himself. He turned his attention to the pages of numbers and after studying them for a few moments, decided to see if his contacts in the National Security Agency could come up with a match or perhaps might even decode it. He'd give them the rest of the pages too, just in case this was the decoded version itself. It bothered Deiter that someone would have both the encoded version and the decoded version in their possession…that just didn't seem to make much sense and even though the NYPD may think so, Deiter doubted it. The fax also included a brief rundown on the results of the autopsy and the lab findings on the corpse's clothing. What was an old guy from the Soviet Union…or Russia…or wherever, doing here and why had he been so badly mistreated? An amusing thought crossed Deiter's mind and he smiled. The guy had to leave the beneficiary of the Evil Empire to come to the Land of Opportunity and Freedom to get cut up and killed. Some guys don't know when they're better off. It wasn't funny, but the irony of all made it seem so.

Deiter picked up the phone, checked a list of numbers on his desktop and punched one set into the machine.

"Henderson." The voice had the bark of authority and Deiter knew it was Hank's way of intimidating anyone who would disturb his last few minutes of the workday with a telephone call.

"You don't have to take my head off, Hank," Deiter said.

"Jack, I'm sorry…how the hell are you; and why do you have to call me at this hour?" He then added, "Unless, of course you want to fill a foursome tomorrow."

"Lose any code sheets, lately?" Deiter asked. There was a brief moment of silence on the other end of the line. The answer was slow and apprehensive.

"No, not that I'm aware of, anyway." Hank Henderson had been with the Army Security Agency, Defense Intelligence Agency or the NSA most of his Army career. As a colonel, he now headed up the Encryption and Internal Security Branch of the Agency. The protection of US codes was his responsibility. In the early years, Hank and Deiter had met while on assignment in Europe. Both had been young, idealistic, reckless and full of righteousness about their job. Deiter was with the CIA and Henderson, Army Intelligence; both were undercover operatives. A thought suddenly struck Deiter. The three of them had been in Rome together back then; Hank, he…and Rose. He hadn't thought of Rose in ages; why now should she pop into his head. He shook the feeling off and returned to the conversation.

"Some documents taken from microdots have come into my possession and I'd like you to take a look at them…may help solve a homicide," Deiter said.

"I take it you can get me copies to work from?"

"Can do…I'll use the secure fax and get them to you tonight." Deiter then added, "Say, Hank, do you have a make on Rose Spinelli…know where she is?'

The other man thought it over and then said, "No, but the 'Company' ought to have something. If she's still alive, that is. At least they'll know. Why?"

"Don't really know...I guess there's something about this case...and then when you answered the phone, suddenly I was thinking back to when we were in Rome. She was there too, you remember...that's all."

Deiter hung up the phone and reflected on what had just happened. After all these years, why had he thought about Rose just then and why did he ask Henderson about her? Something else was stirring in Deiter's brain. It was October. Damn it, he hated October. It reminded him of Sally. It was October 28th when she...Oh, hell, when was it ever going to stop hurting? He needed to get over it and he knew it. Rose...he wondered. He also remembered how Rose and he were more than just operatives...more than just friends. Maybe it was the excitement, the danger they shared; never the less, their relationship became mutually protective...and intimate. "That was over twenty years ago," he mused to himself. She's probably married with five kids now; half of them ready for college. Maybe she had gained fifty pounds and...he paused. No, that wouldn't be like her. She would never get that way, or age. What must she be now? Pushing fifty anyway. Suddenly, Deiter felt old. Almost twenty years had passed since Sally was killed. She would have been almost the same age as Rose by now, if she hadn't...Deiter pushed it out of his mind.

Getting up from his desk, he walked down the hallway to the fax machine with the scrambler line. He took out a fax cover sheet and addressed it to Lieutenant Colonel Henry Henderson; EISB; NSA, added a short note and dropped the seven sheets into the bin on top of the machine. Quickly punching in the number he had gotten from his desktop, he pushed the SEND button and waited for the fax machine to process his small stack of papers. When he had finished, he returned to his office, placed the papers inside his classified safe, and locked the door; he then spun the dial twice. Tomorrow will be another day, he told himself and then shook his head. That was stupid, of course it will be. Looking at the list of telephone numbers, his eye stopped at one he had not used in some while and he pondered it for a few seconds. Picking up the receiver, he punched in the number. What the hell, he thought, might as well give it a shot. He knew several people who spoke and wrote Russian and he knew he'd have to get the phrases on the documents translated. But Rose was different; she spoke and understood even the nuances of the Russian language like a native. It's one thing to speak a language, it's quite another to understand its humor and subtleties. Rose could do that; at least she used to and he felt he really needed her...for the case. Why not try to get the one person he knew of who was the best even though it had been a long time ago when he'd known her. Or was this just an excuse to...he dismissed the thought.

His contact at the Central Intelligence Agency wasn't very helpful and sounded annoyed at anyone from the FBI who would have the audacity to inquire about the whereabouts of a prior 'Company' operative. The contact hung up after promising that he would see what he could do. Deiter knew from experience that the guy really wanted to check him out first and was just stalling for time. Deiter walked out of his office and headed down the hallway towards the elevator.

Suddenly, Deiter didn't want to be by himself tonight. Returning to his office, he picked up the phone, and re-dialed the NSA number and waited for an answer. He was about to hang up when the now familiar "Henderson" sounded on the other end.

"Hank, you on your way home," Deiter asked.

"Trying to if this phone will stop ringing," replied Henderson sarcastically.

"Are you doing anything tonight?" continued Deiter.

"No, matter of fact I was going to stop by for a drink on the way home and then get something to eat. Meg is having dinner with a couple of her old college chums and I'm on my own."

"Mind if I join you?" Deiter asked. "I'll bring a copy of the papers I called you about."

"How about *Masterson's*, say in…oh…twenty minutes? I'll meet you in the bar."

"You got it…thanks, I didn't feel like fixing my own tonight either." Deiter hung up the phone, bent down and re-dialed the combination of his safe, opened it and withdrew the papers. He placed them in a leather document folder that he would take with him. Closing the safe, he checked the handle, spun the dial again, turned and left the office turning off the lights on his way out.

Masterson's was an excellent and very well known restaurant in Old Town Alexandria, Virginia just across the bridge from Washington. Deiter knew it well; he lived only a couple of blocks away on Prince Street. The location is a favorite hangout for those in Deiter's and Henderson's line of work. It specialized in ribs,

Memphis Style, but has a quiet and dimly lit lounge…what most people prefer when having a tête-à-tête or just wanting a chance to relax and unwind in private. The Washington area seems to cater to the "unwinding" crowd. That seems to be most people who worked for the Government. It's also known as a place where very private conversations could be had on matters of State or politics, which needed to be held in a secure, but genteel environment.

Deiter arrived first and slipped into one of four overstuffed dark brown leather arm chairs situated around a low round wooden table near the back of the lounge. From his vantage, he commanded the view of the entrance and the bar; the move was instinctive for him. Part of the restaurant could be seen around the corner at the end of the lounge and Deiter observed that it was beginning to fill up with the early diners. This would be the theater crowd, but they would be gone in another half-hour or so. He studied the bar crowd. Three people were sitting at the far end of the bar; there were two men and a woman. He could only see their backs. The woman sat between the two men with a seat separating each of them. It looked as though they were talking, but it didn't appear as though they were there together. Deiter thought to himself that they were probably trying to pick her up. Something about her was familiar and reminded him of someone else. The full head of dark red hair and the way she shook her hair when she made a point. "Good God," he said quietly to himself. "I must be going nuts…Rose?" At that moment, the woman turned and he could see that it wasn't Rose. He let out a sigh, but never the less his heart still raced with the adrenaline flow. Deiter had long ago learned to trust his intuition and what had happen three times within the last hour wouldn't be ignored. He filed it away and returned his attention to the rest of the lounge, it was empty of people. That's the way he wanted it. The bar waitress moved in his direction and smiled as though she recognized him. "Evening, can I get you something?" she asked in a husky tone of voice.

"Yes you may; Jamison, neat, water chaser," he declared. "I'm expecting someone else too." She smiled again and placed a white square paper napkin in front of him, turned and went to fill his order. In a few minutes, she returned and placed the Irish whiskey and a glass of water with ice and a lime wedge perched on the its lip on the table in front of him.

Deiter lifted the small glass, sipped at the amber liquid and then leaned back in the leather chair and half closed his eyes. Although he hadn't seen him for at least six months, he and Hank Henderson had been close friends for years. There once was a time when they were in constant communication. While he was at Annapolis and Hank was at West Point, they conversed by telephone at least twice a week. Whenever possible, they would meet to double date. By pulling a few strings, they had both made the exchange program between the academies. First, he had gone to Annapolis for a month and then Hank had come to West Point for the same amount of time. Looking for females seemed to fill a lot of their time. When Hank was at West Point, they had a virtual string of girls from the "City", that is New York City, who came up to be escorted around for a weekend. It had been simply a wonderful time for both of them to be alive. During the summers, he would join Hank at the Henderson family's estate in North Carolina. That was when Hank truly excelled in providing a wealth of local female companionship for the both of them. Deiter became close to Hank's parents during that time and the feeling was mutual. Major General Hodes H. Henderson and his wife Lois accepted the lone midshipman as one of their own children. Deiter accepted the offer of parenthood and returned the love in multiple quantities to both of these remarkable people; they were his surrogate parents and that made Hank more of a brother than anything else.

Although Hank had spent most of his career in the intelligence field, there was a point at which he forced his own desires. In 1967, he pressured the Intelligence career team to send him to Vietnam as an infantryman. He got his wish and joined the 3rd Battalion, 187th Airborne Infantry of the 101st Airborne Division at Fort Campbell, Kentucky. In October, they left for Vietnam and a place called Phoc Vinh. Hank was a Captain then and in command of "C" Company. At the end of a year, he returned to the States with a solid career as a combat veteran, the Combat Infantryman's Badge, and a Silver Star for Gallantry in Action.

A movement at the entrance to the lounge caught his attention and he saw the unmistakable silhouette of Colonel Hank Henderson. He was about six–two and built like a linebacker…which he had been. Deiter was surprised to see him in uniform, but guessed this was one of the "dress up" days the Army liked to perpetuate solely to remind them that they were still in the Army despite being on Washington duty and in "civvies" or civilian clothes most of the time. Deiter lifted his arm and gave a brief wave of recognition. Henderson nodded and maneuvered through the tables and chairs over to where Deiter was seated.

"Couldn't see you in the dark," Henderson remarked as he reached Deiter.

"Nice to see you," Deiter said. "Formal day, huh?" Henderson smiled understandingly in return.

Henderson tossed his green uniform hat with the gold "scrambled eggs" on the visor onto the table, unbuttoned his jacket and plopped into a chair next to Deiter; he also sat facing the entrance to the lounge.

At the new arrival, the bar waitress moved over towards the two men. "Good evening, Colonel; what can I get you?"

Henderson looked up at her; his soft eyes framed in a square and rugged face. He smiled warmly. "Dewers, rocks," was the abbreviated response. "With a twist." She smiled and almost blushed, then quickly turned and went back to the bar. Neither man said anything until the bar waitress returned with the scotch. Henderson then raised his glass toward Deiter in a toast and said with a smirk, "Na zdroviq!...(*To your health!*). Whatcha got, Jack?" Under the circumstances, he thought that it might be an appropriate toast. Deiter reached into his document folder and withdrew the sheath of papers, handing them to Henderson. Henderson didn't say anything, but took his glasses out of his inside jacket pocket, put them on and began leafing through the package studying each page. When he had finished, he placed them upside down on the table, leaned back and let out a sigh.

"Well?" asked Deiter.

"I'll run them through the system, of course" he shrugged, "but my guess is that they're fakes or something else entirely."

"What makes you so sure?" replied Deiter.

"Well, there's no reason I can think of for any Russian documentation as a lead in, first of all," he explained. "If these were legitimate documents, they wouldn't have anything else on the page at all, it would be purely code. That's just the way we do it." He thought for a short moment as though putting the next into logical words. "Second, it doesn't have the right feel. I know, I've seen thousands of them." Then he concluded with, "But, just to make sure, I'll have my people see if they can come up with any likely translation or alternative."

"Appreciate it," Deiter said. What his friend had just relayed to him only convinced him that this wasn't something as simple as someone getting their hands on a US coded message…or trying to pass it on. Henderson's "or something else entirely" fit with his suspicion, but for the life of him, he couldn't guess what that might be. Oh, well, maybe the NSA could come up with something…at least a guess. The conversation took a lighter turn as Henderson elaborated on his wife's college "chums," as he called them, and the two began to enjoy the evening. They were tonight, just two old friends reminiscing about old times. Although Henderson had attended West Point and Deiter had attended Annapolis, they had become close friends during their stay at the Academies. They talked about the exchange weeks when they had roomed with each other; this led them to reminisce about the summers that Deiter had spent on vacations with Hank and his parents in North Carolina.

After a pleasant dinner and a longer time relaxing in the lounge, the two parted. Henderson had parked next to the restaurant. He climbed into his car and drove up King Street towards the lights of the Washington Masonic Memorial which he could see ahead of him on Shooter's Hill. Deiter knew that he'd swing around in front of the Alexandria Metro Station, get on Duke Street and turn on Telegraph Road which in turn led to where Hank and Meg lived. Deiter watched him until he was out of sight. Earlier, Deiter had parked his own car in front of his town house before going to the restaurant, so he turned to retrace his steps down Fairfax to Prince Street and home. The evening had been enjoyable as far as he was concerned and he was feeling good. Maybe it was the several "Jamison's" he had consumed that helped him to relax and being with an old friend was entirely enjoyable. Anyway, there wasn't anything to do until tomorrow. Hank was going to do what he could about the papers and he had left his inquiry about Rose with the guy at the CIA.

It took him only five minutes to go the few blocks from the restaurant to his townhouse. He hunched his shoulders against the wind, his hands in his pants pockets. He hadn't worn an overcoat that day, but October in Northern Virginia could still be chilly, especially at night. It was about nine–thirty when he turned left down the cobblestone street that fronted his townhouse. The cobblestones glistened in the light of the street lamps along the street and it seemed to transform him into another century, one that seemed to be more gentle and peaceful. As he passed by his Jaguar XK8 convertible parked just up the hill from his doorway, Jack glanced at it to see that it was secure. He turned into his doorway and fumbled for the keys in his pant's pocket. The building was one of about a dozen on that side of the block and was the same age as the others. It was two and a half stories high, brick, with black working wooden slatted shutters on the windows. The door was heavily carved dark natural wood with highly polished brass fixtures and a heavy brass knocker in the center fashioned as the head of a fox. An oval plaque identified it as an original registered house in the Colonial section of Alexandria. The flickering glow coming from the brass lantern styled lamps on either side of the door was warm and inviting. He had bought the house back in the seventies when he was first assigned to the Washington area; later, when he and Sally were married, she had moved in with him. Those were happy and wonderful times he thought as he slid the key into the brass plate in the door.

Deiter unlocked the front door, stepped inside and headed quickly for the alarm shutoff switch located down the hallway and around the corner. He disabled it and went back to the door to pick up a stack of mail that lay in a pile on the floor. A few catalogs…a couple of bills and some political advertisements…nothing wonderful here, he thought. He closed the door, locked it and went through the pocket door on the left, which led to his walnut paneled study. He switched on the light, his stereo and computer in the process.

Deiter's private sanctuary reflected the personal tastes of its owner. In the center of the room was a large carved, double-pedestal walnut desk. Between the two windows that looked out onto Prince Street, was a scale model of a four-masted man-o'-war that Deiter had made from original plans years before. Otherwise, the room was sparsely furnished as befitting the age of the house. An Oriental rug covered most of the polished hard wood floor. Shear curtains hung over the windows set off by a dark crimson velvet cornice and floor-length drapes that could be closed during the winter months to keep out the cold wind that sometimes blew down the cobblestone street toward the Potomac River.

On his desk, the telephone's answering machine blinked at him with a red number one. He hit the small blue button on the machine and waited, meanwhile tossing his mail onto the desk.

"Jack, Don Adams...you know where," the machine said. "What's this about Rose? Call me tonight, I'll be here." The voice gave a telephone number and the machine added its own message in a metallic voice, "End of messages." Jack flopped into his chair suddenly exhausted. He hadn't expected a reaction from the "Company" so soon and he hadn't heard from Adams since he had left the Agency years ago. Deiter played through the tape once more to get the telephone number and scribbled it down on a notepad on his desk.

Trying to quickly think about what he was going to say, Deiter picked up the phone, punched in the numbers he had written down, and waited while it rang. A voice answered with the last three numbers that he had just dialed. Deiter said, "Adams? Deiter."

"Nice to hear from you, Jack...been a long time," replied Adams in a deep reverberating voice. Don

Adams had been a recruiter for the CIA and was Deiter's
original contact with the Agency just after having finishing up law school. At that time, most of the European
operatives were first contacted by Adams. If he were still
with the Agency, he must now have a much more
important job and Deiter wondered why he deserved
such personal attention.

"What's this I'm being told about you wanting to
know the whereabouts of a previous employee?" Adams
said in a slow and very deliberate manner. "You must
know that such information is not readily available to
just anyone," he continued.

"I'm not exactly Joe-Shit-the-ragman, you know,"
retorted Deiter. "I have a good idea you know exactly
what the hell I do now and who I work for. By the way,
how come this is so important that you're calling me at
home?" he paused and added for good measure, "And on
an unsecured line." Deiter had never really liked Adams,
but before now he had always responded to him in a professional way. This time, it was different. Deiter wasn't
working for Adams anymore and the demeaning manner
of his tone of voice bothered him.

"No need to get testy, Jack. I just wanted to know
whether this was personal or business," Adams said. So
that was it; Agency policy didn't allow for personal
attachments while on assignments and word had gotten
back to Adams that Deiter and Rose had become an
item while they were working for the Agency.

"Strictly business," replied Deiter. "And unless she is
back working for you, if anything personal develops,
you'll be the last to know." Deiter could sense himself
losing it and wished that the conversation would end

soon before he burned all his bridges. He had been known for not only burning bridges, but also blowing them up at times.

"Why don't you drop by tomorrow morning, Jack, say about…Oh, nine–thirty and I'll see what I can do. Ask for me at the front desk and I'll send someone," he added.

"Nine–thirty it is," responded Deiter and hung up. "Damn him," Deiter muttered under his breath. He knew that in the end Adams would tell him what he wanted to know, but would make it unbearable in the process. He promised himself that he would be very professional and pleasant tomorrow, even if it killed him.

Deiter finished sorting though his mail and looked up only when he sensed movement in the room. A series of yowls introduced the familiar sight of his only companion, Sam, swaggering through the doorway. Sam…like in Sam Spade, whom he was named after, was a large black Persian cat that had been Deiter's confidant for over a decade. He was totally independent and constantly reminded Deiter of that fact. "Well, good evening, Sam; what the hell have you been up to?" Deiter asked as though expecting a reply. The cat jumped into his owner's lap to be reassured and settled himself down as Deiter finished opening his mail. Deiter thought that without Sam, he'd lead a lonely existence indeed.

CHAPTER TWO

▼

CENTRAL INTELLIGENCE AGENCY

Langley, Virginia
Friday, October 24th 1997

The way to get to Langley, Virginia and the CIA Headquarters from Old Town Alexandria is to drive north up the George Washington Memorial Parkway along the Western bank of the Potomac River. Deiter decided to go there first before swinging over into Washington and FBI Headquarters in the J. Edgar Hoover Building. He climbed into his Jaguar parked in front of the house, drove around the block and headed up King Street for the GW Parkway. For Washington, the traffic seemed light and he made good time. He passed by Washington National Airport just as a lumbering 747 was taking off in the same direction and straining for altitude. The drive was relatively pleasant and gave Deiter time to consider what he would say to

Adams and just how much he would tell him about the matter of the torture murder and files on microdot. He knew of course that the missions of the FBI and the CIA were very specific as to where each could ply their trade. The Bureau was strictly internal to the Country; the CIA was *supposed* to conduct its activities outside the territorial boundaries. He also knew that at times, and when they could get away with it, their territories mixed. He guessed that the amount of information he would give Adams depended on how much it took to locate Rose. Deiter drove past nearly a dozen joggers who were exercising on the trail that paralleled the highway, passed under Chain Bridge Road and came to the Turkey Run turn off opposite the entrance to the CIA campus. Turning right and around the jug-handle, he followed a half-dozen cars as they approached the main gate leading into the complex.

Deiter stopped opposite the right side of the guard building in the center of the road; a guard dressed in a white uniform shirt with gold badge and a gold stripe down his medium blue pants, stepped up to the car. The guard asked for a pass and Deiter held his Bureau ID up for the guard to see and gave his name, "Deiter, FBI." He waited as the guard moved his finger down a list of names. Deiter's gaze shifted to the twin set of red steel curved barriers across the roadway ahead of him and the double row of tire slicers. Things had changed since he had been in the CIA; apparently they were fully expecting someone to ram through the entrance with a ton of explosives or something equally drastic. "Maybe it's because they're such a friendly bunch here," he mused to himself. The guard's finger stopped halfway down the list.

He grunted and said, "Here it is, thanks Agent Deiter." At a signal, the first of the barriers disappeared into the ground along with the long row of knives aimed at his tires and Deiter shifted into first gear and pulled up to the barrier. As he drove close to it, the second barrier descended into its hole and he crawled past it. He could see in his rear view mirror that both barriers had returned to their original position. The sprawling expanse of the Central Intelligence Agency Headquarters complex can't be seen from the main road. Deiter drove up the long rise in the road leading to the center of the complex, ignored the directions to the expansive parking lot that rivals the Pentagon and drove up to and parked in the "visitor" area in front of the Administration Building. He then proceeded up the walk and through the main entrance. The Building itself gave the appearance of a bird in flight; the architecture consisted of a series of curved roofs. His guess was it was supposed to be an eagle. He stopped momentarily at the statue of Nathan Hale outside the Old Administration Building and then walked briskly to the main entrance of the New Administration Building and into the reception area.

At the reception desk sat two women. One was in her early fifties and the other must have been no older than 35. Both were rather striking and it somewhat amused Deiter that the Agency had a way of selecting people for the most menial positions using criteria of their own invention; hardly an equal opportunity employer. The older woman had a full head of brunette hair and she was in full makeup. She was also very attractive and was the first to notice Deiter. "Yes sir?" It was a question not a statement.

"John Deiter, FBI to see Don Adams," he said.

She read down a list of names in front of her, came to Adams, and picked up the telephone. She waited a few moments for someone to answer and then said, "There's a Mr. Deiter from the FBI to see Mr. Adams." She paused. "I'll tell him." She hung up the phone and looked up at Deiter.

"Mr. Adams is sending someone for you; you may take a seat over there," she said motioning to a set of four overstuffed green armchairs around a low rectangular table. It sounded more like a command rather than a request.

"Thanks," Deiter replied trying his best to sound indifferent. He didn't immediately move over towards the chairs, but wandered around the Atrium. He didn't like taking orders from receptionists and this was his way of demonstrating his independence...and establishing his authority. Overhead were suspended two airplanes, a one–sixth model of the U2 and a full sized SR 71A reconnaissance aircraft. He knew that the U2 model had been made for wind tunnel testing purposes. He kept his attention focused out the front window and periodically would look expectantly towards the double doors behind the reception desk counter. This was the only other way out of the lobby and Deiter knew that his escort would be entering through it. After about ten minutes, the door opened and a young woman appeared. She walked over to Deiter and said, "Agent Deiter, Mr. Adams said you were asking for this; he sends his apologies that he can't see you just now, but he is a very busy man."

Deiter recognized the slight and chose to ignore it. He reached for the envelope that the woman was holding out towards him, took it from her and casually slid it into his inside breast pocket. "Tell Donny, thanks...don't think I'll need to be bothering him again." He then added, "The Bureau's director is always appreciative when it comes to interagency cooperation." Deiter knew that the first message would be understood as telling Adams that whatever was going to be transpiring between himself and Rose, at least Adams would never be told. The latter was a reminder that Congress and the General Accounting Office looked askance at the waste of money resulting from the lack of cooperation between the many departments of the Government...particularly in the Intelligence community. Deiter had gotten the information he wanted, but it wasn't due to the good graces of Adams.

Deiter turned without further conversation, exited through the rotating doors and walked down the walkway towards his parked car. He climbed into the driver's seat, buckled himself in, and started the car. He was a good hundred yards down the road when he reached into his pocket for the envelope. He slowed down upon reaching the main gate and stopped to wait for the barrier to drop and then drove through the gate. As soon as he was out of sight and was headed back down the Parkway out of sight, he ripped opened the envelope and pulled out a single sheet of paper.

Typed on the CIA official stationary was:

Information requested by Agent Deiter, FBI: ("Agent," not Special Agent, another slight, he still didn't like Adams.)

Rose Ann McGuire (nee Spinelli)
136 Princeton Court
Upper Saddle River, New Jersey

Adams didn't really outdo himself; this was as little as he could get away with. Anyway, it would do. Deiter could get the rest. He did notice the "nee," though, and her new last name "McGuire." This bit of information didn't really answer one of the questions that seemed to have been on Deiter's mind; even he didn't know it was on his mind until his heart fell at seeing the words on the sheet of paper. That didn't prove anything, though. Rose didn't seem the type, as he recalled, that was willing to settle down, but maybe she did anyway. No use thinking about it…there's time to check it out later.

Deiter took the Chain Bridge exit from the GW Parkway and drove towards Washington. He could have gone straight, but he wasn't in a hurry and needed time to think. The route to Washington from Chain Bridge down Canal Road was pleasant this time of year. The trees were almost at their best color and he could see the canal through the trees and its bank on the other side. Again, he noticed a number of joggers along the path that paralleled the road. Was it only Washington area that had so many people out running? He guessed it was just the times; he also felt an urge to run, maybe tonight, he thought. Passing the turnoff for the Whitehurst Freeway, he continued on M Street through Georgetown, past the Rigg's Bank with its gold dome, and continued on until it changed into Pennsylvania Avenue. He had to swing right and then left around the White House and back onto Pennsylvania Avenue. He sighed, shook his head and longed for a simpler era not that long ago when he had been able to continue on Pennsylvania Avenue in front of the White House. Remembering the barriers at the CIA, he felt despair at the state of affairs in the world today. It seemed that the people couldn't get close to their own government because of others who sought to destroy it. A few blocks further on, he came to the building that housed his office; he turned left and then right into the underground parking area of the J. Edgar Hoover Building. He parked and took the elevator to the third floor and walked down the hallway to his office.

"Any messages for me?" he asked as he passed the secretary's desk.

"A Detective Polk from New York City called; left this number and would like you to call," she replied. Deiter took the message and went into his office. Sitting down, he pushed a key on his intercom and said, "Get Ken for me."

"Yes, sir," she replied. Deiter noted that it was about ten–thirty; it had been only about an hour since he had arrived at the CIA; not bad, considering.

In a few minutes, Ken Stroeman was at Deiter's office door. He knocked gently and said, "Jack, you wanted to see me?"

"Yeah, Ken, I need you to do some quick research; dig up what you can on this person...very discretely. I need to know how to contact her in a way to raise the smallest fuss. She appears to be married, but maybe she works," he added. "And let me know just as soon as you have something."

Ken Stroeman wasn't known for finding a needle in a haystack for nothing. In about thirty minutes, he was back at Deiter's door. "Hey, Chief," he said as he stuck his head around the door. Deiter motioned him in; Stroeman could see that his boss was on the telephone.

"Would tomorrow morning be OK?" asked Deiter. "I'm heading for New York this afternoon."

The answer was apparently in the affirmative and Deiter nodded his head. "I'll see you then...and thanks, Polk." Deiter hung up the phone and looked up at Stroeman. "And?" he asked.

"I think I have what you want; took longer than usual." Both men smiled at the obvious overstatement. "She *is* Rose Ann Spinelli McGuire, or Rose McGuire. But, she is no longer married; divorced some eleven years ago, although she did have one child...grown and in college, a son. She works at a law firm in Upper Saddle River, New Jersey; owns her house (I have phone numbers and addresses for both home and work); no criminal record....,"

"Oh, thank God for that," joked Deiter. "What took you so long? Did you find out if she's free for dinner?" Stroeman was about to answer when Deiter held up his hand. "Don't tell me; there are some things I can take care of myself." Stroeman smiled broadly at the guarded compliment and his boss' obvious confidence in his work; not expecting a reply, Stroeman gave a high-five sign and left.

By car, it was only a five-hour drive between Washington and the New York area. Deiter decided he would drive instead of flying to New York. Besides, he'd need a car to get around and this would be easier on his travel budget...to say nothing about being able to drive his own car; that meant a lot to him. He had agreed to

meet Detective Polk at the 20th Precinct at ten–thirty
the next morning. If he left at noon, he would be up in
the vicinity of New York in time for supper. "Supper
with whom?" he asked himself. Suddenly, he thought he
knew or at least hoped.

Deiter stared at the paper that Stroeman had left him.
There were two telephone numbers for Rose, one for
home and one for work. Deiter looked at his watch.
She'd be at work now. He punched in the numbers and
waited. A recording answered his call saying that Ms.
McGuire was not available and would be out of the
office the rest of the day. Deiter thought about leaving a
message and then decided not to. He hung up.

The drive north from Washington to New York was
somewhat boring and uneventful. Deiter liked to take
books-on-tape with him on long drives and rather
enjoyed the uninterrupted flight into the fantasy world
of a mystery novel being read to him over his car sound
system. He had left the office about one–fifteen and by
the time he had packed and gotten back on the road, it
was past two. That would mean he wouldn't get in until
about seven…too late to call Rose for dinner, but would
try her at home when he got in. He emotionally kicked
himself. Why should he think that Rose would even
have dinner with him. It's been a long time.

As he listened to the latest mystery story over his tape
player, Deiter reflected that he really did appreciate his
car. Although it was to all appearances a stock 1997 dark
green Jaguar XK8 convertible, he had it modified shortly
after he purchased it. Following some rather uncomfort-
able experiences in which he had almost "bought the
farm" as they say, he installed special equipment in the

car to preclude being caught unprepared again. These installations included a full set of radios capable of communicating with every law enforcement agency in the Country. It also had telephones, night vision devices, two light-weight, slim-fitting protective armor vests, satellite location and guidance systems and a weapons cache. Here, he stored two scope-mounted Armalite AR-10A4 Carbines which fired a.308 Winchester cartridge, a shotgun and a high-powered sniper rifle with a daylight and night scope as well as several assorted smaller handguns each equipped with lasergrips for easy target acquisition especially at night. He was also stocked with sufficient ammunition to sustain him comfortably. Although he financed the modifications himself, its existence was condoned, if not specifically authorized, by the Bureau. The V8 engine had been upgraded as well as the transmission and was better than any police cruiser in existence. In normal mode, the ride was extremely comfortable; he could, however, at the press of a button on the console, stiffen the struts and snubbers to provide a racing suspension. Although few people knew of these modifications, and it looked like a standard make of car, Deiter felt a great deal of quiet pride in his special set of wheels. Any comparison to a vehicle belonging to the literary spy hero, James Bond would have embarrassed Deiter no end. He looked at it simply as protection when he needed it.

Deiter arrived a little after seven and checked into a Sheraton Hotel not too far from the Lincoln Tunnel. This gave him quick access into the City, yet was quite convenient to drive to where Rose was living. He unpacked, pored himself a Jamison over ice and leaned

back on the couch in his hotel room. On an impulse, he
picked up the TV remote and pressed the ON button.
The hotel had a news channel and it was set to the local
area news. A TV reporter was standing on the sidewalk
next to an alley and was commenting on a killing that
had taken place two nights ago, but the information was
just now being released to the press. "Actually," Deiter
said to himself, "it was released last night, but not in
time for your program." The reporter was speculating
on a "mob hit" with rumors of body mutilation. The
reporter next went through a list of all the mob figures
he knew of with tales of past misdeeds of the nefarious
crime lords, proposing that this action was little different. "Good of you to solve the crime for me," quipped
Deiter to himself. Suddenly, Deiter didn't feel much like
going out to eat, but did feel hungry after the ride. He
hit the numbers listed on the telephone for ROOM
SERVICE, gave his order and was told that it would
take a half-hour to forty–five minutes. Deiter hung up
the phone, climbed into his running clothes and went
down to the lobby. He asked the desk clerk where there
was a good running path near by, got instructions and
left the hotel.

It was about thirty minutes later when Deiter arrived
back in his hotel room and after five minutes in the
shower, he dressed himself, pored himself another drink
and sprawled back on the couch. There was a knock on
the door and dinner was served.

At a little past nine, Deiter tried Rose's home number
and when receiving no answer, tried the one which was
her work number. The phone rang three times and he

was about to hang up when a woman's voice answered in a weakly whispered question, "Yes?"

CHAPTER THREE

ROSE

The Law Offices of Symond, Hennessee and Smith
Upper Saddle River, New Jersey
Friday, October 24th, 1997

Rose McGuire was working late on a project synopsis for Aldridge Mason's negotiations with a businessman from the city of Bryansk in Russia. Although it meant spoiling a Friday evening, Aldridge would be furious if she didn't complete it before the weekend. Aldridge's idea of a pleasant Saturday or Sunday morning was to come to the office and work. He was only an associate in the firm, but he held a great deal of power...over the firm and, she had to admit to herself, over her. She sat back and stretched her arms out in front of her, wiggling her fingers. Looking at the clock on her desk, she noted the time and was glad that she was just about through with the brief. It was in Russian; the English version was written by Aldridge. Rose was looking forward to going home; it had been a long week and she yearned to stretch out in her tub and thoroughly relax.

She glanced around the office in an attempt to relax her mind so as to formulate the last few lines of translation in the brief. If the quality of an office's furnishings reflects the success of a business, then the law firm of Symond, Hennessee and Smith could be classified as being successful. With over fifty associates, partners and clerks, it was very successful. The décor was heavy walnut, black leather and brass...brass lamps, brass nameplates, brass handles, and even brass signs saying GENTLEMEN and LADIES. There was a smoky glass partition that separated the offices of the associates from the open reception area and waiting room. Plants adorned the table tops and ivy curled around the window frames in a tasteful manner. The partners, of course, had private, separate offices down the hallway. It was late and most of the lights had already been turned out by the cleaning crew. Hers was the only office where a desk light still burned; when the clicking sounds of her computer keyboard ceased, she seemed to be able to hear the absolute silence in the remainder of the office complex. Rose was alone.

The name Rose suited her and she knew it. She had a thick full head of hair cut below shoulder length; it was the delight of every hairdresser. She particularly liked men to do her hair; the feel of their hands on her scalp, neck and face were complementary and sensuous to her...and yet safe. Although she now dyed it a dark red to hide any telltale gray, as a teenager it was called auburn, but it was still as full now as it was then and she wore it attractively. At a full five foot eight, she presented herself as a tall and striking beauty that graced many a party given by the firm. It was easy to spot Rose in a crowd of people; she was personable and seemed to attract people to her. Seldom would she be standing alone. Rose wore mostly designer clothes...those in good taste anyway, and only good jewelry...mostly gold; she would also wear rings on either hand, not caring if it looks as though she were wearing an engagement or a wedding ring even though she's now divorced. It tended to keep men guessing, even those men with whom she may be involved. With an enviable figure of 36–28–37, she looked great in clothes; her legs may have been a bit too thin, but no one except her seemed to have ever minded. Her face was pretty in a coquettishly childish way and wonderfully photogenic. She had high Germanic cheekbones and a straight nose; her complexion was smooth although she now used full makeup to cover what she perceives as creeping age. Although forty–nine, Rose sometimes looked thirty–five, unless she was tired or worried, then she fully looked her age. Rose's lips were not as full as she might have liked them to be, but enhanced with lipstick...usually red to dark reddish purple shades...they were acceptable. At times she would wear lipstick only a shade away from black when she wanted to challenge the prim and properness of the world, or when she felt naughty or angry. Her eyes were dark...almost black...with dark lashes; they were large, liquid pools somewhat too close together, but in an alluring way...one of her best points and what seemed to draw men to her. Hard to explain men sometimes, they become attracted to the strangest things.

Rose had a lilting giggle that was reminiscence of a little girl. She would shake her head and the abundance of her hair would swirl around her face. She would play with her hair and run her fingers through it when she wanted to flirt; she knew it seemed to turn men on...and she liked that. Sometimes, Rose would bend her head down and stare into her glass of Absolute, hum quietly to herself and then quickly turn her head to look at her companion with a quizzical smile...as though she suddenly knew what sensual thought was on his mind. She knew what effect this had and she had practiced it to perfection.

Rose had been born Rose Ann Spinelli, the only daughter of Antonio Spinelli and Katherine Mueller Spinelli. Her parents were of Southern Italian and Germanic origin. Her mother, Katherine Mueller Spinelli was the matriarch of the family and second generation German; Rose found that she could gain her grandfather's attention by speaking his native tongue to him. Not that Rose ever had any trouble getting attention from males at all. Her father too, was an immigrant American. He had come to this country when he and his brothers were in their early teens. He had been betrothed to a young girl just before the family had left the little village in Eastern Italy to come to America. The family of his wife-to-be considered that the Spinelli family had broken the contract when they left Italy. It was in New Rochelle that Antonio (Tony, as he preferred to be called; it was more American) had met Katherine Mueller. They were married as soon as they had graduated from high school. A few years later, Rose, their third child, was born. At home they spoke the language of their new country as well as the languages of their forefathers, both Italian and German. The Spinelli family savings were used to send their only daughter to get a college education. She would, of course, become a teacher…an appropriate profession for a girl…until she could be married, anyway.

When Rose was growing up, her mother had instilled in her the need for security in her life. It was what a woman needed in order to survive, she was taught. There were certain ways a woman could assure it, too. Rose was always headstrong and knew what she wanted. On occasions, she used others, mostly men, to assure she had position, if not money. Rose had always known that she was attractive to men and she used what wiles it took to secure them to her. To increase her effect on them, she many times resorted to using body language. She might show a little more leg then usual…just to gain their attention or by leaning forward, she would shrug her shoulders to give them a bit more breast to view. If the effect wore off, she might rarely, and if absolutely necessary to secure her position, use her bed with devastating and long lasting effects. The men who had participated in this delightful endeavor were captive to her charms forever…joining a very small, but exclusively loyal and secret fraternity. She sometimes had to make use of those talents during the years that she spent with the CIA.

At a quarter past nine o'clock, she had just finished the brief when the double chirp of the telephone disrupted her in the middle of pulling her coat on. The ringing startled her as it was unusual for a call to come in on her private line this late at night and not on the firm's main number in the outer office. The personal lines were universally used by close friends or relatives, members of the firm or other employees. She hoped it wouldn't be Aldridge Mason, she wanted to be alone tonight. She picked up the phone and answered tentatively, "Yes?"

"Rose?" the voice on the other end of the line inquired.

"Yes, who is this?" she asked.

"Rose, it's been a long time I know, but I hope you'll remember me, it's Jack...Jack Dieter. He paused, "You remember, your contact in Rome in...oh, '72 or '73, I think; yeah, that's it, 1973. We were recruited at about the same time by Don Adams."

Rose let him ramble on, all the while glowing in the impossibility of what she was hearing. A smile eased across her face as she slowly sank into one of the overstuffed leather couches in the office. It was Jack...*John Remington Dieter III*. The "third"...Rose had always wondered what the other two were like; Jack seemed to be one of those kinds of people who had the mold broken when they're born. Suddenly, old memories began to flood back to her...good memories, anyway, none of the bad ones. Was that really the way it was? She knew it wasn't, but in her present state of mind she also knew now what she wanted. "Jack, you old scoundrel," she bantered, "Where have you been?"

"Me!" he exclaimed, with a touch of exasperation in his voice. "Do you know what I've been through and how much it's cost the Bureau to locate you?" "The 'Company' isn't very cooperative in helping us locate some of their past, and...uh, best operatives. One has to do a lot of arm-twisting. Say, Rose...can you spare a few minutes? I need to talk with you. I've got a proposition you might be interested in that goes back in a way to the old days, but a hell of a lot more promising and financially more productive. How 'bout dinner tomorrow night? Your place? You used to do a great stromboli."

She suddenly felt as though things were beginning to happen faster than she could think. The excitement was there again too, maybe it was the adventure. My God, it was like a dream. Just when she had wanted something to happen, it happened. The frightened feeling was there again too; the reason she left the company in the first place. Somehow, though, it wasn't unsettling to her this time and she wore it more comfortably. Maybe she had matured. She didn't have the slightest idea what Jack was doing now or what her part might be, but a feeling close to euphoria began to sweep over her and she was on a high. Maybe those were good days after all. "I'd like that, Jack...and Jack...it sure is good to hear your voice again; you don't know how much I've missed it...and I need...Oh, never mind...tomorrow night. Six? I'll be looking forward to seeing you." The phone went dead and she sank back into the couch exhausted. She hadn't told him where she lived, but if Jack could get this number, he already knew where she lived...and probably a lot more.

Unexpectedly, the tune to "Miracles Can Happen" began flitting through her mind and she smiled to herself. Suddenly, she felt she wanted...no, she really needed a drink. There was a cozy, familiar bar only a couple of blocks away...a place she often drifted to when she needed to be alone with people or needed time to think. She hurriedly placed the finished brief on Aldridge Mason's desk, turned the lights off and left the office. The cool air hit her face as she pushed open the door that led to the street. Within a few minutes, she had slipped into a booth at Dinty's Tavern and was sipping on an Absolute. Her thoughts strayed to Aldridge Mason. In light of what had just happened, the thought of him made her face flush; but embarrassment then gave way to anger. What was he turning her into? She felt as though she were a prisoner...even a slave...her life, her entire being had slipped out of her control...at least until tonight. How had she gotten into this prison?

As Rose relaxed and sunk into the booth, she twisted the glass in her hands and began to reflect on how her life had changed since she left the "Company's" employment. She recalled that it was a telephone call that first brought her into the excitement of that life style...she smiled...and now perhaps it was to be another phone call that might return her to it.

It was during the last semester at Kent State when most of the soon-to-be graduates were sending newly fashioned resumes off to school systems near their homes...or as far away as they could get from home. It was a time for interviews when each one of her classmates would rush off to this district or that to sit nervously waiting to be called upon to enter into that office where a superintendent of schools (or more usually, the screening assistant superintendent) would ask the appropriate questions to draw the victim-of-the-moment into what appeared to be innocent conversation; but in reality it was to see what real reason there was to reject this person who was taking up their time. Rose didn't want any part of that.

She recalled that it was on a day like this when she was once before mulling over her life's situation, when the phone call came. The person on the other end of the line had said his name was Mr. Adams and he was interested to know if she would like to work for a large company that would promise a great deal of overseas travel. The position was in what could be termed the Human Resources area, he had said and would include interviewing prospective foreign employees. Her interest in languages and psychology, he said, was what first interested him in her qualifications. Well, that was right, anyway. Rose took to languages well. Early on, she had thought of teaching in primary school, later it would be secondary, and finally, on the advice of her language professors, high school or college. She thought about teaching either German, which was more popular and besides was her grandfather's tongue, or Russian, in which she was fully fluent, or even Italian; in which she had been mostly fluent from childhood. Not many people took Italian in college, though.

Mr. Adams had said that the pay and benefits would be commensurate with those received by all but a very few new graduates and better than most. He would meet her at the Hilton Hotel in Philadelphia that Friday at six o'clock in the lounge if she were interested. She was. The thought of travel was intoxicating to Rose. It was strange, though, that an interview would be held somewhere other than on the campus or at the business location.

She remembered that the thought temporarily unnerved her. This *was* really strange; what kind of employer would interview young women in a bar? A pimp? A white slaver? Maybe he's some kook out to entice women into his clutches. She laughed to herself at the thought...he'll find the worse end to that deal; she hadn't taken Taek Quan Do for nothing, and she was pretty good at it, at least that's what her instructors had told her...and there were those awards she had earned. Oh well, at least it would be in a public place and she was fairly sure of her own ability to handle herself in most situations. The intrigue had been somehow pleasing to her and for the time she relished in it.

The meeting with Mr. Adams did in fact change her life. For three years, she was to live in another world, one completely out of touch with the one she had known in New Jersey. The Central Intelligence Agency sometimes had a strange way of selecting their employees, but now Rose Spinelli was to be a spy for her country. It wasn't until much later, however, that she would know the exact dangers that she would have to face.

The training at the Central Intelligence Agency's center and school at Langley, Virginia was intensive and demanding on Rose, but she was fully up to it. She was an attentive student and made an excellent agent. Her good looks and quick mind interacted with her command of Russian and Italian to make her quite believable in the eyes of the Russian agents in Europe and she blended into the scene of Rome as though she were a native Roman. Her ample dark red hair and her jaunty walk habitually elicited whistles and catcalls from that city's would-be Romeos. She delighted in it and it made her feel comfortable to reaffirm her effect on men. It was an exciting time, but the years still left her exhausted. There were also the times that she had to do things that left her feeling violated and dirty. But she kept telling herself that it was for the right cause and most importantly, it kept her alive and still in contact. She could get the information she needed to pass on to her contact and eventually back to Langley, but then in the end, it still left her empty. Rose was good at what she did and both she and the "Company" knew it.

In 1974, Rose left the Agency. At the time, there were no regrets. To her acquaintances throughout Europe, Rose had just vanished. To some, a disappointment and loss; others just expected that she ran afoul of someone or something that she couldn't handle or had just gotten into too much trouble and ended up as one of those forgotten statistics. Which side was responsible would have been anybody's guess. Only Jack Deiter knew the truth; for the rest, the "Company" covered for her.

Rose raised her glass and shook it, signaling to the bartender for another Absolute. She then took stock of the bar for the first time since she had arrived. There were only two other people there besides herself and Max, the bartender. One was an old man huddled over his beer at the far end of the bar. She had seen him there before in the same seat and she wondered if he had ever left. The other person was a well-dressed middle-aged man in a dark suit. He appeared to have dropped in for fortification before heading for home to what she guessed was to face the realities of an unhappy domestic existence. "Better get out before it kills you," Rose murmured to herself. The man in the dark suit turned to check out Rose and she turned away showing her intention to remain alone and her lack of desire to make idle conservation. His eyes dropped and he turned back to his drink, regretting the lost hope that he might have found some new excitement in his life, but had to return to the mundane. Rose realized that this wasn't like her; she always was on the lookout for someone who would listen to her and appreciate her good looks and witty conversation. There wasn't time for that tonight, though, there was only time to look at her life and herself and take stock of where she was going and what kind of difference tonight's telephone call might make.

Rose returned to her memories. After leaving the Agency, she had returned to Upper Saddle River and had regained an acquaintance with a high school classmate, Bill McGuire. They were married in June of 1975. It wasn't really that Rose wanted to spend the rest of her life with Bill (or anyone she knew, for that matter) but it was kind of expected of her by her parents. There didn't seem to be any other alternative at the time and then she was 28 years old, her biological clock was ticking, and this was not the age to pass up the "chance of a lifetime" for…who knows what. It was a mistake and one that she realized almost as soon as she was married. Bill was full of himself and the importance of his family…and his work. His work was always first and he traveled constantly. She wasn't used to that…to having someone leave her. This was the Rose who strolled the streets of Rome and the rest of Europe as though she belonged there and constantly faced dangers her old classmates would never have dreamed of doing. Staying home alone was not her style. After Rob was born, it became worse and the boredom became routine. First it was caring for the baby; Bill was away most of the time and when he was home, he had his cronies from his boyhood days who demanded his time. There also was golf, and fishing of course and just hanging out. Rose wanted him to spend more time with Rob, but Bill would get angry whenever she mentioned it to him.

As soon as Rob was able to go to a day care center, Rose started looked for a job. She was approached one night in the summer of 1982 at a cocktail party put on by the Allen's over on Cross Turnpike Road. Walter Allen was with an Upper Saddle River law firm that specialized in corporate law, but he also had connections with other law firms in the area. His wife, Allison had been Rose's roommate in college and tended to look out for Rose then, as well as now. Walter wanted to know if Rose would take on a position as law clerk with his firm, Symond, Hennessee and Smith. She would. At first she started out as a secretary and clerk, but it didn't take long for the most demanding of the lawyers to find out that beneath those good looks was a talent and a brain that would make their life a lot more ordered. She learned fast and soon it was Rose whom they turned to when they needed some expert research…not just a law clerk. She had a phenomenal memory and could locate the most minute of references to establish a point of law needed to turn a case. Her ability to speak and write in four languages made her invaluable in the firm's new international business ventures. There was more to Rose; they all knew it, but they didn't quite dare to get to know her on a more personal basis. It was undoubtedly the "Handford" effect that caused so much reticence and caution. That had been Sally Handford and her affair with one of the junior partners of the firm that gave rise to the expression. It was a long time ago, but all the new members of the firm were told the story in exquisite detail to make sure that there would be a lasting impression. Such behavior was simply not tolerated! Even bachelors were warned not to fraternize with "the help."

Bill wasn't happy with Rose working and showed it constantly. If it wasn't for Bill's family, she knew that she would have left him long before she eventually did. Rose liked his family and was fully accepted as a member. What amused her was that even after the divorce, she still was part of the family. Especially when Bill moved away and left her the house. Actually, she had to buy out the mortgage...Aldridge Mason, of course helped with that too. To both sides of the family, nothing had really changed. They still counted on Rose to do all the holidays, to drive them to the doctor, and to bring them dinner when they were sick. And Rose did it; it made her feel wanted in some way. She did have a compassion for people, and it showed.

She remembered how Aldridge Mason had first maneuvered his way into her private life. At first, he had seemed to be so paternalistic, so helpful, yet authoritative; so much like a father figure. He was in his mid-forties when she first began working for the firm. In the beginning, Rose was pleased with his attention and saw nothing offensive or dangerous about it; in fact, his approach made Rose realize that she missed the comfort and security that could be provided by an older man...the security she used to feel when her father was alive. Soon, however, it became apparent the many "gifts" he showered her with were not out of any fatherly compassion, but a very deep seated passion instead.

Mason wanted something very specific in return for his generosity to Rose. By the time that Rose had realized the situation, it was already too late. She was indebted to him for a great deal of money...and Aldridge was not about to allow her to forget it. He demanded...and got...time with her alone. When he went to Europe for consultations, he of course needed an assistant. It always turned out to be Rose. It wasn't that Aldridge Mason was necessarily unattractive, he could charm almost anyone when he wanted to...when it would benefit him. In fact, Aldridge rarely gave anyone his time unless it was beneficial to him. But he was generous to Rose, almost to a fault. She knew deep down that all his generosity came at a price. Finally, she had given in to his insistence...and their times of intimacy together became more frequent and following her divorce, became routine. In many ways, she needed him as much as he needed her; at least in that period of her life. She liked to spend and he was willing to pay the bills...again, for a price. Young Rob was able to attend the best schools, and it was Aldridge that assured Rob's acceptance at Princeton and the promise of graduate school following. She didn't consciously think of herself to be a "kept woman." It was one of those things that life dealt...take it or leave it. Someday, though, it would all come to an end and she would be rid of the necessity of giving in to him, of being dependent upon him. Once in awhile, she actually began to believe that there might be some sort of love between them; there certainly had been a lot of intimacy...sex, that is. But real love wouldn't force those types of demands on another person and she knew it. When she tried to exert her independence from Mason, he would threaten to withdraw his support; he would treat her as though she belonged to him the same as any other of his acquisitions. She would always and finally beg him to forgive her. She somehow desperately needed his approval and he would withhold it until she was again contrite. The access to real money, however, had become as much an aphrodisiac to Rose as she was to Mason. It was a boost to his ego to see men faun over Rose…all the while knowing that, although they flirted with her and desired her, later that night it would be he who would have her. It both amused him and aroused him to think about "those poor fools" wasting their time and money in vain; it gave him a sense of power over them and over Rose.

Now though, that telephone call from Jack Dieter…what might it mean? All of this could change and she might be able to separate herself from Aldridge Mason once and for all. Maybe she would have financial security too. With luck, she might even disappear and Aldridge would never be able to find her. The thought delighted her and she remembered the times she and Jack Dieter spent together in Rome and she wondered if he was married now.

Rose looked up to see the man in the dark suit pull on his overcoat and stroll slowly towards the door. Before he put out his hand to grasp the latch, he turned to look at Rose. It was as though he wanted to give her one last chance before he walked out of her life forever. He saw no sign from the woman in the corner booth, shrugged and put his weight to the door as he went out into the night air. She felt a twinge of regret and sorrow for the man...and herself. She sighed and looked into her empty glass.

The mirror over the bar was at an angle and Rose could see herself sitting in the corner booth. She wondered what others might think when seeing her there. All in all, she was satisfied that her appearance was acceptable to others and to herself, but the other part of her life, the financial and personal side, certainly needed some attention. Maybe something was beginning to improve in that area. She pulled a bill from her purse and easing out of the booth, she slipped on her coat and started for the door. As she passed the bartender, she slid the bill across the bar. "Thanks, Max," she said. "See ya." Outside, a cold October wind almost caught her breath away as she turned right and headed up the sidewalk. A sudden gust blew her hair as she walked up the street towards where she had parked her car. She pulled her coat closer around her, grasping her purse under her left elbow. "Miracles Can Happen" began to run through her head again and she smiled and started to hum as she walked rapidly up the street, her heels clicking on the sidewalk.

Rose McGuire went to sleep quickly that night and slept through until late the next morning. That hadn't happened for years, and she felt a comforting newness; she was completely refreshed when she awoke. Her first thought was that she needed to go shopping for the makings of her special stromboli that she would make for Jack that night; maybe...yes, maybe an especially good red wine as well.

CHAPTER FOUR

▼

NYC & ROSE TOO

New York City
Saturday, October 25th 1997

Jack Deiter woke up just after dawn, put on his running clothes, left the hotel, and followed the same trail that the hotel clerk had described to him the night before. It was six–thirty when he returned to the hotel room. He quickly showered and dressed. Although it was Saturday morning, he knew that traffic might still be a problem getting into the City if he delayed too long; besides he wanted to get business over with as quickly as possible so that he could find where Rose lived to keep from being late that evening. He also had some shopping to do first.

After a quick trip to the FBI's New York Field Office to check in and inform the Assistant Director in Charge that he was in his territory, Deiter headed for the 20th

Precinct Station House. The street in front of the office
building that houses the Precinct was filled with parked
cars. Deiter went around the block once and finally spotted a car pulling out of a space not too far from the
entrance steps to the Precinct. "My lucky day," he said to
himself. Deiter didn't like to park his Jaguar in the City,
but considered that the Precinct entrance couldn't be
that dangerous a place to be. He pulled into the newly
vacated space. As he walked towards the entrance, he
turned and pointed his alarm activator at the car and hit
the button; a "beep" assured him that it was activated.

The desk sergeant indicated to Deiter that he was
expected and asked a plainclothes officer to escort him
up the flight of stairs to the Homicide Bureau and
Detective Sergeant Kenneth Polk's office. Polk was
seated behind his desk and looked up expectantly when
the officer and Deiter came around the corner; he obviously had been pre-warned that Deiter had arrived. As
Deiter came into his office, Polk slowly rose to his feet
and extended a hand and a smile to the FBI Agent.

"Special Agent Deiter, I presume," the detective said,
"I'm Ken Polk."

"It's Jack Deiter, Ken, glad to meet you."

"Maybe you won't be when you see what we turned
up here," replied Polk extending his smile even broader.
"After that we should go to the morgue to see the mystery man."

"Although the murder is in your jurisdiction, we may
have considerable interest in this one for other reasons."

"I 'spect you might," replied the detective, "lots of
strange things turning up here. Have you made anything of those codes yet?"

"Not yet, **if** that's what they turn out to be; we're still working on it. I ran a copy to the NSA to have them check it out. If it is a code, they'll find out whose it is and when it was sent or received."

"Come on, let's go by the evidence room, I'll give you what we have and then we'll drop in at the lab to get the microdots. I've got to admit, our guys did a helleva great job finding them."

"You may be surprised at just how important that is, if I don't miss my guess," replied Deiter.

Polk led the way downstairs and into the evidence room. He explained to the officer at the desk what he wanted and was asked to wait. In a few minutes, the officer came back with several items in his hand. "I think this is whatcha wanted, Sarg," he said. He produced a cane with a brass falcon's head and a large plastic bag containing a sports coat, pants, underwear, shoes, a shirt and a tie. Polk handed the parcel to Deiter and said "Sign here and you can rid the City of New York of a problem." Deiter signed the form on the clipboard that the clerk handed him. He then picked up the items and both of them left the room, Deiter carrying the cane and package.

"The lab's on the fifth floor," said Polk. They headed towards the elevator and Polk pushed the up button. "The lab is run by Joyce Higgins," explained Polk. "She's a bit cheeky, but smarter than hell. I try not to let her know she's good; it'd go to her head...she's bad enough already."

Deiter smiled at what he had deduced from the description. "You like her," he stated.

Polk grinned, "It shows, huh?"

The elevator opened and both men stepped inside. Three minutes later they were walking into the Police Lab. "Joyce, this is Special Agent Jack Deiter of the FBI," said Polk as they entered the double swinging doors and came face to face with a smiling young woman about thirty–five years old with short blond hair and dressed in a white smock.

"Dr. Higgins…Joyce," she said offering her hand to the FBI man. "Detective Polk isn't very good at introductions."

"I understand that you're the one credited with finding the microdots," he said shaking her hand.

"He told you that?" she asked. "My goodness, I didn't know I was allowed to share in the glory. Come over here and I'll show you what we found," she added.

The microdots were in a clear plastic box about the size of a pack of cigarettes. Against the white background, Deiter could make out six small dots, each about the size of a typed "o." As far as state-of-the-art in microphotography, they definitely were not. The technology must have been at least ten years old. Both FBI and CIA versions would be able to put all six inside a typed "o" with plenty of room to spare.

"Oh, I see you've got the cane," announced Joyce. "Let me show you where the microdots were hidden. Deiter handed her the cane and she unscrewed the brass falcon's head handle. Turning it over, she held it out for Deiter to see the inside of the handle. "They were under a black disk which was attached here," she said, pointing to a place on the inside of the hollow handle.

"You certainly are thorough," Deiter remarked.

"We try to be," she replied with a smile. She looked up at Polk as though begging a reply. He didn't seem to have heard the exchange.

"Let me show you what they look like on screen," she said moving over to the computer. She punched out a series of numbers and the first of the sheets appeared on the screen. "This was the one we first saw and it suggested a code sheet,"

"That was our first thought too," Deiter replied.

"And now?"

"We still haven't figured out why our code sheets should have Russian notes on them."

"Yeah," she commented, "Good question. Not my expertise, though; but I'm sure you have someone that can figure it out."

"We're working on it," Deiter concluded.

Joyce brought up the rest of the sheets on the screen and printed two copies of each. She slipped one set of copies in an envelope and dropped the other set in her hold basket on her desk.

"Here is a fresh copy to go with the dots," she said. "I don't think we'll need them anymore, we have the information and their existence can be verified if we need them in court." She laid out a paper on the desk and indicated that Deiter should sign for receipt of the items. He did so quickly.

"Thanks," said Deiter "I think I've got everything you turned up. If you need anything for court, the Bureau will get it or a court-acceptable version to you," he added. "I'm very glad to have met you, Joyce," he added extending his hand.

Deiter gathered up the bag of clothing and the cane; the plastic box with the microdots, he dropped into his inside coat pocket, and started out of the room. "Thanks again for the help," he said over his shoulder. Polk held the door open for him and the two of them walked down the hallway to the elevator door, pushed the down button and waited. In a shorter time than expected, the door opened and they were on their way to the front desk of the Precinct.

Polk turned to Deiter as they were walking past the Precinct front desk towards the entrance. "If you'd like, you can follow me to the morgue, I've got something to do afterwards and it might be more convenient if you use your own car." Deiter agreed and they left the Precinct.

Deiter walked to the rear of the vehicle and threw the cane and package of clothing into the trunk of the Jaguar and then slid behind the driver's seat. Polk was pulling out of his parking space up the block and Deiter followed him. The trip to the morgue took about 15 minutes and Deiter parked next to Polk near the entrance to the New York City Coroner's Office. Deiter joined Polk and both of them entered the Office.

"Hi, Doc, I'm back again," quipped Polk.

Deputy Coroner Willard Hastings had just finished completing an autopsy and was preparing a corpse to be returned to the holding cabinets. "You back again, want to see your old friend or a new one?"

"This is Special Agent Deiter from the FBI," Polk said gesturing towards Deiter. "He wants to see the same guy."

"Hang on," Hastings replied, "I'll roll him out." Hastings pushed a cart containing the body of an extremely corpulent male covered with a green sheet against the far wall and crossed the room to a set of panel doors. Opening the middle panel door, he pulled a tray out until the top half of a form was apparent under the green sheet. "He's all yours, let me know when you're through." Hastings left the two men and sat down at the desk. He started to thumb through a small stack of papers.

Polk grabbed the top edge of the green sheet and uncovered the body down to the navel. The upper portion including the head showed obvious signs of torture with either a sharp knife or a razor. Deiter noticed that the eyelids were missing. "The only reason I can think of why someone would cut off eyelids is to expose the victim to a strong light," he observed. "The American Indians as well as other cultures sewed or propped open the lids when they stretched someone out in the sun as torture or execution."

"It also prevents sleep," replied Polk. "Helps to encourage the memory, somewhat."

"You through?" asked Polk.

"Yeah. Have you taken pictures of him yet?"

"In my office. I'll have 'em faxed to you," Polk promised.

Back out on the street, Polk and Deiter shook hands and separated. Deiter sat in the Jag for awhile pondering what his next move would be. The killer might still be in New York, but it wouldn't do any good to stay if there weren't any better leads than what he had right now. "What was the motive?" he thought out loud to himself. Clearly, someone wanted information and wanted it badly. What information could that old guy with a cane have that would be that important? "The Cane," Deiter

exclaimed. He got out of the car and opened the trunk
and took out the cane. Deiter unscrewed the falcon's
head and looked inside. The section below the brass
handle had been hollowed out. "Why hollow out an
entire section if it was only going to be used to hide
microdots?" he mused. Polk had said something in the
report about paper fibers inside the cane. There must
have been something else hidden in there...the killer
had overlooked the microdots, but he may have been
satisfied with something else...or thought he had the
real thing. Could there have been a full-sized copy of the
microdots? If so, then why microdots and the copies?
No, that didn't make sense. Deiter threw the cane back
into the trunk, returned to the driver's seat, and started
the Jaguar; he pulled out into traffic and set his thoughts
on the rest of the day. He headed for the Lincoln Tunnel
and New Jersey.

He had been given Rose's address by Adams, but he
wanted to check out exactly where it was and how long
it would take him to get there, he didn't want to be late.
He withdrew the sheet of paper from his inside pocket
and checked the address again. A look at the map last
night had told him approximately where Upper Saddle
River was. After exiting the tunnel, he followed the signs
to the Garden State Parkway. Off the Parkway, he took
the Ramsey Road exit and then turned right on West
Saddle River Road. Deiter pulled into a Gulf station and
asked for directions to Princeton Court. In another five
minutes he was cruising slowly by a brick ranch style
house near the end of a cul de sac. The number on the
door read 136. Deiter noted the time and headed back
towards his hotel.

The question had been in his mind since he first started to think about Rose again. What do you say to someone whom you had known in a very special way over twenty–five years ago and two marriages...hers and his? Does one bring flowers? Deiter decided against that; this was going to be a business deal. "Yeah, right," he said to himself. A bottle of wine in exchange for a dinner might be appropriate. If she fixes stromboli, a red wine...perhaps a Chianti would be right. Her Italian side would be able to tell a really good Chianti, however. Deiter spotted a liquor store and pulled off the road. In ten minutes, he had thoroughly interrogated the store-owner on the attributes of Chianti and had come away with the best bottle that the store could produce. It was three–thirty when Deiter returned to his hotel room. He changed into his running clothes and left the hotel to run the now familiar circuit. When he returned, he showered and changed into more casual clothes than he had worn that morning. Deiter was partial to black. He chose black pants with a black turtleneck sweater under a charcoal blazer. It seemed to fit his style and he felt comfortable dressed that way. He sat down to watch television...a rerun of Mad Max...somehow Deiter related to it. At five–fifteen, he put on his blazer and headed out the door. Why was he feeling apprehensive? "I guess it's seeing Rose again," he said under his breath.

Even on a Saturday, the roads were filled with cars, but it was just six o'clock when Deiter drove up to the brick split ranch at 136 Princeton Court. He tucked the bottle of Chianti under his arm and walked up the walk-way to the front door.

Rose McGuire had just shoved the stromboli into the oven when the doorbell rang. She quickly ran water over her hands and applied some hand cream, rubbing it in fanatically. She looked up at the kitchen clock; it was exactly six o'clock. "I think I remember that about Jack," she said to herself. "Right on time." Rose headed for the door, stopping to take a last brief look at herself in the hall mirror. Although she knew she looked wonderful, including her recently coiffured hair and newly done nails, to herself she said, "It'll have to do." She stopped at the door and took a slow deep breath to calm herself. "Stress management...basic step one," she thought. She reached out and swung the door open wide. The man standing on the other side was a more mature version of Jack Deiter than she remembered. What did she expect...time to stand still? It was Jack, never the less.

"My God," Deiter exclaimed, "do you just get more beautiful? When'll it ever stop?"

"Jack, you'll never change; at least not that part of you, thank God." She smiled broadly and stepped through the doorway toward him, throwing her arms around him. Their lips met in a long kiss, arms tightly around each other and for a moment the years since their last meeting vanished as though it were only yesterday. Jack needn't have worried about how a re-acquaintance with Rose would play; it played very well. He was glad he had made the inquiry, even if she didn't participate in the game again. He hadn't felt this way since...Sally.

As Deiter lounged back in the overstuffed leather love seat in what, he supposed, was a small family room or den of Rose's home, he felt very satisfied, The dinner had been absolutely scrumptious and he felt well rested and at ease. There was a fireplace across one wall; the love seat in which he was sitting was in front of it; the fire was warm on his face. On either side were matching overstuffed single chairs. Off to the left was a sliding door to the patio. Rose had lit a fire and the coolness of the night made it comfortable...and romantic, he decided. "Hell, what could be more so," he mused. Rose was busying herself in the kitchen, cleaning up after the dinner meal. Deiter was savoring a glass of Remy Martin Cognac and felt in a particularly peaceful mood. He hadn't approached Rose on the purpose of his trip to New York or her proposed part in all of this, but he knew it was about to come up as soon as Rose finished cleaning up and returned. They had talked about so many things, people they knew, places they had been...even things they had done together...especially that last week in Rome. Deiter didn't know what the rest of the evening might bring...so he decided to just let it take on a life of its own.

Rose walked down the stairs to the den with a glass of Absolute on the rocks in her hand. She slid into the seat beside Deiter, placed her drink on the table in front of the love seat and snuggled down under his arm. The two of them didn't speak for several minutes, they just stayed there close together.

"Well?" Rose finally asked.

"Well, what?" Deiter replied.

"Well, why this meeting after all this time, and what kind of proposition do you have? That's why you came here, wasn't it?"

The question came too suddenly for Deiter and he wasn't prepared for it yet. For all he knew at this point, he had only come to see her. "Sorry, Rose, I guess I was just reminiscing." He took a sip of his cognac. "We have a situation that you may be able to help us with; that's why I contacted you." He paused, looking into his glass. "No, God damn it, I contacted you because I kept thinking about you and seeing you everywhere and couldn't get you out of my mind."

She put her hand on his cheek and looked into his eyes, "Always the honest one; I like that, Jack, even though it may hurt you to say it."

"Damn it, Rose, I didn't realize it until now how lonely I've been. Oh, I knew I was alone and unhappy, but not truly lonely. You made me realize that. Not that I'm blaming you or anything, it's just that seeing you again has made me realize how much I've missed some-one who was close to me."

"Sally?" she asked.

"Yeah, Sally, but more than Sally. I remember a time when you and I were inseparable and happy, in love, and alive."

Rose felt as though her heart would burst through her chest. She stared deeply into his eyes and finally, moved her head up and slowly kissed him. It was deliberately slow as though to express the emotion she was feeling at that moment. She knew that he felt as strongly about her as she did of him. She could have floated around the room if she wasn't surrounded by his arms in a tight embrace.

Deiter knew he wanted to spend the entire night there; he wanted Rose so badly. It would have been a natural, yet quite extraordinary ending to this perfect evening, but...and he couldn't really put words to it. It would come in time, but not tonight. He owed Rose that.

"Rose," he whispered quietly. "You know what I desperately want to do right now. But I don't feel either of us is in a logical frame of mind at this particular moment. I think I'd better leave, but I do need to talk to you about how you can help us." He paused, then added, "Meet me tomorrow for lunch...please. My treat, this time."

Rose had been ready for almost anything, but not this. She stumbled over her consent. Her head was down and she didn't want to look into his eyes.

"Sure." The word was filled with emotion, almost a desperation she hadn't intended. She rapidly tried to recover her composure. She was facing away from him and she quickly raised her head up and sideways; she grinned an impish smile, the kind that she gave men that silently said, "I know what you're thinking." Again she said, "Sure!" except this time it was full of confidence and a note of finality. "Call me in the morning," she added cheerfully. They kissed goodnight at the door and Deiter waved as he climbed into the Jag. It had turned cold and a wind had picked up. Deiter shivered.

The ride back to the hotel left Deiter in a lonelier mood than he could remember in a number of years...ever since Sally. He almost turned the Jag around twice to retrace his way back to the brick split-level at the end of the cul de sac, but he fought it both times. He pulled into a parking space in front of the Sheraton and shut off the Jag. As he got out of the car, he slammed the door. "Damn!" he exclaimed to no one in particular.

New York Metropolitan Area
Sunday, October 26th, 1997

Although he was in bed before midnight, Deiter didn't get to sleep for hours, so it was almost eight–thirty the next morning when he finally woke up. He didn't feel either rested or refreshed. He didn't know what his mood or his temperament was…he guessed it was the stress and occurrences of the night before that concerned him. Was he too blunt with Rose; did he turn her off, or worse did he embarrass or hurt her. Although they had spoken at great lengths of their time together twenty–five years ago, he didn't know what her circumstances were now. He mentally kicked himself. How could he have been so insensitive as not to ask about everything she was doing. He wouldn't have blamed her if she decided not to go to lunch today. "Lunch!" Deiter exclaimed as he bounded out of bed. He needed to call Rose…but first he needed to find out where to tell her to meet him for lunch. Would he pick her up instead? He decided to play that by ear and see how she reacted when he called. The call shouldn't be before nine o'clock though…but not much later than that. At fifty–five years old it was too late to be playing the dating game, he thought.

Deiter donned his running clothes and headed down to the lobby. At the desk he inquired of the young woman on duty if she knew of a particularly nice restaurant for lunch or brunch on a Sunday. She indicated several and Deiter made a mental note to look them up in the phone book when he returned from his run.

The morning was decidedly chilly and Deiter had wished he had worn a heavier jacket. There appeared to be a difference of at least three weeks in the seasonal change between Washington and New York and Deiter had not prepared for it. He cut his run short; he needed to get some things done before noontime anyway. After showering and putting on a fresh set of slacks and a shirt, he sat down to study the reading material that the hotel had placed in the drawer of the bedside table. It included the descriptions of many of the local eating establishments. Deiter wasn't impressed. He wanted something special for Rose. Something to impress her, he guessed. "New York," he thought. "What would be something that was very special in New York that would surprise her...something she'd never done?" He looked at a series of advertisements in the folder that he held in his lap. "Hudson River Cruise" read one advertisement. Suddenly, he knew what he wanted to do. It also meant that he would not be at work on Monday morning in Washington.

He made two calls. One call he made to the operator to get the telephone number and one to the hotel to make a reservation. When he had finished, he felt like he had just accomplished something spectacular. It was nine–fifteen when he dialed Rose's number.

"Hello?"

"Morning, Rose, it's Jack. Didn't want to call you too early."

"I've been up for hours, Jack. How are you this morning?"

"You still free today?"

"I said I would be...for lunch, you said; so you can tell me why you really came to see me."

"I know, and I will; do you have the whole day free?" he asked.

"Yes, I guess so."

"I want to take you to a very special and somewhat private place. Do you mind?"

"Just what have you got in mind, Jack Deiter?" she asked with a hint of suspicion in her voice.

"Just a quiet place to talk," he replied.

"Do I trust you?"

"With your life and your happiness and your future, Rose." He almost regretted it after he said it; but her reply was worth it.

"I believe you, Jack Deiter, I believe you and I'd go with you anywhere."

Deiter was stunned. He didn't know what he expected and he knew he had let his feelings loose when he had said that, but the response was like a warm comforter suddenly being wrapped around him. All he could say was, "I'll pick you up at eleven sharp."

"Great," she replied with quiet enthusiasm.

Deiter had some shopping to do and not much time to do it. He hoped there was a mall open someplace. He put on his black sweater and sport coat, picked up his hanging bag and stuffed a few items in it and left the room. Following the directions of the desk clerk, Deiter pulled into a nearby shopping mall. The fashionable designer section of Macy's had a good selection of women's clothes and he picked out several casual as well more formal dresses. His next stop was the cosmetic counter where he explained to the clerk, somewhat embarrassed, that he needed an emergency supply of lipsticks, makeup, or anything else a lady would need if she were "staying over." He told her it was for someone with dark red hair. On his way out of the mall, he passed a Victoria's Secret store and went in. It only took him five minutes to select a shear and lacy teddy and some other silk intimates. That kind of shopping made him nervous...and he knew what the pretty brunette sales clerk was thinking. He paid for the purchases with his VISA Card and left the store. He would pick up the toothbrush, comb, and other things at a drug store on his way. Deiter was extremely pleased by his purchases and his clever imagination. There could be one big problem in his plan and he knew it...she could decline his offer. He'd have to cross that bridge when he came to it. This was better than lunch, anyway.

"Lunch!" Deiter almost forgot, how they were going to do lunch. Then he knew. He stopped at another store in the mall and acquired a small picnic case that had a place for a bottle of wine, two glasses, napkins, utensils, and a compartment to store food. After leaving the mall, he stopped at a deli and a liquor store and ended up with French bread, cheese, assorted meats to include a delicious looking *pâté de foie gras,* mustard, and a nice white German wine. Next door was a drug store at which he completed his purchases.

At eleven o'clock sharp, Deiter pulled up in front of the brick split-level on Princeton Court. He walked up the pathway to the front door and rang the doorbell. The door opened almost immediately, and Rose was standing in the doorway. "I can set my watch by you, Jack Deiter," she said. Jack walked through the doorway and kissed her.

From Upper Saddle River, Deiter and Rose drove east to pick up the Garden State Parkway and followed it until it changed to Interstate 87 and then to the Palisades Parkway. The trip through the New York highlands was beautiful this time of year and he knew a particular place that would make it seem like a wonderland. They rode in silence for awhile, looking at the magnificent scenery. The magic fall colors stood out against the bright blue sky. Deiter had put some classical music on his Boze sound system and the Jag glided along the highway effortlessly. They had passed Bear Mountain before Rose interrupted the silence to inquire of her companion, "D'you have a destination, Jack?"

Deiter smiled. "When I was a midshipman, I spent a few weeks at West Point in the Autumn. I was on an exchange program. I stayed with Hank, Hank Henderson; you remember him, don't you?" He paused. "I've always wanted to go back there at this time of year. The Highlands of the Hudson River have a very special place in my memory and though I can't explain why, I thought maybe you might enjoy it too." He then added, "There's one particular place overlooking the river that's just beautiful." He smiled again, suddenly recalling the times that he and Hank Henderson had gone there while double dating at the Academies.

Rose seemed to remember something unique about Jack. He had a deep sense of history and liked to go to those places where great historic events had happened. He truly was a romantic, despite himself.

"You really are something, Jack. I appreciate what you're doing, and why."

The trip up the Hudson River to West Point wasn't that long and it was only twelve–forty–five when they entered Highland Falls, the town that bordered the United States Military Academy. After passing through the main gate, Deiter headed up the hill towards the main portion of the installation. At one point, he pulled off towards the right and down into an area that included several parking spaces. It was Sunday, so there were still spaces available. He parked the Jag and grabbed his newly purchased lunch box from the trunk of the Jag. He and Rose then started walking up the roadway between gray granite buildings rising like the sides of a canyon on either side. It gave the appearance that they were entering a large fortress. They had gone about one hundred and fifty yards when Deiter took a trail behind a large monument to General Koskiusko, a Polish Revolutionary War hero. The trail led along the river, but at a somewhat higher elevation. When they had arrived at a bend in the trail, he stopped. The view of the Hudson River was beautiful through the gold, orange and red foliage. There was a large rock on the right side of the trail and Deiter motioned that they should sit on it. The romance of the moment and the scenery made Rose's heart pound and her breathing come more quickly. This was something that had not happened to her in many years and she became caught up in the moment. The years melted away and the two of them were young again and in love. A sudden cool breeze came off the river and she shivered. Deiter placed his coat over her shoulders and put his arm around her; she snuggled close to him. For awhile, there didn't seem a need for much conversation between the couple seated on the rock overlooking the river. Both of them were caught up in the moment and the splendor of the view, and there was just nothing to say. The noonday sun was warm on Rose's face. Deiter broke the spell by opening the container of lunch he had brought; with a corkscrew that had come in the case, he opened the wine and filled the two glasses. Next he produced an assortment of meats, the *pâté*, cheese, and bread to make sandwiches.

"I can't believe you, Jack, you really know how to throw a feast," she remarked.

They toasted their first glass of wine and then ravenously attacked the food. With the last glass of wine and their appetite satisfied, they resumed their previous positions with his arm around her.

"This is truly spectacular," Deiter thought to himself. He looked down at Rose and thought that she too seemed to share the moment.

After a while, Rose looked up at Deiter and asked, "Are you ready to tell me what you want of me?"

"Okay," he said, "I've put it off long enough; now's a good a time as any." He paused. "Rose, we've run across a set of documents that belonged, we guess, to the previous Soviet government. A man's been brutally tortured and murdered and we don't know why. Someone wanted desperately to find out what this man knew. A group is about to be formed that will include a number of people who are intimately familiar with the Russian language. The nuances of the writing and the coded portions of the papers need to be deciphered. That's where I really believe you can help. You know Russian like a native."

"Oh, there are better people than me, Jack, its been years since I've been into this sort of thing," she said. "Why me?"

"I think you may know the answer to that," replied Deiter. "There is, of course, the reason I told you earlier. I don't know why you came into my mind, but you have and I'm very glad. It's been a lot of years, but...there it is. I can't ignore it. One has to go on intuition."

Rose thought for a moment and decided that Jack was right...go with intuition. "I'm in," she said suddenly. "But you didn't need to transport me up to a romantic place like this and try to seduce me to get me to agree," she continued.

Deiter placed his hand on her cheek and turned her face toward him. "I think you know that's not the reason," he said. Suddenly, both embraced and their tongues sparred in a warm and passionate kiss. After a moment Deiter asked, "Do you need to get back tonight?"

"No, not really," she answered almost breathlessly. "Why?"

"I made reservations at the hotel," he replied.

Sitting up straighter, she turned to look up at him and replied, "You scoundrel, what do you take me for?" His eyes took on a hurt look, but she kissed him once again fervently to erase any misunderstanding that her remark might have caused. They sat there together in the sun, luxuriating in the moment.

The thought of them working together was intriguing to her. What would she tell Jack about Aldridge Mason...and their relationship? It would have to come out sometime. Mason would be furious. Why not just disappear? Would Mason try to find her? She knew the answer to that. He would move whatever mountains were necessary in the process. She knew that Mason considered her his private property, his investment. What could he do to Jack professionally? She knew about some of Mason's past vendettas and didn't want to subject Jack to one. Not that Jack couldn't take care of himself...she was sure of that. Perhaps turnabout was fair play after all, she thought. The idea of just disappearing sort of intrigued her. Could Jack fix it so that the local law enforcement wouldn't react to any inquiry from Mason? She guessed he could. People drop out of sight all the time. She would tell Jack the whole story; she would have to...but not now...tomorrow, maybe. This time was too precious and too romantic to be ruined. She had needed this and she felt warm in Jack's arms.

It was almost four o'clock when Deiter finally suggested that they should start back. They had left the rock after about an hour and had walked up the trail ending up at Trophy Point, the location of Battle Monument, a memorial to Union soldiers killed during the Civil War. They had walked, hand in hand for almost two hours and had sat on an old cannon overlooking the river. It took them less that fifteen minutes to walk back to the car and another five to drive to Thayer Hotel at the Main Gate.

"I've never stayed here," remarked Deiter. "The last time I was here, cadets and midshipmen were barred from going anywhere except the main floor."

"No girls in rooms?" she teased.

"No, no girls in rooms," he replied.

"Guess this is going to be a first then," she retorted.

He smiled down at her and said, "A very big first, in a long time." He kissed her again as he was getting out of the car. Going around to the rear of the Jag, he opened the boot (Deiter liked to use the British term for the car's trunk…after all, it was a British car) and took out his hanging bag, two large bags from Macy's, and the one small one from Victoria's Secret.

"I think I have everything we'll need here," he remarked as they headed for the hotel entrance.

"You really did plan this, didn't you?" she said a voice filled with amazement.

"Yup," he replied with a smug grin.

"I don't know whether slap you or kiss you."

"Want suggestions?" he asked as they made their way through the hotel's front door.

She looked up at him, smiled and grabbed his arm

Deiter checked in at the desk while Rose looked over the displays in the lobby. The decor was definitely gothic with heavily paneled walls of dark walnut. Flags were displayed overhead and there was no mistaking the military flavor of the place. The bellboy picked up the bag and Deiter came over to her.

"Ready?" he asked. They crossed the lobby towards the elevators following the bellhop. The elevator stopped at the third floor and he led them down a dark scarlet carpeted hallway with the same wood paneling as the lobby to Room 318. After showing them the attributes of the room sufficiently to deserve a tip, the bellhop turned to Deiter and asked if there would be anything else. Deiter said, "No, thank you." The bellhop accepted the folded bills that Deiter held out to him, left the room and closed the door behind him. It wasn't until then that the awkwardness of their situation hit them both at the same time. Deiter thought to himself, oh well, when in doubt, punt. He took Rose in his arms and she returned his passionate kiss with equal ardor. Supper would have to wait awhile...first things first.

CHAPTER FIVE

▼

ALDRIDGE MASON

The Law Offices of Symond, Hennessee and Smith
Upper Saddle River, New Jersey
Sunday, October 26th, 1997

Aldridge Mason sat behind his sumptuously appointed walnut desk in his office at the law firm of Symond, Hennessee and Smith. He was only an associate of the firm, but exhibited more power than most of the partners, not because he was more important, but because the partners were basically very gentle men. Aldridge, on the other hand, was ambitious and arrogant, but he was good and he knew it. He had gone through a stack of paper in his hold-box to determine whether there was anything that he might have overlooked during the week. Sunday mornings were a good time to catch up on such things. He then turned to his in-box. On top of the pile was a translation of a contract with a Russian firm.

Rose had apparently finished it up the day before. He picked it up and scanned it; he didn't know any Russian so couldn't tell if it was right or not. He did know that there were delicate parts to it that must be just right…in Russian, to protect the company. He had to make sure that Rose had translated those correctly.

Mason picked up the telephone and selected "6" on the console, Rose's home number. The line rang four times and an answering machine responded. After the introduction and the tone, Mason left a message, "Rose, I'm going through the translation of the contract and have some questions. Let's get together at your place later on this afternoon…say about four. We can spend the evening discussing it over dinner. If you really want to go out, I suppose it'd be all right and then we can continue later back at your place." He hung up the phone and smiled to himself. Life was good for Aldridge Mason. After his rather messy divorce, he had considerable freedom. That included Rose. He was pleased that she had seen fit to understand what he could do for her. It did his ego good to be seen with her. He may even have loved her, but the important part of it was that she made him feel good. She could be very difficult at times and he had to discipline her when that happened. Eventually, she would come around, though and he would be generous to her once more.

Aldridge R. Mason was a successful lawyer. He was of average height and somewhat overweight. Physical conditioning was not a big thing with him. If he had to play golf with someone who could benefit him, he would and pretend as though he was very competent at the sport, but just off his game. His normal dress was a wrinkled blue blazer with khaki pants...even in the winter. Normally, he wore a white shirt with a red striped tie. One could say quite honestly that he dressed like an unmade bed. Although quite wealthy, he bought cheap clothes from discount dealers. He had a puffy white face...his jowled cheeks could sometimes get quite red; he had thin lips that sometimes twisted into a sardonic smile; his hair although dark, was thoroughly laced with white and he wore it relatively long to best show off its curly waves. He had slate blue eyes that usually showed either an accusatory or disdaining look. His waist was larger than his chest reflecting that lack of concern for the physical appearance of his body. At sixty, he had managed to control the world he lived in and was contentedly assured with his life. He was second generation Irish; his father having come to this country in the early thirties and worked hard to support his new wife Mary. He passed on to his only child, Aldridge, the belief that it didn't matter who needed to be pushed out of the way to get what was due them. He hated his father for his arrogance, but didn't realize that his own arrogance was even worse. After graduating from law school at Seaton Hall in 1964, Aldridge never again contacted his parents; he was ashamed of them for their low status in life. Although brilliant as a lawyer, Aldridge Mason became a rather pathetic man obsessed with his own insecurities, desperate, weak and vindictive to the extreme.

He stopped reading and set down the papers in his hand. He looked at his watch. It was nine–thirty on Sunday morning. Where was Rose? She should have been home. He knew she had worked late on either Friday or Saturday night and might have been sleeping in. Curious, he thought; perhaps she was still asleep or had gone to church this morning. Yes, that had to have been it; he dismissed it from his mind for the time being.

At four–fifteen, Mason turned his El Dorado left into the cul de sac of Princeton Court and pulled up in front of number 136. He smiled to see Rose's car parked in the garage; he climbed out of his car and strolled up to the door. On trying the doorknob, he found it locked. Grunting, he pulled out his key and unlocked the door and went inside. He called out, but the house was empty. This was strange, he thought. It's not like Rose to be gone at a time when he was suppose to be there. He walked over to the answering machine and punched the message button. His message to her started to play. Rose hadn't been there to receive it. He became more suspicious and concerned. He went into the casual room and reaching behind the bar, brought out a bottle of Scotch and pored himself a drink. He'd wait for her. On a hunch, he checked the closet, but her overnight case and suitcase were still there in the corner. At ten–thirty he went to bed; she must have been out with girl friends and not realizing the hour and decided to sleep over.

Mason awoke at six o'clock and immediately began calling for Rose throughout the house. He was still alone. It was Monday morning and Rose hadn't come home. He waited until seven o'clock before he showered, shaved and then stormed out of the house, slamming the door behind him. He was furious at Rose, how dare she treat him this way. He drove to his office; he had to do some thinking and he did it best there.

When he arrived at the office, he first checked Rose's desk to find it neat and unoccupied. Periodically throughout the day he would walk out to check the desk again. Still Rose didn't show up. He dialed her home number and received the same answering service message. Mason asked the senior secretary if Rose had called in. He was told no, she hadn't. The rest of the day was spent in Superior Court with a client.

At six that evening, Mason again dialed Rose's number. Again, it rang four times and the answering machine responded. He slammed the receiver down. Where was she? As he sat leaning back in his chair, a realization came to him. She must have been out with someone. Not only that, she must have spent the night with him. He could feel the blood rise in his neck and head. This was unacceptable. Who did she think she was? She belonged to him...he added quietly to himself, bought and paid for. He could give her anything she wanted...hadn't he already? He would wait until tomorrow when she came to work. Yes, that's how to deal with it. He would call her in and explain the "facts of life" to her. He smiled to himself; things like this...although not as serious, had happened before...when he had confronted her, she had begged him to forgive her. That would be satisfying, yes, satisfying indeed. And then afterwards...afterwards, he would spend the night with her and she would make it up to him. Mason sighed...yes, that's what he'd do. He felt better now.

Thayer Hotel
West Point, New York
Monday, October 27th, 1997

The sun streamed through the window of the hotel room and onto the large double bed. The two figures who lay there under the covers were quietly sleeping. Jack Deiter was the first to move and without opening his eyes, he stretched first his arms and then his legs as a cat would do. Then he quickly remembered where he was, opened his eyes and looked over at his companion. Her head was snuggled into the pillow and her face looked as though she was totally at peace with the world. There was the hint of a smile on her lips. Deiter stared at her and sighed. It was a bit more audible then he had intended and she stirred. Her eyes opened and the smile grew wider. "Hello Jack Deiter," she whispered.

Her smile was infectious and he returned it with, "Good morning, Rose McGuire; did you know that you are the prettiest girl in this county?"

She giggled and said, "Small county."

Deiter reached out for her and brought her in close to him. He could feel her bare legs and breasts against his skin. Her back was cool to the touch. They kissed gently and he slid his knee between her legs. She reached up and placed her hand on his cheek and slid it to the back of his neck, all the while remaining in the kiss, their tongues seeking each other once more. He smiled while kissing her as he recalled that the teddy he had bought for her the day before had been discarded early in the evening and that the two of them had made love several times, ending up sleeping in the nude. So much for buying night clothes when you're going to shack up. They made love quietly and slowly, enjoying every moment of each other, not being frantic in their lovemaking. The act was more of a mutual giving and sharing with the purpose of providing pleasure rather than taking pleasure.

Rose finally pushed herself away and said, "We...I have a problem. I should be at work in an hour."

"You...we don't have a problem, because you won't need to go to work there anymore," he replied. "Send a letter with your notice later today and pack up; I'll drive you to Washington...you can stay with me...unless you want to find a place of your own."

"Jack, I have to be honest with you and I hope you won't be angry with me," she said almost pleadingly.

Deiter went cool for a moment, her words striking a cord of fear somewhere deep within him. "What is it, Rose?"

Rose sighed. "I suppose I should say 'There's someone else,' but that's not quite it except that it's partly the truth. Let me start from the beginning."

Rose told Deiter everything about her relationship with Aldridge Mason; how it begun, how it progressed and what she had done. She told him about the house, Rob's education, the demands that Aldridge made on her, her feelings of hopelessness...everything. When she had finished, she buried her head in his shoulder and began to sob quietly. "I never thought I could find love again; I didn't have it with Bill, and certainly not with Aldridge...I had felt betrayed by life and alone. If you hadn't come along, I don't know what I would have done."

He took her face in both his hands and kissed her. "But I did come along," he said, pausing for a moment.

He then continued, "It was impossible for me not to."
He told her of the times when the memory of her had
suddenly occurred in the last few days and how it
seemed to follow an inevitable plan. They were destined
to be together again. It was what should have happened
in the first place...it just took longer to happen.

After showering and dressing, they went down to the
hotel dining room. Over breakfast, they discussed in
more detail what they would do. It was not wise, Deiter
had decided, for Rose to return to her job at the law
firm; too much of a chance of running into Mason.
Rose had described Mason's possessiveness to Deiter earlier. They instead would both go to her house and collect whatever clothes and other belongings that she
would need for the next few months while they would
be working on the case. She'd call Rob and tell him not
to contact Mason and if he were called, would say that
he didn't know where she was. That would be the
truth...she would contact him without letting him
know where she was. After the case was finished, they
would decide what to do next.

The drive to Upper Saddle River and then to
Washington and Old Town Alexandria was as pleasant
as Deiter could ever remember. For awhile, they kept up
a continual conversation of places and people they had
known, of times of dangers and times of fun. They
talked of global warming, of Washington politics, and of
educating children. Most of the subjects, they agreed
on. Rose felt as though she were in a dreamland. She
couldn't remember when she had been so happy. During
parts of the trip, they would just listen to music and
watch the scenery. The gold and red foliage seemed to

decorate their own feelings and mood. When they arrived at Deiter's house on Prince Street, she was not only impressed by the elegant comfort of the house, but was deeply moved by the openness of her partner to share it with her and to make her feel that it was her home as well. She had known about Sally and the pain it must have caused Jack when she was taken away from him. She didn't feel that whatever ghost of Sally remained in the house was antagonistic to her, if anything it seemed friendly.

That night while both of them lay close to each other in Deiter's bed, Rose reflected on what was happening in her life. She guessed, anyway, that perhaps there was a God who cared for them. How else would one ever explain what had happened these last few days. How could something so vile and sad as this murder result in something so wonderful and good for her? She went to sleep with that thought.

The Law Offices of Symond, Hennessee and Smith
Upper Saddle River, New Jersey
Tuesday, October 28th

Aldridge Mason arrived at the office earlier than usual this morning. He wanted to be relaxed and unhurried when Rose arrived. Although she missed yesterday at work and had not called in, he was sure she would be there today and he didn't want to seem too concerned. Throughout the night he had planned every word he would say to her and how he would play each of her reactions. This had happened several times before, and although she had not been out of his control for this long, he didn't see why today should end up any differently. He was pleased with himself. He knew that the times when Rose was contrite were some of the best times for him in their relationship. He busied himself editing the various briefs that he had written and preparing himself for the cases that he would present later in the week.

At eight forty–five, Mason put down the portfolio he was reading, looked at the clock on his desk, and stood up. He opened the door to his office and looked down the hallway towards Rose's desk. The desk was empty. He wandered through the office complex trying to look nonchalant. Rose was nowhere to be seen. He stopped by the desk of the firm's senior secretary and casually asked, " Did Rose call in?"

"Why no," she replied, "I haven't seen her this morning."

Mason humpfed and returned to his office. As he sat there, he slowly started to seethe. He had lost control and was furious. By noontime, he had worked himself into a virtual fever. He grabbed his coat and walked out of his office telling the senior secretary that he didn't feel good and would be gone the rest of the day.

Climbing into his El Dorado, he drove to 136 Princeton Court. He pulled up before the house and parked. He sat there for a few moments studying the house; Rose's car was parked in the garage as it had been earlier. Nothing seemed to have changed. He walked up to the door, unlocked it and walked in. He began searching the house, room by room. In the bedroom, he noticed that most of Rose's clothes were missing includ-ing all of her lingerie. He looked through the desk in Rose's office and found the checkbook was missing as well as certain pictures and other papers. He looked in the metal file box and discovered that her passport was also missing. These missing items were not the result of thievery; Rose had intentionally taken them and had left without telling him. His anger rose and a burning sensation moved up the back of his neck and manifested itself in the narrowing of his steel blue eyes. He was being betrayed and he didn't like it. He sat back in the overstuffed leather chair next to Rose's desk and closed his eyes, breathing deeply and slowly. When he opened his eyes, he knew what he had to do. He had friends in the Upper Saddle River Police Department, the State Police and the Federal Bureau of Investigation. He would find out where Rose had gone and with whom. It really shouldn't be hard to do. Feeling more relaxed, he locked up the house and drove back to the office.

Upon settling down at his desk, Mason's first call was to Mort Kinder, a private investigator whom he had previously hired on several occasions. Once, he had his exwife followed to see whether there was some way he could counteract her claims that he was the only unfaithful partner. That didn't work out, but the man had done a through job. He did have Rose followed on several occasions when he suspected that she had found a new boy friend. There would be no need for him to pass on much additional information about Rose to Kinder; he had most of the background already. Mason placed the call and gave the PI what he had learned and instructed him to get on the trail. The next call was to a Police Lieutenant from the local police department. He had defended him in a rather dirty bribery case even though Mason didn't usually take trial cases. He was successful in getting the man off and of course earned the guilty man's undying gratitude. The next call he made was to a law school classmate now working in the State Justice Department with the State Police. His last call was to an FBI agent he had worked with in uncovering a scam involving international business price fixing. When he had finished, he leaned back in his chair and smiled. He was back in control and all he had to do now was to be patient and the solution would come to him. He picked up a brief from his basket and went back to work.

CHAPTER SIX

▼

"CHARLIE" WAGGNER

Washington, DC
Monday, October 27th 1997

It was only a fifteen-minute walk the back way from her apartment to her office in Chevy Chase, Maryland, and Charlie could have easily walked it if she'd wanted to. Today, though, she was in no particular hurry and decided to take the long way around and drive instead; she thought she might do some shopping after the workday was over...besides, she loved to drive her car. Charlotte Ann Waggner preferred to be called "Charlie"; she never was a "Charlotte," that's too feminine for her. Although there is nothing necessarily to denote masculinity about her, Charlie's interest in physical exercise always provided her with a tomboy appearance and outlook at life. From rock climbing to skydiving, flying to gymnastics, she was always a "Charlie."

Charlie's condominium, Bedford Towers, rose 14 stories over her right shoulder as she pressed down the accelerator causing her brown 1976 Morgan Plus 4 to roar into life. It jumped ahead and forced her back into the rich brown leather seat as she snaked down the tree-lined road, which led to the Washington beltway. The weather was pleasant, especially for the last week in October, and the trees were just coming into full color; the reds and yellows dominating the landscape. The coolness of the morning air felt brisk and refreshing in her face; her barely shoulder length blond hair blew out behind her as the Morgan weaved through traffic. She realized that it wouldn't be long now before the top would have to go up on the Morgan and with it the freedom she felt even now as she wound her way through traffic and finally raced down the entrance ramp and out onto the beltway and into the early morning traffic.

She turned off at the third exit from the beltway and took the first right turn. The "tank," as it was called by some of the old-time residents where Charlie worked, was at the end of a long divided road through a corporate park with ponds and trees gracing the entrance road. On the surface, it looked like any other business with manicured lawns and a parking lot spanning the length of the four-story building. The sign read "Jonathan Banks, Inc.," and gave the impression to those who didn't know any better, that it was some sort of financial investment firm. Jonathan Banks had started the firm as a think tank back shortly after the Korean War and contracted primarily to the Federal Government. It specialized in Russian and Eastern European political, financial and military affairs and advised their clients as to appropriate strategies. The long list of clients included the National Security Agency, the Federal Bureau of Investigation, the Central Intelligence Agency, the United States Department of State and the United States Army. They also did some research work for private manufacturing firms, but without the government, there would be little other interest in what the firm produced. Charlie had been fortunate in several ways to land a position with JBI. It helped, of course, that her father, John Waggner, worked on the staff of the Senate Intelligence Committee and knew of the firm's existence in the first place. Neither should it come as a surprise that the daughter of one of Jonathan Bank's closest friends would apply for a job with the firm. He had known Charlie ever since she was born and had followed her as she grew up, including her successes in academia. Charlie's easy acceptance of foreign languages impressed the firm's CEO and filled a need in his organization. When it came time for Charlie to find a job, Banks was prepared to offer her an opportunity she couldn't refuse. Charlie was everything a man could want for in a daughter, he supposed. Oh, it was true that Banks had never married and as far as he knew he had no children, much less a talented daughter like Charlie, but he was continually amazed and delighted with how his friend's daughter had developed into such an exceptional young woman.

Charlie parked the Morgan next to the entrance to the firm's building, zippered up the tonneau cover on the car and headed for the front door. As a sign of independence typical of her, she shook her nearly, shoulder-length blond hair quickly to both sides and squared her shoulders as she left the Morgan and headed up the sidewalk. Charlie Waggner was confident, clear-eyed, and absolutely in charge of her life; in short, she was totally competent. At 5 foot 7 inches and 125 pounds, she was, at the grand old age of 35 years, firm, athletic, strong, yet not muscular, at the prime of her life, a challenge to the world, brilliant, and she knew it. Her routine at the gym kept her in top shape, which was a perfect 36–26–36. A female with masculine interests, she could be one of the guys and most alluring at the same time. She kept her blond hair cut short; it fit her lifestyle better. Her high cheekbones and a pretty slender nose that was almost on the verge of being turned up were inherited from her mother. Her straight and sensitive lips, which seemed to always contain the hint of a smile or smirk as though she was hiding some seductive secret and about to let it out in delight, was a copy of her father's.

As the only child, Charlie was both doted upon and challenged by her parents. She had attended private schools while growing up; was a Girl Scout, which she enjoyed, and played soccer throughout her secondary school days. At George Washington University, she became a gymnast and placed first in overall competition during her junior year, but had to drop out after breaking her left arm in an unfortunate fall during practice the first part of her senior year. In compensation, her father taught her to fly and she earned her private pilot's license before graduation. Her love for her father made it easy to share his interest in sports and the excitement of life.

She wanted to carry on in her parents' tradition by attending GWU; she lived at home throughout the years of her college life. The influence of her parents inspired her to want the Foreign Service. She majored in Political Science while minoring in Modern Languages; and graduated in 1984. She went on for a Master's Degree in Political Science, completing it in 1986. She speaks Russian, Greek and German fluently and is conversant in most Slavic dialects. Languages always seemed to come easily to Charlie. Perhaps it was because her mother frequently spoke in the languages she knew and loved; Charlie simply mimicked her.

As Charlie swung her weight against the revolving door leading into the lobby of the firm's office building, she glanced back at the brown Morgan she had just parked in front of the building. Just seeing it caused a self-satisfied smile to spread over her face and caused her eyes to sparkle. The car was the love of her life. It was a graduation present from her father. He had developed a fascination for the Morgan ever since he had gone to Europe with a Senatorial fact-finding mission in Germany in late 1978. Her mother had filled her in on most of the details of the incident not long before she died. According to the story, he had met a beautiful blond woman driving a brown Morgan and the fascination had remained with him since then. There had been a whirlwind romance, which ended almost as soon as it had begun. John had been honest with his wife about the affair and it was forgiven, if not totally forgotten. At one other time, while on another fact-finding trip to England, he had visited the Morgan factory in Malvern Link, Worchestershire. Here the Morgan sports cars are still built by hand as they always had been. Later, he had brought Charlie there on Spring break just before she graduated and they had picked out the car together. By pure coincidence, the car had been brought back to the factory for reconditioning by the original owner, a Baroness Maria Sergeievna von Klauss. She remembered that her father asked no questions about the owner as though he already knew who she was, but instead spent his time examined the condition of the car. He was delighted to learn that the car was indeed for sale by the owner and after reconditioning, would be as good as new and much less expensive than a new one. Both of them fell in love with it, her father for the fantasy it held for him and she for the love of her father.

Charlie sailed through the lobby of the firm and clattered up the stairway to the second floor of the JBI office building. She passed the firm's conference room and stopped at the doorway only long enough to wave to two of her fellow employees who were filling their coffee mugs in preparation of the morning's work. "Hi, all," she said and disappeared two doors down the hallway into her office. Charlie swung her light jacket over a peg on the coat rack, hit the computer's on switch and sank into her chair behind a glass topped oval desk. Her computer and printer began to flash lights and groan into life. She thumbed through the "in" box on her desk to see if anything would pop out at her to grab her immediate attention. Nothing was there of importance. By this time the computer had warmed up and completed it's boot. She "clicked" to go on-line and using her password was given authority to enter. Clicking through the various selections, she finally came to the choice she wanted and proceeded to check her e-mail. Only one message came up.

The message began with a red lettered classification and condensed lettering reserved for classified documents. It read:

C-O-N-F-I-D-E-N-T-I-A-L

Subj: Special Assignment
Date: 97–10–26 23:42:37 EST
From: J. Banks
To: C. Waggner
Charlie;

Received a call late tonight from a friend of mine in the National Security Agency. An incident happened in NYC several days ago that may relate to something we have been researching for NSA. The FBI is doing the investigation of the incident in connection with the NYPD.

We will be coordinating work on this situation and setting up a task force to work with all participating agencies. I want you to join the task force. There will be reps from NSA, FBI, and possibly CIA. Your knowledge of Russian will be of great value. I will inform your father to assure that the Senate Intelligence Committee is up to speed. Expect to have our first meeting this week…will let you know time so you can set up. JB

C-O-N-F-I-D-E-N-T-I-A-L

"That's interesting," Charlie thought to herself. If she was going to be on a special task force, why couldn't it be in Paris or Bermuda…just her luck. She printed out the e-mail and picked up a stack of documents to be translated. Charlie Waggner started another workday.

▼

CHAPTER SEVEN

ANDREI MIKAILOVITCH KILYAIKIN

Kharkov State Institute of Measures and Measuring
Instruments (KhGIMIP)
Division of Internal Security, Technology Applications
Grozny, The Chechen Republic of Ichkeria
Thursday, March 7th 1996

The office of the Chief Scientist/Physiologist of Technology Applications was sterile and devoid of any personal possessions. Besides the bed in an alcove behind the curtain, a wooden desk and a barrel-backed wooden office chair, there were no other real pieces of furniture in the room. On the desk was an ancient black telephone of obvious Russian origin and a green shaded banker's desk lamp. Against the left wall, a wooden bookcase stood suffering from a bad case of overstuffing;

an antiquated steel safe with a large dial on the front squatted next to it. A wooden coat rack stood at the right of the only door to the sparsely furnished office. An iron stove against the far wall was sizzling in a feeble attempt to stem the cold, which seeped through the window frames; a half-empty bucket of coal had been placed next to stove. The office had two windows behind the desk that looked out onto a cobblestone street leading into the center of the city. Square gray buildings lined both sides of the street; some of them were now empty…the people had gone further south to escape the threat of Russian artillery bombardment. Few cars now traveled this stretch of road. The four story stucco building that housed the Kharkov Institute in Grozny was built in the late 1940s, but the black soot pollution from the factories and cooking hearths of the Chechen population of the city gave it an appearance of age far in excess of its fifty years. For months now, there had been a continuous tension in the air even though at times statements from the Russian Government and President Boris Yeltsin seemed almost conciliatory towards the Chechen "rebels." In the distance the sound of artillery fire could be heard periodically followed by explosions somewhere in the city. Most people didn't dare venture out for fear of being shot by Russian snipers or killed by the harassing artillery.

The purpose and operation of the Technology Applications Group, like many bureaucratic organizations created in the Soviet Union, was not what it appeared to be on the surface. Working under the Division of Internal Security, (an arm of the KGB) the group was afforded protection from any interference by the Institute and worked independently. It was an excellent cover for the operation officially known in Moscow as "Rasputin." Aside from the official office in the Kharkov State Institute building consisting of three clerks and the Chief Scientist, the group also used a large house on Beslan Place at the edge of the city. The house officially was considered a "halfway" house where agents spent at least six weeks between their training and their departure for the United States and Great Britain. There, they were kept apart from any contact with Soviet citizens, and spoke only English. Their US passports were prepared, personal history of their cover personality was memorized, and the transformation from Soviet to American or Englishman was completed. It was also the location where "Rasputin" was initiated by the office of Technology Applications.

On this late afternoon, the lone inhabitant of the office sat at the wooden desk pouring over a stack of papers, intent on comparing a list of numbers on several lists to those on a master list. The light from the desk lamp shone through the shade and gave a strange green tinge to the man's face making his studious concentration almost comical. His hair was long for a Russian, and was white and thick. At the back of his crown it had started to thin and some scalp showed through; his eyebrows were thick and still retained some of their original black color. He would be celebrating his 68th birthday in a month. Not that he would really celebrate anything. That wasn't like Dr. Kilyaikin. A tweed jacket showed under his white lab coat, a plaid shirt with blue tie and unpressed brown nondescript pants completed his ensemble. The man was of medium build with a somewhat thicker midsection; his face was somewhat puffy and might have been quite pale except for the green tinge now caused by the lamp.

Andrei Mikailovitch Kilyaikin thought of himself as a dedicated Communist and loyal Soviet citizen...even though the CCCP no longer existed...officially. Several highly-placed people in the Government of the Soviet Union had shown their appreciation for his contribution to the country by placing him in the responsible and important position he now occupied. Although there had been little or no direct communications with Moscow since the breakup of the Soviet Union, he was still loyal to his work for that Country and of course the Communist Party. The program had been his idea and creation, and he alone was now responsible for its continued oversight and continued existence. Finally, Andrei leaned back in his chair. He removed his eyeglasses, placed them on the desk and brought his hands to his face as though to relieve the tension in his eyes by rubbing them. He sighed and looked over his shoulder through the dirty window at the darkening street. He could see the Avenue of Lenin a block away; the snow had been cleared and he was relieved that it would be easier to walk to his apartment this night. He was almost through, but he'd have to wait until the staff went home to use the typewriter to copy over the lists. He wanted to be sure that no trace of the copy could be determined. This project was his and it would die with him if the Soviet Union were not restored. In the meantime, he might still be able to serve the party in another way. Andrei had time to think now and he reflected on what had happened.

For the first time in months, Andrei thought of his
father. Although he was of Russian heritage, Andrei had
grown up in Grozny. His father, Mikhail Sergeiovich
Kilyaikin was born in 1907 and grew up during the First
World War and the beginning of the glorious revolutionary years from 1917 to 1921. In 1924, Mikhail as a
very young man joined a Cossack regiment of the Red
Army fighting the Naqshbandi in Chechnya. During
that first winter, the Red Army disarmed the Chechen
population and liquidated the "bandit's nests" of
Naqshbandi guerrilla fighters in the high mountains and
the underground Qadiri. The uprisings still occurred
from time to time during the years that followed. In
1927, Mikhail married Valerie Kochenko who had
moved to Grozny from her home in Rostov near the Sea
of Azov, a lake that empties into the Black Sea. They had
met while he was still in the Red Army and had joined
him when he was ordered to occupy a position in
Grozny. Mikhail had been given a house there by the
Soviet Government as part of the Russification process.
Andrei, their only child, was born in April of 1928. He
recalled that his father was tyrannical and abusive; his
mother tearful and afraid. Andrei had been served with
demands that he must do well in school or be
beaten...his father held a fierce loyalty to the Red Army
and the Soviet Union. He was also instilled by his father
with a hatred for the ethnic Chechens and the
Moslems...not that he shared any love for Christians
either, he preferred the Communist doctrine of atheism
when it came to religion.

Andrei left home as soon as he was able to earn an
appointment to the Lenin University of Science in

Volgograd from the Science Educational Union of the
Russian Republic of Chechnya. He remained single and
rarely dated or associated socially with women. The only
exception was his much younger cousin, Maria
Sergeiovna Kochenko who as a young girl was attracted
to him and the feeling was reciprocated. Andrei graduated from Lenin University of Science in 1955 with a
Bachelors Degree in Electronic Communications and a
Doctorate in Bioelectronics. He was considered brilliant
by his professors and upon graduation was given a position at the University. After four years, he was invited to
accept a position at the Academy of Sciences in Moscow.
At that time, Maria, then sixteen years old, left her
home in Nadterechnaya and joined Andrei in Moscow.
Andrei's mother was a sister of Anna Kochenko, Maria's
mother. Sergei Kochenko, her father, had been an army
comrade of Andrei's father and also participated in the
Russification process carried out by the Central Soviet
Government. The time with Maria in Moscow had been
a happy memory for Andrei; as happy as he could ever
remember. He had achieved greatness, or so he thought,
early in life and was living with a beautiful and exciting
girl. Those times could not have been better for Andrei.

Andrei, just for a moment, reflected on those days and
compared them to the conditions in which he now lived;
he frowned. His two-room apartment was on the fourth
floor of a drab-gray, stucco building on Brovneff Street in
Grozny. It was Spartan to a fault. He only returned there
to sleep, but frequently he simply stayed at the institute.
He preferred the bed in his office; it was close to his work,
and he didn't need to walk in the city to his apartment in
the cold...or lately during the bombardment. The bus

system was notoriously bad in Grozny and recently it had become nonexistent. He took all of his meals at the Institute...sometimes in the cafeteria, but because of his position, he could get them delivered to his office, which he preferred. He rarely, if ever, went to a restaurant...only when he was invited to go to one by a very infrequent visitor from Moscow; more recently, none had arrived. His creation...the project...was his life and his superiors were delighted with his progress. Andrei became obsessed with his work and never took advantage of the benefits offered to him by the thankful Soviet bureaucracy...vacations on the Black Sea Coast, a kiosk in the mountains...his work was sufficient; it was his creation and his gift to the entire Communist cause.

Kilyaikin had been devastated by the downfall of the Soviet Union and Communism. His ties to the new Russian Government were not strong...the new rulers were a weak substitute for the Communists. The idea of unsupervised and uncontrolled elections, embracing a capitalist economy, or allowing a decentralized leadership were abhorrent to him. He continued his work, but no new "clients" were made available to him. He monitored the location of the agents already in place in the United States and Britain, but no missions were conducted. He feared that his continued presence may ultimately become an embarrassment to the new Russian leadership in view of their Western leanings. He feared that he might even be terminated...either from his job or permanently to silence him. As the time passed, he had became increasingly apprehensive.

He had been in a quandary until THEY came to him, those despicable Cheshens whom Yeltsin had called "mad dogs." These were of the worst sort; they were the criminals often called the "Russian Mafia." They had contacted him about his ties to the former Soviet government. Someone from Moscow (he suspected an ex-member of the KGB) had sold them information about a large cache of money in US banks...indicating that Kilyaikin might know how to get access to it. They had told him that they would provide him with money and all the equipment he would need, as well as forged passports and other identification. They wanted him to locate the accounts of the deep agents and transfer the assets to a separate account that could be accessed by the Mafia. In turn, he could retain 10% of the total amount he "liberated" from the American banks. He was shocked by two things, first that anyone else knew of his operation...knew about "Rasputin." He, of course, wasn't sure how much they really knew, but most repugnantly, he had been asked to commit treason. Later though, he began to see certain advantages that might result from using the knowledge he possessed...knowledge that he had developed, for another purpose. Perhaps this wouldn't be treason; the old ways, the old government no longer existed. Suddenly, he saw a very different life for himself. The thought of enormous wealth of course did have its appeal...and the years of his devotion to a now lost cause, his life's work now seemed somehow wasted. Before there was always the devotion of a thankful and all powerful government...now that government might wish to destroy him, unless he acted quickly. The fools who were sent to the United States and Britain...after he performed his work...were of no real importance to him and certainly not to a nonexistent Soviet Union that he had served so well. They may yet be made to serve his ends, however, and should Communism return, he would be declared a hero for saving the fortune that languished in the United States banks. He may even use the money to encourage the return of his country to its rightful status; that made it almost a patriotic thing to do...yes, he decided, he'd do it. But, on no account would he share it with those filthy, greedy criminals...he would keep it all for the future of the cause. The thought intrigued him. How much was $180 million worth now, twenty, thirty years later? Quick calculations using an average amount deposited at reasonable interest made it almost...$800 million...that amount was beyond his capacity to even imagine...but it was possible. He remembered how the Nazis has stashed away millions before the end of World War II and were using it to attempt reestablish their old empire...why not the Communist party and the Soviet Union. Of course afterwards he would have to get rid of the fools that might betray the cause before they could report him and ruin his plan. He knew he'd have to kill most of them after he found out their part of the code; to let them live would be to invite disaster. No one knew how easy it would be for him, no one. He may well be the last of the great Heroes of the Soviet Union. The thought pleased him. Ah, yes, his creation, "Rasputin." Andrei Kilyaikin smiled to himself.

The noise of the typewriter in the outer office had ceased for almost five minutes and there had been no other noises since he had heard the outer door close. Andrei was alone. He slowly raised himself from his chair, grabbed his cane and limped to the office door. He opened it and looked out; the outer office was empty, as he had expected. He went to the outer door and assured himself that the lock was secure. Returning to his office, he picked up the six pieces of paper he had been studying and placed the remainder in the safe against the wall. He then went into the outer office and placing a clean sheet of paper in the typewriter. Andrei began to painstakingly copy the corrected original; it had to be perfect. It would include the numbers of only those who might be suspected of defection, not the solid agents. He had already microfilmed the entire list...in case he needed backup.

That night Andrei Kilyaikin didn't stay in his office, but went back to his apartment to sleep. He needed to rest and prepare himself for what was going to happen. From the Institute, he followed the Avenue of Lenin to where it crossed the Sunzha River. He passed the marketplace, but no one was selling and the booths were tightly shut. Turning onto Chicherina Street, he walked a block to his apartment building. He entered the doorway and slowly made his way up the stairway to the fourth floor. It was almost midnight when he finally climbed into bed. In the morning he would make the contact once more with those people...how he despised them.

That night his dreams were of Maria...they were back in Moscow again; she was so lovely.

Grozny, The Chechen Republic of Ichkeria
March 8th 1996

Andrei woke that morning to the sound of aircraft flying low over the city. He quickly threw some water on his face and hacked at the stubble of his beard until it was satisfactory enough to pass in public. Nobody worried too much about personal appearances these days. He was fortunate enough to be living in the one part of town that still had a semblance of running water. It was cold, but water, never the less. He ran a comb through his hair and dressed. He would meet his contact at eight–thirty at a boat house along the West bank of the Sunzha River, just North of where it flowed under the Gudermes–Beslan railroad bridge. There would be Russian roadblocks somewhere along the way; exactly where, it wasn't possible to predict. His status, he was sure, could get him through the Russians, but he was not so sure about the rebel Cheshens. Andrei pulled on his long coat, placed his dark brown fur hat on his head and walked awkwardly down the dreary stairway to the street below; his leg hurt him more in the cold. He caught his breath as he stepped into the early cold of Grozny's late winter morning. There was still some snow on the ground; the wind caught the side of his face and he was glad for the fur hat that protected his head; Andrei pulled his coat closer around him.

It was not too far to the railroad bridge over the Sunzha River. Andrei walked through the market where some vendors were just setting up their shops. He noted that he should stop on the way back to pick up something for dinner. He turned left and followed the street until he came upon Boevaya Street and turned left following it to the river. The boathouse was off to the left and he walked to it slowly leaning on his cane. He had seen no Russian patrols or roadblocks as yet today. The boathouse was made of plank lumber and its walls were gray from the natural aging of the wood and the ash that was always present in the air. A door was at the rear of the house, and Andrei tried the door handle; it was open. He went inside. Despite the brightness outside the building, in contrast, the interior was dark; soot covering the windows allowing very little light to come inside. He could see where two boats were tied up and could just make out some oars and rigging hung on the walls, but little else. He stepped in and shut the door behind him. The slow slopping of waves on the boats was the only sound to break the heavy silence. He must have waited for about five minutes before a voice came from the end of the building saying, "Privet, tovariw. Kto tam?" (*Hello, comrade. Who is there?*) Is your name Andrei?"

"Yes," he replied.

"You have made a decision?" the voice asked.

"Yes, I will agree to what you have asked," he said.

"Good, we will do well working together."

"How do we proceed?" Andrei asked.

"Provide us with a list of the equipment you will need and we will make sure it is delivered to you when you get there. We will arrange for papers and American dollars as well."

"How soon do you need the list?"

"It must be within the week, the situation here in Grozny is too unstable."

"I will have it for you tomorrow."

"Good, I will be here at the same time; Do svi-daniq, tovari]!" (*Goodbye, Comrade!*)

Andrei left the boathouse and started to retraced his steps to his apartment on Chicherina Street when he stopped. He knew that he could have his contact arrange for the transmitting equipment to be "stolen" from the house on Beslan Place, but that might only bring suspicion on himself. No, it was better for them to buy new equipment, perhaps in the United States and have it ready for him when he arrived. It would then be of the latest design and more dependable than that he now had. Although it was a Saturday and he normally did not go into the office, he had done so on enough occasions not to raise suspicion. Besides, no one would be there. He turned and started walking along the railroad bridge towards the Avenue of Lenin. In just over twenty minutes, he arrived at his office.

Andrei spun the dial on the ancient safe in his office and retrieved the inventory list of equipment for which he was responsible. Sitting at his desk, he slowly moved his finger down the list. He stopped at each item that was a part of the transmitting and receiving station located in the attic of the house on Breslan Place. He copied each description on a separate piece of paper. On the typewriter in the outer office, Andrei copied the specifications for each item of equipment he might need. When he had finished, he placed the original document back into his safe and left the office. As he walked through the snow, he heard artillery again firing from across the hills to the North. He had to make his preparations quickly and leave Grozny, it was no longer safe here, either from the Russian Army or the local rebel Cheshens.

It was now late in the afternoon and suddenly he felt hungry. For the first time in months, he stopped at the local tavern. Inside, it was warm and the light was low; a musician was playing the accordion. He ordered a glass of vodka and a bowl of soup. He sat there for a while waiting for his soup to be delivered and listened to the music. Maria and he had done this on a number of occasions in Moscow. The vodka tasted warm and sweet on his lips and burned as it slid down his throat. It took the chill away finally. A heavyset pleasant looking woman wearing a simple print dress and a white apron brought him his soup and a plate with a large portion of bread. Tomorrow, he thought as he broke off a piece of the half-loaf of dark bread and dipped it into his soup, I will begin the process. As soon as they can get me papers and the money, I will leave. He thought to take the train to Moscow and from there by Aeroflot he would go to Frankfurt and then on to New York. Tonight Andrei was not in a hurry and he relaxed over his vodka. How long ago had he ever spared time for himself? There was always his work. He remembered again those times in Moscow with Maria; they had spent many such evenings in the local taverns. Now, there was nothing like that left in his life. But, perhaps he did have a new mission; maybe that would be his crowning achievement. He felt good in himself when he left the tavern and walked the rest of the way back to his apartment.

Later that night, as he tossed restlessly in his bed, he began to remember; perhaps it was the vodka, but nevertheless he remembered. Maria had indeed been beautiful.

Where was she now? He could see her long blond hair in his mind. Those days in Moscow when they had been together were exciting, happy, and wonderful. Whatever happened to those days? It was only, he thought...thirty–seven years ago...no, it couldn't have been that long ago. Had his life been so wasted on his work? As he drifted to sleep, the full memory of those years in Moscow come back to him.

Moscow...

CHAPTER EIGHT

MOSCOW

Moscow, The Soviet Union
Thursday, August 14, 1959

Andrei didn't even take notice of the sidewalk perform-
ers as he hurried along Slavanskaya Place towards the
Metro station at Kitay-gorod. He was excited and
wanted to get back to the apartment to tell Maria what
had happened. He was going to be in charge of a project
of his own; one which would be of importance to the
entire Soviet Union. In a few years, he could choose
where to set up his project permanently and they could
even to go back to Grozny. He ran down the steps of the
Metro, put a kopeck in the slot and pushed the turn-
stile. He looked for a train to Tekstilshchiki, it was as
close to Gravornovo and their apartment as the Metro
went; he waited impatiently on the platform, pacing
back and forth. The first train went only as far as

Volvogradskiy Prospekt. After what seemed an interminable delay, the next train arrived; the sign in the
window read "Vykhino." Good, it would go through to
the end of the line; he waited until the door opened and
then quickly stepped aboard and found an empty seat in
the middle of the car and sat down. The ride was only
four stops, but the distance to the first stop at the transfer station at Taganskaya was long…more than half the
distance to his stop. When the train stopped to pick up
transfer passengers at Volvogradskiy Prospekt, the car
suddenly became crowded with people with parcels
under their arms; some were carrying luggage. He was
jostled several times and was growing more irritated by
the minute. Finally he pulled himself to his feet and
maneuvered his way through the crush of humanity
arriving at the door just as the train pulled into his stop.

Relieved of the mass of people on the train, he walked
quickly out to Lyublinskaya Street and looked down
towards the open market at Zhdanovkiy. Maria might
be on her way home from the market and he would join
her walking to their apartment. He cursed under his
breath. No such luck today, he had missed her. Andrei
turned and headed up the street toward Gravornovo.
Soon the streets would be crowded with spectators who
were on their way to the soccer match at Moskvich
Stadium across Volgogradskiy Prospekt.

Their apartment building was about half a kilometer
past the Molodezhnly Cinema. It was not far to walk and
had been a good location despite the closeness to the railroad tracks and textile factories. Maria and he went to
the cinema as often as they could afford it. They had
been so fortunate to have found the apartment. It had

only one bedroom, but they did not have to share it with anyone else. It was one of the benefits of his position and of course the kindness of the manager of the store where Maria worked. The manager's brother was the caretaker for the building, and his fondness for Maria brought them the courtesy and convenience of this apartment. It really was quite large for just two people.

Andrei entered the front door of the building and ran up the dark stairway to the fourth floor. He was winded when he reached the door to the apartment. He tried the door to find it unlocked; Maria would be there. He burst through the door. Maria was sitting at the table in the kitchen area peeling potatoes with a small knife. Her long blond hair was done up in a kerchief. She put down the knife and looked up and smiled as Andrei was turning to close the door.

"Andrei, I heard you running up the stairs, what is it? Is everything all right?"

He was beaming as he came over to her. "I have a new appointment," he explained still out of breath. "Maria, this has to be the greatest day of my life."

"Tell me," she said beaming at the possible good news, he seemed to have.

He plopped himself down on a chair at the table next to her and reached out with both hands to cup her head and leaning forward, kissed her on the mouth. "My idea, my project, has been given approval at the highest levels of the Soviet Union; I can establish my own program...and I will be in charge!" he exclaimed proudly. "It will mean, of course, a promotion," he bragged. "It will mean that we will have vacations on the Black Sea

and a kiosk outside Moscow and..." he quickly added,
"and more money,"

"I'm proud of you, Andrei," she returned, smiling at
him and grasping his hands in hers.

Andrei leaned back in his chair and looked at the ceil-
ing, his face beaming. "Maria, this is also the happiest
day of my life,"

"What did you propose to them that they were so
happy with you?" she asked

He looked at her for a moment, considering if he
could or should tell her; it was very much a state secret.
Yet, he felt that he knew this girl, this woman, well
enough to trust her with his life. Wouldn't they always
be together; didn't they share everything? He decided to
tell her.

"You must not breath a word of this to anyone, it
would mean my life...and perhaps yours too," he
warned.

"Andrei, is it that serious?" she asked with a questioning smile.

"Yes," he retorted with a frown. "Yes, it is...many
lives could be forfeited if it were known."

The smile vanished from her face and was replaced by
an expression as somber as Andrei's.

"Of course I won't say anything," she said solemnly.

Andrei wrapped his arms around her and kissed her.
"I must tell someone, I am so excited. Thank you for
wanting to listen."

Andrei stood up and walked around the table. He
chose his words carefully. "Do you know that we have
some of our people living in the United States?"

"Our people?" she asked, "Diplomats?"

"No," he replied, "Spies. Not just regular spies, but those called 'deep agents,' ones who are Soviet citizens yet are so well trained and speak English...American English...so perfectly that they blend into the American culture and are given even the most sensitive of positions." He paused and then added, "They are very valuable to our efforts in the world, and to the country's security as well."

"I think I can understand that," Maria said.

"Well, for the past few years we have lost many of them."

"How, what happened to them, were they killed?"

"No, they either defected or dropped out of sight...just disappeared; obviously they took on new identities. Never-the-less, they became of no value to us." Andrei stood up and began pacing back and forth across the apartment.

"I see," she replied.

"There's more; the Chairman wants to establish large bank accounts in the United States and Great Britain for use by our operatives should certain missions become necessary," he continued. "Especially in case of a nuclear war. With our people defecting, the availability of large amounts of money would only encourage more defections or disappearances."

"Of course."

"I was the one to introduce the solution to their problem," he said proudly, looking over his shoulder to see her expression. "My work in bioelectronics produced a microchip so small that it could be embedded permanently in a person and by the use of special satellites we can locate every one of our agents." He beamed and kneeling down in front of her he reached out and grasped Maria's hands in his. "We will never again lose an agent, we will know their exact whereabouts at all times."

Maria smiled and kissed Andrei, "Oh Andrei, you are so brilliant."

Andrei could not contain his pleasure at having Maria share in his triumph. He took a breath and continued. "There is still more," he began again and then paused. "Never repeat what I am about to tell you now," he admonished her. "Never."

"You know I won't, Andrei."

"The chip also contains an embedded charge of electricity," he began slowly. "Enough to kill yet make it look like a natural death."

Maria was startled at his revelation. "But, why...?" she began.

"It's better that the agent be dead then to betray the Country," he replied in explanation. "There is a lot of money at stake as well."

"Would you be the one to...to..," she stuttered.

"If need be, but there would be others who would have to order it, it would not be my decision. It would be as though I were a soldier...that sort of thing," he said.

"Oh," she replied unconvincingly.

"I did not tell you how much money was going to be involved," he went on. "Each agent would have a million dollars deposited in an American bank...a million dollars, Maria."

Her eyes widened, and she looked into Andrei's eyes. "Why so much?" she asked.

"What they would have to do in case of the nuclear war would cost a lot of money, money that we would not be able to provide them from here…especially in a short period of time. Besides, it will be gaining interest at very good rates, in hard currency. The Soviet Union will loose nothing…it will gain, in fact."

"How many agents will there be?" she asked.

Andrei hesitated and then went on, "I was told to plan on a hundred, but if the program is successful, there may be many more; perhaps twice as many. They have given it a name, the project, I mean; it will be called 'Rasputin' after the Mad Monk. They were trying to make a bad joke, I think."

For a moment there was silence between them. Maria was the first to speak. "When I first moved here with you, Andrei, you said that I would be able to resume my studies," she began. "Would it now be possible for me to begin that? I have not said anything because I know how hard you have worked and how much we needed the money that I made. Will there now be enough money to allow me to become a student?"

Andrei smiled broadly. "Yes, of course," he said. "The new semester begins at the University next month. I'll see to it that you are entered." He kissed her again and asked, "What do you want to study?"

"I want to learn new languages, Western languages," she replied. "You remember."

"Yes, of course, and it will be helpful to be here in Moscow, after you finish. There are many positions for translators here. Yes, that will work out perfectly, of course you must start next month." Maria smiled and took Andrei's hands in hers and kissed them. "Thank you, dearest," she said. She couldn't bear to tell him that staying in Moscow or the Soviet Union was not what she had in mind at all. Returning to Grozny was, of course, totally out of the question. Maria had dreams, too.

CHAPTER NINE

▼

SEAN STEVENSON

Watergate Apartments
Washington, DC
Wednesday, October 29th, 1997

It was almost 5:30 AM when the phone rang in the Watergate apartment of Sean Stevenson. He tried to ignore it at first, but then rolled over, fumbled around in the darkness and finally grabbed the receiver. "Yeah," he grunted. "Good morning Sean," said the low and husky female voice on the other end. "We finally have a break." Suddenly, he was wide-awake. "I'll fill you in on the details when you come in,"

"Be there in 45 minutes," Sean replied and hung up the phone. He looked at his hands; they were trembling. After all these months, maybe the time had come; he was alive with excitement. Sean quickly showered, combed his hair and trimmed his neat and stylish black beard, dressed in his usual black suit with striped tie, grabbed an overcoat and left his apartment.

Sean Stevenson had a passion in life. It wasn't just a job at the National Security Agency, it was also his past, present, and…so he guessed anyway, his future. At 40 years old, he had done more and been more places than many men; he was, in fact, more than just one man. It was his secret and that of the NSA. The initial deception of his new land and then the betrayal of his heritage he felt deeply; it burned in him and he yearned to find satisfaction in bringing the whole episode to a close.

In the early morning traffic, it took Sean only a half-hour to get from his apartment in the Watergate to Fort George G. Meade, Maryland and the Headquarters of the National Security Agency and the Central Security Service. He turned onto Savage Road and entered the large parking lot in front of the fenced-in building complex of NSA/CSS. Sean parked his car in the lot, locked it and started to walk toward the entrance gate. Behind him he could hear the drone of airplane engines and turned to see the silhouette of the tail assembly of a C-130 cargo plane against the pre-dawn sky; it was sitting, almost as though it were crouching at the end of the taxiway, its engines turning lazily. As he approached the double row of cyclone fencing topped by concertina wire, the plane's engines suddenly revved up and it started taxing slowly down the tarmac towards the runway. Sean watched it over his shoulder as he walked quickly to the gate. The silhouetted tail assembly disappeared behind a row of tall conifers and only the sound of its reverberating engines left any hint that it had ever been there at all. He passed through the checkpoint at the gate and headed for the main door. Sean pushed open the double door at the building entrance and virtually glided through the reception area. He murmured a greeting and waved his badge at the guard at the desk as he headed for the elevator. Within three minutes, he was at the office of the Deputy Director. Although it wasn't even six–thirty in the morning, NSA/CSS Deputy Director, Shirley McHendrie's secretary was at her desk. "Good morning, Mr. Stevenson, she's expecting you," she said as Sean entered the office reception area. He waved a "thanks" and knocked on the dark walnut paneled door to the Deputy's office.

A woman's voice called, "Come," from somewhere behind the door and Sean let himself in.

Shirley McHendrie was sitting at her large mahogany desk in the center of the room. The paneled walls were covered with frames holding her various degrees interspersed with tastefully selected examples of art. Behind her on the left stood a set of flags; the US Flag and the Agency's together between the two large colored plaques containing the seals of both the NSA and the CSS on the wall. She had a quiet confidence about her which spoke of intelligence and an understanding of the intricacies of the world in which she worked. At 52, she had spent most of her life in the intelligence community. Her earlier years had been in the employment of the CIA as had many of the current employees now under her. She was quite attractive in a quiet and serene way; she was dressed in a dark, navy-blue suit with a white blouse and a simple, but expensive gold band for a necklace. On both wrists, she wore gold bangles. Her dark brown hair was worn swept up on the right side and contained a one inch streak of gray. Sean wondered how she could look so elegant so early in the morning. She appeared to have been at work for hours…maybe she had never been to bed, except she looked too fresh for that.

She smiled when she saw Sean and beckoned him in as she stood up and moved around her desk to sit in one of two large brown overstuffed leather chairs which were strategically placed to face the front of her desk. Between the chairs was a small table containing a tray with a carafe of coffee and two mugs.

"Coffee?" she asked.

"Thanks."

She began pouring coffee into both mugs and motioned Sean to sit in the other chair. He seated himself and waited for her to begin; he could see that she was pondering what she would say and was trying to select her words carefully.

"Late yesterday," she began, "I was informed by COL Henderson that he had been contacted by a member of the FBI about a particularly gruesome murder in New York City. What was of special interest to us, however, was the discovery of several lists of numbers resembling code sheets. The lists were on microdots hidden in the shaft of a cane found next to the body. The lists resembled an old version of our code, but the titles and notes were all in Russian or so we thought."

"Were we able to decipher them?" interrupted Sean.

"That's the strange part," she replied, "we thought it was just another SIGINT breach and were confident that we could identify the message origin and time of transmission and we'd find where the breach was."

She hesitated. "It wasn't our code or anything like any other codes we've ever encountered. We couldn't make anything out of it...and our computers went through their entire cycle."

"I'm not sure how this relates to me," Sean quietly interjected.

"Sean, as you well know there's a network of deep agents of which you were one and they're somehow connected. We also know that there's a system of checks on each one of them to keep them in line. How they're controlled and by whom, we don't entirely know...anymore than we know about the chip we found implanted in you; but we do believe that the chip has a lot to do with it."

"How does the dead guy fit in?"

"I don't know for sure, but we do know he was a Russian and he was tortured extensively for some very important purpose; that's obvious."

"Could the codes be a list of deep agents?" Sean asked.

"That's why I called you."

Shirley McHendrie shifted in her seat. "We know that since the breakup of the Soviet Union, the whole espionage setup has been in disarray. We know that communications has been almost nil to a particular sector of that group." She paused. "In one area, lately, signal communications have increased. It has to do with several of the Soviet communications satellites that were sent up initially in the early 60s and eventually replaced a decade later. We've been monitoring their transmissions and have wondered why they were silent for so long. Periodically, they would transmit, but why they did so was a real mystery. The Soviets claimed that these satellites were for 'peaceful' mapping purposes, and the others were low frequency seismic disturbance detectors for use in predicting earthquakes. We didn't believe either story."

"I know I may be looking at the negatives," Sean interjected, "but why would a list of deep agents be duplicated and brought to this country? It would seem to be the last thing that any government would do...even the current Russian one."

"You're absolutely right," Shirley responded. "If this is so, then it must be initiated and financed by someone else in the previous Soviet Union...NOT the current government."

She shifted in her chair once more. "Sean, there's more; some of the numbers that were on the list matched three of the receptor frequencies on the chip that was implanted on you."

"Then that proves it!" he exploded.

"We think so," Shirley replied slowly. "But we have to be sure. What this can mean is that we may have a list of all of the Soviet deep agents in the United States—and perhaps even more." She hesitated again and then satisfying herself that it would be safe, said, "I think that there was something else in the coded list; I think that it has to do with the last of the three coded numbers on the list."

"What's that?"

She hesitated again. "When we removed the chip from the base of your skull...and you probably were never told, but it was attached to your basilar artery...we subjected it to various frequencies. At 328.165 megahertz, it sent out a relatively strong electric surge of current when the signal was modulated in a certain way. The current would have been sufficiently strong to have initiated a stroke in your basilar artery, if it had still been implanted. That exact frequency showed up on one of the lists as well as that of the modulating signal. That number was referenced to a list of what appeared to be names on the last list. We couldn't make sense of any of the Russian printed there except it was printed in the Cyrillic alphabet."

Sean sat there motionless. Finally he spoke. "That very well could have been my fate, then?" he asked.

"I'm afraid so, Sean, had we not removed it. I'm sorry."

"They never did trust any of us, did they?"

"I'm afraid not," she replied and then added, "I must be frank about this, Sean, they were losing agents right and left; what do you think they should have done about it? The entire system was unworkable and could never compete against a free democracy. They were desperate."

"Why didn't they tell us about the implant? At least the locator part, if not the…destruct mechanism?"

"You know the answer to that as well as I do. It isn't the culture; it still isn't. For what it's worth, my guess is that they still don't know you located the chip or that you defected; if they did, the chip would have signaled more than the one time it did. We're still monitoring it to see if it reacts."

"What now?" he asked.

Shirley sighed, which was unlike her. She thought for a moment and said, "We're forming a task force to track this thing. I've asked Jonathan Banks to provide a place at his facility to house the task force until we find out what's going on. It's too important to chance identifying it with the Agency and housing the task force here." She paused and then continued, "Hank Henderson will be a part of it...you know him. The FBI will have their counterespionage chief, Deiter there plus a contact of his who has a good background in the Russian language and has some background in Soviet affairs as well. I believe that Jonathan has also assigned one of his area experts to it. The smaller the group, the better; I don't want it to be compromised...it may mean the lives of a lot of people."

Sean nodded, "I agree. Thanks for counting me in."

Shirley smiled. "I don't want anything to happen to you, Sean, it was you that brought us this jewel in the first place...you're important to us."

Sean stood up, nodded to the Deputy Director and walked towards the door. He grabbed the handle and started to open it. Turning towards Shirley, he smiled once more and then went out closing the door behind him. When he had left, Shirley McHendrie sighed again; she leaned back in her chair and raised her eyebrows. It's now up to her trust in the human equation...and the "Great Jehovah," she thought with a grin. The magnitude of this discovery might either be a tremendous asset for the Country...or a great calamity.

CHAPTER TEN

▼

TASK FORCE IVAN

Jonathan Banks, Inc.
Chevy Chase, Maryland
Friday, October 31st, 1997

Charlie had attended to the details of preparing for the first meeting of the task force. Coffee and sweet rolls were laid on to be delivered at seven–thirty sharp in the rooms that had been set aside at the firm as the control and communications center of the group. Over the weekend, equipment and furniture had been delivered to the large conference room on the top floor. A security system had been installed to prevent any unauthorized entry to that floor and cameras had been set up to monitor various entranceways. The communications and computer equipment were of the latest vintage. Several desks with terminals were set up in the room as well as a conference table. There were to be seven members of the

task force. Besides Charlie and her boss, Jonathan Banks
who with the NSA/CSS Deputy Director, Shirley
McHendrie, would kick off the project, there was COL
Henderson and a Sean Stevenson from the NSA, John
Deiter from the FBI, and his Russian speaking col-
league, Rose McGuire. Charlie didn't really have an
appreciation for what part some of the other people
played in this scenario, but was sure that after the first
meeting, this would all be made clear. At eight o'clock
all of the participants were suppose to be there. Charlie
suddenly was hit by the thought that this was
Halloween; no strange omen attached to it, she hoped.

Shirley McHendrie arrived early and was in Jonathan
Banks' office with the door closed. One by one the rest
of the team arrived. Charlie had met Hank Henderson
before and periodically had seen him with Banks.
Henderson had with him Sean Stevenson, whom
Charlie had never met before, but after introductions,
the two of them seemed to take to each other easily.
Charlie thought to herself that sometimes you meet a
person and although you know that it's for the first
time…it seems like you've known them forever. The last
to arrive was the FBI counter espionage chief, John
Deiter and his Russian speaking associate, Rose
McGuire. Charlie sensed that these two had known each
other well for a long time, although they tried not to
show it. Sometimes, that's a bit hard to hide. Deiter was
a striking man with strong features accentuated by his
shaved head and black arched eyebrows. He looked to
be in his fifties yet still had the physique of a cat that
was apparent under his close-fitting tailored black suit.
The woman had a fierce head of dark red hair cut below

shoulder length. She was nice looking with a good figure, well dressed and very personable. As they entered, Charlie walked over to them extending her hand to Deiter.

"Mr. Deiter, I'm Charlie Waggner. I work for Jonathan Banks," she said.

"Glad to meet you, Charlie...and its Jack. This is my associate, Rose McGuire," he replied motioning to the woman next to him. Charlie turned to her and extending her hand said,

"Zdravstv$te, Roz Mikgur?" (*How do you do, Rose McGuire?*)

"Cpasibo, xoro]o, Carli Uaggnor," (*Thanks, very well, Charlie Waggner,*) Rose replied.

As Rose and Charlie conversed in Russian near the entrance, on the other side of the room Sean at first perked up at hearing the exchange of greetings in Russian and grew more interested as the conversation continued. He interrupted his discussion with Hank Henderson and walked over to where the new arrivals stood. He spoke directly to Rose and said, "Where do you come from in Russia?"

Rose smiled and said, "I'm American, born and bred. I've visited Russia, but I was born right here in America."

Sean was astounded. "I've spent years learning American English, so I appreciate how perfectly you speak my mother tongue."

"That's a compliment indeed," replied Rose smiling broadly, yet inquiringly.

"I'm sorry, I didn't introduce myself, my name is Sean Stevenson...it is also Stephen Chandler and Stefan

Cheklenov. I was born in the Ukraine, not far from Kiev. I was a deep agent for the Soviet Union."

Charlie was visibly shocked by Sean's revelation. She turned towards him and was about to speak, but Sean put his hand on her arm.

"What's happening here has to do, in part, with me. I came here as a deep agent, but was disenchanted with my assignment even before I arrived. I believe that Shirley McHendrie will explain everything…as far as we know it. Please wait until she has her say."

Colonel Hank Henderson had followed Sean Stevenson across the room and looked on at the exchange with Rose McGuire with some amusement. After Sean had finished talking, he stepped forward and threw his arms around Rose. "Rose, you haven't changed a bit…beautiful as ever," he said as he lifted her up in his arms. There aren't too many men that could lift and swing Rose McGuire about, but the former linebacker did it as though she was a feather. He gave her a big kiss on the cheek and finally dropped her again. Both Charlie and Sean stood there speechless at the unexpected greeting. Henderson turned to them and said, "Oh, we're old friends…you know, CIA."

Rose was about to say something when the door opened and Jonathan Banks and Shirley McHendrie walked in. Banks was first to speak as he entered the room, "Please, everybody sit down, we have a few things to say before the work begins." He escorted Shirley McHendrie to the right side of the conference table and stood next to her at the head of the table. The rest of the group came over to the table and sat down. Sean sat

down next to Charlie and across the table from Deiter
and Rose McGuire.

Jonathan Banks began by thanking everyone who was
present at the gathering, introducing first the Deputy
Director of NSA/CSS and then the other members; his
face then took on a serious look. "We are now in a very
different situation vis a vie the powers in the Eastern
block than we were a decade ago. At that time, there
were specific programs set in motion when the Soviet
Union was in a confrontational mode with the Western
world. Some of these programs still exist today, but now
are only a minor problem to the Country itself. During
the sixties and early seventies, the Soviet Union sent a
great number of deep agents into the United States.
These agents could pass for any American and were in
possession of documents that substantiated their credibility. They could, and the intent was, that they should
infiltrate the highest places of government, both state
and Federal. If and when they were needed, they would
be able to perform any act that the Soviet Union
desired. They were of great danger to the nation. But
that's now in the past, at least for the present. There are
forces that would still want the Communists to regain
control of what is now the remnants of the Soviet
Union. What is particularly disturbing at this point, is
that the people who were sent to this country are now
themselves in danger of their lives by someone who was
suppose to be their mentor. We know of several of the
deep agents who have been, we suppose, murdered. Of
particular note are those who have defected. Their life
span has been especially short beginning in about 1960
to 1975; as soon as they either disappeared or defected,

they died, killed by what we suspect was a transmitted frequency which made it seem as though they died as the result of a stroke.

Deiter squirmed uncomfortably in his chair. For some reason, he thought of his parents and their unexplained coincidence of death. Why should they have anything to do with this? It didn't make sense, so he dismissed the thought.

Banks continued, "In the early 1960s, the Soviets were experiencing a mass defection of their best trained deep agents. They would either defect or simply disappear. After all, they had been trained to do that very well. We highly suspect that a project was initiated by the Soviets which included implanting a microchip at the brain stem of all of their agents." Banks waited until the impact of what he had said was appreciated by his audience; he was an excellent craftsman when it came to impact speaking. He then continued, "You have all met Sean Stevenson. Forgive me, Sean, but I must explain what has happened."

"Of course, I understand and insist," responded Sean.

"I thought so," Banks paused. "Sean first came to our attention about five years ago when he underwent an MRI scan trying to find any possible physical cause for his migraine headaches. The scan showed what is called a UBO or unidentified bright object and appeared to be a foreign object adjacent to a cerebral artery. The neurologist was a friend of mine and one night over supper he casually described what he had found, simply as a point of interest. He was intending to surgically remove the object. I asked him if the location was that in which strokes often occurred. He said yes, and I urged him to let me attend the operation as it reminded me of several recent 'natural' deaths of defecting agents from the Soviet Union."

Banks could see that three of the group seemed somewhat bewildered by what he was saying. He realized that they had no idea that the documents passed on to the NSA by the FBI pertained to the topic he was discussing. "Bear with me for a few more moments; I'm sure you'll see the relevance of all this," he said smiling gently. "As soon as the object had been removed, it was placed under a microscope. It turned out to be a bio-electrically powered microchip." He paused and then continued. "I informed Shirley McHendrie and her people went to work trying to determining the origin and purpose of the chip. I also had a talk with Sean to determining if he knew of its existence or purpose. I was convinced that he knew nothing. He then revealed his identity and purpose of his assignment to me. I was convinced he was sincere."

"Since that time," McHendrie interjected, "we've worked closely with Sean. During the past few days, we've been processing a number of disinterments to repeat autopsies on certain individuals. We have come up with astounding results."

Sean turned to look at the Deputy Director with a questioning gaze. She acknowledged his look and continued. "Those who either have changed allegiances, left their control or were identified for some other reason, died from what is termed 'stroke,'" she said. "In fact, they were murdered by their control."

After a moment, Deiter cleared his throat and said, "Could you clear up something for me?"

"Of course," McHendrie replied. "Everything has to be completely clear for us to work together and get to the end of this thing."

"How does the FBI and my current case have to do with all of this talk of deep agents and implanted chips? I was led to believe that we were working on the same project and I don't see the connection right now."

"Jack, I'm sorry that I failed to give credit to you and the FBI; without your contribution, we would have never realized the whole story. The microdot documents that you found in the cane have given us a great deal of information. They also have given us a source to be able to identify all of the deep agents that have been sent to the United States. The repetition of 181 sets of numbers on four lists seems to indicate that it may pertain to 181 deep agents. They fail to tell us who is eliminating those agents, especially the ones who were in hiding or defecting and why."

"Do you have any idea who the murdered guy in New York was?" asked Deiter.

"No, that's still a mystery;" replied Banks, "not only who he was, but why he was tortured and what he might have had in his possession to cause it."

"We certainly might assume that it had to do with the lists," interjected Shirley, "but why would one have both microdots and hard copy of those lists?"

"I think," Banks drawled on slowly, "that we will find the answers to those questions when we find out who feels these killings are necessary and what it would profit them by doing so. I think we can be somewhat assured that it is not the present Russian government; there seems to be nothing to be gained."

"Who else would gain?" chimed in Hank Henderson. "It could have to do with someone who's very sympathetic with the Communists, a total psycho, or the criminal element."

"Now, that's a novel thought, Hank," said Deiter. "Is there any money involved?" There was silence around the table for a few moments.

Finally, Sean cleared his throat and broke the silence. "I don't know if I mentioned it before, but I suppose that there could be money involved. I don't know how someone could get their hands on it, but if it were possible, for more than a hundred agents, it could be a sizable amount."

"What is it?" asked Shirley McHendrie.

"There was a bank account established in case it would ever be needed to perform a mission ordered by the Central Committee," he continued. "I was required to memorize a number and was told that the KGB would give me the second portion and another party, who I didn't know, perhaps a control or someone from the Central Committee, would provide the third and final portion. Together it would identify the bank and the account number; the name on the account was my cover name. It was felt that this would facilitate the transfer of money that way."

"How much was in the account?" asked Rose.

"I don't know exactly, but it was suppose to be enough to carry off any mission."

Henderson reached over and switched on a slide projector that had been placed in the center of the conference table. On the screen at the far end of the table, the first of the pages of microdots appeared. He clicked the

remote until a three-column list of what might have
been names preceded by a number appeared. Halfway
down the third column was the number 135. With a
laser pointer, he highlighted the line. "This is what we
have so far," he explained. "The number represents the
location on the list where we recorded the frequencies
that showed a response on the chip. We think that these
words in Russian characters are in reference to Sean, but
although written in the Cyrillic alphabet, it makes no
sense in Russian."

"I'll vouch for that," said Rose.

"The frequency that was found to respond to the
interrogatory signal on the chip and the bank number
we know," interrupted Charlie, "what do they have in
common?"

Henderson clicked the remote and backed up two
frames. "Here is the first list," he said. "The frequencies
were 765 and 432; the bank number was 709863."

There was silence around the conference table as the
group studied the list.

"There it is," shouted Charlie, "In the top row, third
column, next to the last set of numbers."

"Right on!" remarked McHendrie, " I think she has
it." The others laughed at the humorous reference to *My
Fair Lady.* "That list must be the contact list."

"Try the next list," said Banks. Henderson clicked the
remote and the next list appeared on the screen. For several minutes, no one said anything.

Henderson said, "The large print at the top and bottom indicates that it is a highly protected document,
that's KGB Secret."

"I don't see any correlation," said Banks, "go on to the next list."

Henderson clicked the remote and the third list appeared.

Henderson said, "Look in the top row, the third column over and the fifth number set down. That's the frequency that Sean's implant reacted to by emitting a signal."

"Not only that, but there is a parallel there," said Deiter. "It is in the first row, third column and fifth number...one, three, five...the number that precedes this crazy Russian-non-Russian writing on the next list. This has got to be a code of some sort, anyone have an idea?"

"That's part of the answer," Banks exclaimed. "The number on the last list may have something to do with the information on the other lists."

Rose thought for a moment while studying the words at the top of the first list. Something was familiar. "Look at the two letters following the first set of numbers at the top of the list." She took the laser pointer from Hank's hand and highlighted it on the screen. "If these two letters were something else instead, like the abbreviation of megahertz, that is, MHz, maybe we could get a start on the translation of the code," Only Rose, Sean and Charlie knew Russian and they all studied the text. Rose continued, "Charlie, Sean, do you type in Russian? I mean on a Russian typewriter."

"Yes," replied Sean, "But I only hunt and peck on an American one, that's a bit beyond me."

"I do a little," replied Charlie.

"Pretend that you are typing some of that text on the screen. Then look at what you have typed in English," she went on. "I chose the 'MHz,' which comes out to be the 'MHz' that appears on the text. What if this was in English written on a Russian typewriter?"

"Hank, can you get this transcribed on a Russian typewriter?" asked Banks.

"Better than that, I will put this in a word processor and just select the Cyrillic basic font. That would give it to us."

"What about the KGB list?" asked Rose.

Henderson clicked the remote back to the previous list.

Sean remarked after a few moments, "These number sets are nine digits long rather than six; what information responds to that?" No one responded to his question immediately.

Finally, Deiter asked, "What information don't we have?"

"The bank name," replied Rose.

"How many digits are in a bank identification number," asked Banks.

Rose dug into her purse and pulled out her bankbook and her eyeglasses. She opened her bankbook, put on her glasses and studied the check. "Nine digits!" she exclaimed. She looked up at the screen. "The same number as each one of the sets; that must be the bank identification."

"See why I brought her," Deiter remarked with a shrug. "She has this...thing."

Everyone laughed, but the magnitude of the discoveries was not lost on them. They had not only the key to the identification of all of the deep agents, but also all but six digits of the bank account numbers that had been set up for them; and they possibly had even that for one person…Sean.

"This has been a good session," concluded Banks. "We'll continue to meet here until we have all the answers; Hank, get us that translation and I want you to all look at it. We'll meet here the day after tomorrow at eight AM; thank you all for coming." He and McHendrie got up to leave. As they were heading for the door, Banks turned to Deiter and said, "I hope you and Ms. McGuire will be able to continue to participate with us, you both have been a great asset."

"I've been assured that we'll be in this until we find out what's going on," replied Deiter.

"I'm glad," said Banks, Shirley McHendrie smiled her concurrence and they both left the conference room, closing the door behind them.

"Well," exclaimed Hank Henderson, "we're into a puzzle; we're going to try to save the lives of spies from a nonexistent country who are in danger from their own control…ever done that before?" He looked over at Sean and quickly added, "No offense, Sean, just an observation."

Sean grinned, "It's OK, that's very Russian, you know…how does it go, a puzzle inside of an enigma…something like that."

▼

CHAPTER ELEVEN

PROJECT RASPUTIN

Moscow, The Soviet Union
February 15, 1960

Andrei sat leaning against the window of the train with his briefcase on his lap; he looked out at the lights of the Metro stations as he passed them. Snow had covered the streets of Moscow and by the light of the street lamps he could see that it was beginning to snow once more. He had done something today that he had never done before and he didn't know how he really felt about it. It had been his duty, yet it still scared him. He had received his orders from the Central Committee. Why did he feel so worried, even sad about what he had done? They had defected, after all. Wasn't that betrayal...treason? Of course it was. Then he was truly justified...and besides, he was following orders. Why then, did he feel so badly? He hadn't pulled a trigger or stabbed them with a knife; he didn't see blood and there wouldn't have been any. It may not have even been successful…yet he knew deep inside, that it had been. Maria would know what to say to comfort him. Why doesn't the train move any faster?

The Metro finally eased into the station at Tekstilshchiki and the doors slid open. Andrei stood up and slowly walked out into the station. As he climbed the stairs leading to Lyublinskiaya Street, he could already feel the cold. Snow covered the pavement and was piled high on both sides of the street to a height of almost three meters. The wind was blowing towards him and the snow blew into his eyes; the flakes were hard and stung his face. Even the elements are against me today, he thought; is it because of what I've done? He shook the thought from his mind.

It took him a little longer this night to walk the half-kilometer from the station to the apartment. By the time he arrived and had climbed the stairs, he was chilled to the bone. He brushed the snow from his coat and stomped his boots before he tried to open the door. He pressed the handle and then silently swore under his breath; it was locked, Maria wasn't home yet. He dug into his pants pocket for the key, fumbling it while holding his gloves under his left arm. The key finally turned and the door swung inward. As he went through the doorway, he carefully removed his hat to keep the snow from falling to the floor. Maria would be angry if there was water on the floor. He carried it to the sink, carefully brushed it, and returned to hang it on a peg next to the door.

He returned to the window over the sink and looked out at the snow-covered street below to see if he could catch a glimpse of Maria walking home. He saw no one. He sighed and physically drooped; then reaching into the cabinet next to the window, withdrew a bottle of vodka and a small glass and sat at the table placing the bottle and glass before him. Maybe what he needed was a drink to make him relax and think more clearly. He filled the glass with the clear liquor, threw it down his throat and filled the glass once more.

As he stared at the glass of vodka, the events of the day began returning to him slowly. He had arrived precisely at eight o'clock at his laboratory and sitting at his desk, he was rechecking the design improvement to the latest version of the microchip. At a noise, he looked up to see Colonel General Boris Ivanovich Ulanova of the Central Committee standing just inside the doorway to the laboratory. Andrei jumped to his feet and exclaimed, "Comrade General, someone should have told me you were to visit." Andrei hurriedly pulled a chair towards the center of the room, indicating with a gesture that it was for the General.

"No need, Andrei Mikailovich, this must be a private meeting; that is why I didn't inform anyone that I would be here today," he said. "We have a problem and for the first time, we must exercise your project."

"What's the problem?" asked Andrei with a slight wince, thinking that he may have done something wrong.

"The first married team, the one who was called back for your 'treatment;' their control has lost contact with them and we need for you to locate them for us."

"Of course, Boris Ivanovich, I will do it immediately," replied Andrei somewhat relieved. He crossed the room to where the electronic modules lined the far wall of the laboratory. "They only returned to America last month," he observed absently.

Andrei turned the dial on a safe located below the array of electronic displays until it opened. Drawing out an envelope, he sat down at one of the displays and withdrew the contents of the envelope. He studied the lists and finding what he was searching for, underlined the entry. He next typed in the numbers from the list on the keyboard and entered the information into the computer. A display appeared on the monitor in front of him with the information he had typed. He checked the numbers again against the list he had spread out in front of him; they matched. He pressed the ENTER key again.

At an altitude of 200 miles, the Soviet satellite, *Rastof* which had been launched into orbit the previous December activated, processed the information it had just received and transmitted a modulated signal in the low frequency range. *Rastof* had been advertised as a peaceful mapping satellite when it was launched. Within thirty seconds a weak, but readable signal was received on another frequency. Simultaneously, a second satellite, *Prodjnya* (ostensibly a low frequency seismic disturbance earthquake predictor) received the same signal, processed the information, and compared it with slave signals from five other satellites; it then signaled *Rastof.* There was a pause of about two minutes while the triangulation was computed; it then transmitted the results back to Moscow.

The screen in front of Andrei showed a set of numbers and Andrei copied them down. He walked over to a map of the United States on the adjoining wall and measured the horizontal and then the vertical coordinates. "The man is located in the Washington area. I will check the woman now," he said. Repeating the procedure, he walked over to the map again and placed a pin just north of Washington," The woman is apparently at the same location," he remarked.

"They are not where they should be," replied the General. "They should be in Boston."

"Perhaps they are on vacation," offered Andrei.

"I would not think so," said the General with a sneer in his voice. "Can you get a precise location?"

"But of course Boris Ivanovich," replied Andrei walking over to a cabinet with wide, but narrow drawers. He opened the top drawer, closed it and opened the second. A stack of maps lay in the drawer and Andrei started to finger through them. Finally, he drew out a map about a meter square and laid it out on the top of the cabinet. The map was of the Washington, DC area. Andrei measured the longitude and latitude carefully and marked the location at which they intersected. "Here is the exact location, Comrade General. It appears to be north of Washington, DC and on the perimeter of their Fort Meade military installation."

The General nodded, "The United States National Security Agency, of course."

"Is there something else that I should know, Comrade General?" asked Andrei.

The General closed his eyes as though considering the question carefully. He placed his hands together in front of him as though he were praying, then spread his fingers apart. "Operatives do not lose their controls," he said slowly. "Good agents always tell their controls where they are going and what they are doing...these people did not. Now we find them at the headquarters of the highest American security organization."

"Do you think they may have defected?" asked Andrei.

"That would be an obvious conclusion," said the General. "They are in Washington without an apparent reason. I doubt that they were uncovered by the Americans."

Andrei went quiet and pale. After a few moments, he asked, "And what is to be done?"

The General turned his head towards Andrei and said, "You have already devised the solution. It must be carried out, otherwise the whole program is a farce and I must report that to the Central Committee."

Andrei suddenly knew why he had paled. It was up to him to destroy the two people whom he had met at the halfway house and in whom he had implanted with the devise of his own creation. This was the time when he was to be tested. He had not killed a living soul in his entire life. He was not a soldier; no one was shooting at him; his life was not endangered.

The General sat very straight in his chair and looked directly at Andrei; several moments passed without a word being exchanged between them. Finally, the General sighed and stood up. "Andrei Mikailovich," said the General very slowly, "please show me as you activate the termination instructions for John and Constance Deiter." The next few minutes passed as though Andrei was in a dream. He mechanically typed the code and carrier wave on the keyboard and entered the information into the computer. In two minutes, the confirmation appeared on the monitor screen. "TERMINATION INSTRUCTIONS COMPLETE." Andrei slumped in his chair. The General turned on his heel and left without a word. It seemed as though there was silence everywhere in the world to Andrei; he sat there staring at the screen for almost a half-hour before gathering his briefcase and leaving the laboratory. The rest of the day, Andrei wandered through museums and the Moscow Library. He wasn't looking at anything in particular, he was just thinking. Then, he found himself at the Metro late in the afternoon.

Andrei was startled from his thoughts by a noise at the door. Maria was home. He looked at the clock and at the darkened window. She was very late; it was dark outside now; he noticed that he had not turned on the light and the bottle of vodka was now only half full.

"Maria," Andrei shouted as she came through the door. "Where have you been?"

"Why studying, what else?" she replied. "You know that I will be taking my exams in two days."

"I'm sorry, I just needed you, that's all," he said softly.

She dropped her books onto the sofa and took off her coat, hanging it next to the door. Then she turned to Andrei. "What's the matter with you, Andrei?" she asked. "You look as though you've seen a ghost."

Andrei slumped into his chair, his hand on the glass of vodka. "Made them, most likely," he replied.

Maria came over to him and sat at his feet. She reached up to place her hand on his face. "Andrei, what's happened to you?" she asked.

He pondered for a moment and then slowly said, "Do you remember how I told you about the part of my program that could destroy an agent?"

"Yes," she replied.

"Today...today I had to do that; and not with just one agent, but a married couple," His head fell to the table and he sobbed."

Maria reached for his hand and grasped it between both of hers. "Did you know them?" she asked quietly.

"Yes, they have been agents for a long time and were brought back to be 'conditioned' in the laboratory," he replied. "I have spoken to them on several occasions. They have a teenage son...had a teenage son."

"Why?" she asked.

Andrei was silent for several moments; then he replied, "The General, Colonel...General Boris Ivanovich Ulanova came to my laboratory this morning. He told me about the two deserters." He looked into her eyes for the first time. He wanted to see forgiveness, compassion, or understanding. He saw a questioning glance and a waiting instead. He continued, "He said that I had devised the solution and that if it was not used, then he must explain that to the Central Committee. I was scared, Maria, I was scared. I have never killed a single person in my life, to say nothing about a man and woman with a child."

Maria let her hands slide away from Andrei's hand and she placed them in her lap and looked down. They stayed that way for several moments, Andrei looking down at Maria with a pleading look on his face…she continued looking at her hands. Finally, Maria stood up and turned her attention to making dinner preparations.

After dinner, they sat at the table, neither one looking at each other. Finally Andrei said, "What am I to do?"

"Do?" said Maria, "Do?" "You've already done what the powers have wanted you to do. I was afraid of this when you first told me of it. Are you a killer, Andrei?"

Andrei slumped in his chair. "What am I to do?" he asked again.

"That's something you must deal with; it's between your conscience and God," she replied.

Maria finished washing the dishes, put them away in the cabinets and went to bed. Andrei sat at the table with the bottle of vodka.

In the morning, Andrei awoke and followed his normal routine of the day. Maria was silent, but that was not unusual, she was never a morning person. When Andrei was prepared to leave for work, he turned to kiss Maria and mention that perhaps they could go to the tavern tonight and enjoy the music. After they kissed, Maria said quietly, "I won't be here tonight."

Andrei stared at her, but she turned and busied herself at sorting the laundry that she had done the day before. "You have something to do?" he said. "A class, perhaps?"

"No, I will be moving out," she said plainly.

Andrei was shocked. "But why?" he asked grabbing her arm and turning her around.

"Andrei, it's not good. I can't live with what's going on; I must have a time to myself to sort it out." She then put her hand to his face and said, "Let me have room,

Andrei, my dearest, let me have room for awhile. This whole thing about killing people has me very upset."

Andrei looked at his watch and noticed that it was late and he might miss the Metro. "Don't leave today, Maria, don't leave today, I need you." He put on his coat and hat and opened the door to go. "Maria, not today," he said as he went into the hallway. He closed the door and clambered down the stairs and out into the snow covered street.

Maria sank into the chair at the kitchen table and put her face in her hands. She knew what she had to do. She didn't like leaving Andrei, but her life wasn't to be the one she was now living. It wasn't so much the thing about Andrei killing some poor soul, but it served as a good excuse. For the next hour, she packed all of her belongings in an old suitcase. She placed her key to the apartment on the kitchen table and looked around at the small apartment. As she left the apartment, she felt a sense of sudden longing, but shrugging it off, she closed and locked the door behind her. Maria knew where she would be going and the old life had to be left behind.

That night was to be the worst night that Andrei was to know in his life. The anguish consumed him completely. In a drunken stupor, he had burst from his apartment thinking he had heard Maria returning and tumbled down the flight of steps to the ground floor, breaking his arm and right leg. He soon weakened from the loss of blood where the bone pierced the flesh of his leg and the intense pain had caused him to lose consciousness. It was morning before he was discovered and rushed to the hospital. For six months, Andrei was confined to the reconstructive and recuperative wing of

Moscow's Botkin Hospital next to the Central Airfield. The bone in his leg healed, but persisted in causing him pain when strained. His emotional state of mind never healed. Although he yearned to seek out Maria and ask her to return, he had been powerless to do so at first and then it was too late. He never saw her again.

CHAPTER TWELVE

▼

JOHN WAGGNER

Washington, DC
Monday, November 3rd, 1997

The Senate Office Building seemed like a second home to John Waggner by now. He had walked its halls and served its lawmakers for almost forty years. At sixty–three years old, he was still athletic; at five–foot–ten and 165 pounds, he could still take the steps to the Capital two at a time and spent at least six hours a week in the workout room in that building. His brown hair had been graying at the temples for a number of years now. His face was square and handsome; a slight scar on his right cheek came from a football injury in college. He lived alone now after being widowed a little over three years ago; his only real joy in life was his work in the Senate and his daughter, Charlie. If a father ever loved and beamed with pride for his daughter, it was John Waggner. Everyone whom he came in contact with knew that or soon learned it.

Waggner walked down the wide hallway to the offices of the Senate Intelligence Committee. As he opened the double mahogany door and walked inside, the secretary greeted him and handed him a stack of messages. "Charlie called; she wants you to give her a call at work," she said.

"Thanks, I'll call her; anything urgent?" he asked.

"No, just Charlie," she replied with a grin.

"Thanks," he retorted with a bigger grin. He knew that the staff was aware that he doted on his only daughter and the love that was between them.

John Waggner graduated from George Washington University in 1956 with a BA in political science and took an MBA from Wharton Business School in Philadelphia. For the last 20 years, he had been the mainstay on the Intelligence Committee of the Senate Staff. He had a private pilot's license; he once played football at GWU, still jogs daily and is the source of Charlie's love for physical activity. Martha Horton Waggner, his wife, grew up on a farm in Colby Kansas, the only daughter (among four sons) of Ann and Henry Horton. Martha did very well in school and earned a scholarship to GWU where she met John Waggner. She majored in Modern Languages, easily mastering Russian as well as most of the Slavish tongues and Greek while minoring in History, which seemed to be a natural companion subject. After graduate school, John and Martha were married in the Episcopal Church in Bethesda where they also rented their first apartment. John became a staff aide to Senator Harvey Anderson (R)

Maryland, a boyhood friend of his father from a long line of Republican politicians and a very well known Maryland family. Within two years, they had purchased a spacious home on Conrad Place in Bethesda, MD. It was there that Charlie had been born and there he still chose to live even though he lived there alone. It was a sanctuary to him and he could think of no place else in the world that he would ever call home.

Martha had been able to divide her time between raising Charlie and her work. She was one of the most called-upon translators for the Senate Staff and could, most of the time do the translation at home. Only occasionally did she have to drive to the Hill to do translation on a sensitive or confidential document. Once she was even called to fill in for the White House Russian translator and sat in on a telephone call between Khruchev and Kennedy, translating for the President. In 1994, Martha died of leukemia; John was devastated.

At home, his study was the one sanctuary that John Waggner could count on; it held all of the comfortable and refreshing things in his life down to a picture of Charlie on his desk. He knew he wasn't perfect and had a number of vices. He used to smoke. Cigars were a pleasure to him, but after all the controversy over tobacco and cancer, he thought better of his pleasure and quit. He enjoyed a good drink of Scotch or brandy in the evening. All alone in his study, he often, late at night, would put a favorite classical CD in the player, pour a drink in a snifter and sit back in his black leather easy chair. He would let the soothing music and the velvet of the spirits roll over him and lull him into a more pleasant frame of mind. This was his way of winding down and relaxing after a hectic day...completely alone...and lonely, so very lonely.

Although John drove a very sensible car, he did have his fantasies. In the garage was his toy and his love...and men do love cars, especially John. His love was a 1968 MGB, British Racing Green with a black ragtop. Only when he felt really free and comfortable with himself did he take it out to drive in the rural Maryland and Virginia countryside. This was his car; this was John Waggner. It made him remember earlier days and even though it really wasn't necessary, it kept John Waggner young. He remembered driving one like it in Germany...many years ago.

Although his love for Martha had been genuine and she had been the one who had made his life complete in the early years when he was a young staffer in the Senate, the years in between had brought their marriage to a point that both considered it only a comfortable convenience to remain together; there was little, if no romance left between them. There was, however, their daughter who kept them together. His chance meeting with Maria Kochenko, a Russian, in Germany in the summer of 1978, opened a new, but brief chapter in his life.

John had quickly fallen in love with Maria; he was entranced with her beauty, and the way she showered attention on him when he was with her. It was a new experience for him...he even listened to the words of love songs for the first time in years. He had become somewhat of a cynic as far as romance was concerned. He often said that a cynic is a disillusioned romantic and in his situation, this was probably true. For that short time, however, he was once more a romantic and once more he relished the feeling. But it wasn't to last; he returned abruptly to the States and to Marsha. Maria returned to the Soviet Union and he eventually lost track of her. It wasn't really either his fault or hers, it was just fate.

John Waggner worked hard and felt it necessary to spend long hours making certain that the Senate he served had the information it needed to make the decisions that affected the Country...his Country...it was personal to him. Other than that, he had one overwhelming interest and love in life...his daughter Charlie.

He had arrived at his office at seven–thirty and sorted through his incoming mail for about twenty minutes. Nothing was immediate for a change and it gave him an opportunity to sit back and relax. At eight o' clock, he reached for the telephone, pushed two buttons on the console and waited. Charley would be at work by now. After two rings, Charlie answered.

"Charlie Waggner," she said.

"Hi, Charlie, what's going on?" he asked.

"Hi, Pops," she replied. "How ya doing?"

"I don't know whether to love your familiarity or hate your colloquialness," he replied.

Charlie laughed and said, " Ah, come on Daddy, where's your sense of humor?"

Waggner chuckled and replied, "It's still here; what's going on?."

"Well, has Jonathan briefed you on the microdots?"

"Yes, he called yesterday on the secure phone and gave me a full briefing. I passed it on to the Committee."

"We've established a task force to investigate it," she continued. "I'd like to discuss it with you further, would you like to come over for dinner tonight?"

"Love to; what time?"

"How about six? We can have a glass of wine before dinner."

"Sounds great, I'll be there. See ya at six."

Waggner hung up and started back to work; he felt better now and looked forward to the evening with Charlie.

John Waggner walked into the lobby of Bedford Towers at exactly six o'clock that evening. He was dressed casually since he was to have an evening alone with his daughter. He wore blue jeans and a western shirt and boots. It was chilly so he also wore a soft brown leather jacket and a brown western hat. He pushed the button for the fourteenth floor and waited as the elevator door closed behind him. In two minutes, he was knocking on Charlie's door. From inside came a call of "Come on in, Dad, its open." Waggner tried the doorknob, and let himself in. He caught a glimpse of movement in the kitchen area and headed in that direction, throwing his leather jacket and hat on the back of an overstuffed chair.

"How do you know I'm not a burglar?" he asked.

"Because it's exactly six o'clock and you're always on time," she replied not even looking around. "And besides, burglars don't knock." She was placing a meat loaf, his favorite, in the oven and having finished, wiped her hands on a dishtowel and walked over to her father and putting her arms around his neck, she kissed him. He surrounded her with both arms and returned the kiss. It was unmistakably a serious father-daughter love affair in a family that now included only the two of them.

"So, what are you up to, Charlie?" he asked sitting down at the small kitchen table.

She busied herself with preparations for supper and over her shoulder replied, "Jonathan may have filled you in on some of it…it has to do with some microdots found in the cane of a dead man in New York City. There's something that appears to be in Russian and lists of numerics. We have figured out part of it mostly because of someone that…and get this…is, or was anyway, a deep agent for the Soviet Union. He now works for the NSA. He's also kind of nice," she added in a lower tone of voice.

Her father raised an eyebrow. "Oh?" he remarked, more as a question.

Charlie gave him a smirk, stuck out her tongue, and continued. "There were some other things that I noticed today that bothered me, but we can get into that after supper." Charlie poured two glasses from a bottle of *1995 Barone Fini Pinot Grigio* and set one of them on the table in front of her father. She sat down across from him at the table.

After they had talked of personal things that were going on in their lives and about some news about their extended family, they had supper, finished the dishes together and sat down with a cup of coffee in the living room. Charlie then broached the subject of the project again.

"Dad, when the meeting was over, I took the slides and copied them into my word processor. I then converted them into an English font. The gibberish in Russian was transferred into English. Apparently, the author had written it in English on a Russian typewriter. Not a bad code, actually, and fairly simple to decode if you knew what to do." She looked down at her coffee cup and paused again. "There were two things that bothered me, Dad. First, on the sheet of names, Sean's cover name was there as expected opposite the number that indicated where to find correlating numbers on the previous pages."

"Wonderful," Waggner interrupted. "You cracked the code."

"That's not all. I also saw two names on the list with another special coding preceding them."

"Oh?"

"The names were John and Constance Deiter." She could see that her father didn't understand the connection, so she continued. "The FBI agent with the team is John Deiter. I knew that this could be a coincidence so I did some checking. The agent, John Remington Deiter, III, was orphaned at the age of eighteen. Both of his parents died within a week of each other...of strokes. Their names were John and Constance Deiter."

"What you're saying is that this agent's parents were deep Soviet agents," Waggner observed looking over at his daughter.

"Yes, I suppose so," she replied again looking down at the coffee cup that she cradled in her hands. "But also, if they were killed, it was probably because they defected."

"Yes, of course."

"Dad, I think that I'm the only one that knows this…except you."

Waggner thought for a moment and said, "What else did you get from the translation?"

"Well, there were several references to 'Rasputin;' my guess is that its a code word for some project…in fact two of the sheets say 'Project Rasputin' in the titles."

Waggner repeated the word as a question, "Rasputin?"

Charlie nodded her head in silence, looking up at him.

John Waggner sat back with his coffee cup in his hand. The look on his face was detached and thoughtful. He sighed and shifted in his chair, placing his cup on the table. "Rasputin," he said again almost wistfully as though to draw up a recollection from some fuzzy corner of his memory.

After several moments, Charlie looked up at her father and tilted her head in the gesture of a question. Then she said, "Dad, what is it?"

Waggner had been looking blankly into space and then looking straight at Charlie said, "Something from a number of years ago…someone I knew…and the term "Rasputin."

Now it was Charlie's turn to say, "Oh?"

John Waggner sighed again and looking away from her said, "Charlie, your mother must have told you about the blond in the brown Morgan."

Charlie smiled, "Yes, she did."

Waggner shifted his weight again. "Do you mind if I'm very honest with you?"

Charlie laughed, "I insist," she said, her large eyes now staring fixedly at her father.

"I don't want to repeat any of what you may already know, Charlie," he continued. "It happened on that trip I took to Germany in the summer of '78. We were to meet with a trade group from the Soviet Union. I wanted to make it into a mini vacation as well…no, I just needed some time away from your mother, I guess. It's a long story and I won't go into the details, but I met a Russian woman from the trade group by the name of Maria Kochenko. She was lovely, blond and we seemed to….to enjoy each other's company. When we first met, I didn't realize that she was on the trade group. Her English was excellent and she had a superb sense of humor. I guess you would say that we fell in love."

"I think I know all about that, Dad, but that's all water under the bridge now; where does it fit in with what's going now?" she interjected.

"I'm coming to that. We had many long discussions about what our own life experiences had been and how we had grown up and where. She said that when she first came to Moscow, she lived with a man who was considerably older and came from her home city which was…Grozny…I think. As I recall, she had mentioned that he was a cousin or other relative of some sort…anyway, they were related in some way. Anyway, one night after she had consumed a little too much vodka, she mentioned that he had headed up a project that she joked about because its name was Rasputin. She also mentioned that when her friend began to get into the business of spying and assassination, she left him."

Charlie had been only partially listening to her father, but her father's last statement jolted her. "What?" she exclaimed. "Do you think you could ever find her again? She could be a key to finding out who's responsible for the killings."

"I don't know," her father replied, "but I think I know where to start. Do you still have the original paperwork on the Morgan?"

"Sure, but why?"

"Will you get it for me?"

Charlie went over to her desk, a tall mahogany secretary. She bent down, opened the bottom drawer and thumbing through a stack of papers, came up with a brown folder with the picture of a Morgan Plus 4 on the cover. She returned the rest of the papers to the drawer, shut it and sat down next to her father on the couch. Waggner took the folder and started sorting through the forms and letters until he came to the one he wanted…the name and address of the previous owner. He looked at the name and Charlie thought she detected a barely perceptible sigh escape from her father's lips.

"Did your Mother ever tell you that the woman I met that summer was the previous owner of the Morgan?" he asked.

"No, but I had always suspected it," she replied.

"The Baroness Maria Sergeievna von Klauss," Waggner read from the form in his hand. "Her last name used to be Kochenko," he added. "The address is a

Stuttgart postal box, which I suppose is the von Klauss estate. "

"All things being equal, and no slight to Mom, having a father who had an affair with a baroness is kind of amazing." She paused and looked at him out of the corner of her eye, "I'm kind of impressed." Both of them erupted into laughter.

Waggner finished his coffee and got up to go. "As usual, Charlie, this has been delightful, thanks so much. Tomorrow I'll try to contact Maria; if I can't, I'll find out as much as I can and fly over to Germany and try to talk to her. I'll get what information I can, anyway. Hopefully, we may find out who we're dealing with."

"Anything I can do?" she asked.

"Maybe Jonathan's firm or the NSA can come up with something on Maria; if so, it'll help me get in contact. Can you do that for me early tomorrow."

"Sure, Dad."

Waggner put on his jacket, kissed Charlie, and left the apartment. He had a lot of thinking and remembering to do. He had to remember all that he could about what Maria had said when they were together, maybe some other memories might come back too, he mused. That night, it was John Waggner's turn to dream of the beautiful woman he had known.

The U.S. Senate Office Building
Senate Intelligence Committee
Washington, DC
Tuesday, November 4th, 1997

John Waggner arrived at his office at seven–thirty in the morning. He poured a cup of coffee from the pot set up in the outer office, went back into his office and closed the door. He picked up the telephone on his desk and punched in the Senate's central operator's number. When he received an answer, he asked, "Can you find a party for me in Germany?"

"I'll try, sir," came the answer.

"I am trying to contact a Baroness Maria von Klauss at the von Klauss estate outside of Stuttgart."

"We have a German speaking operator who comes in at eight o'clock," she replied, "if you can wait until then, I'll have her try."

"Sounds great, thank you…when you, or she, gets anything at all would you call me immediately?"

"Of course, sir."

He hung up the phone and picked up the papers from his in-box. All he could do now was wait, and he could get some work done in the meantime.

It was about eight thirty–five when the phone rung on Waggner's desk. He picked it up. "Waggner."

"Mr. Waggner, this is the switchboard; we have some information on the party you wished to contact."

"Yes, of course, what do you have?"

"I'm afraid that the Baroness wasn't there, but I did leave a message that you would like to speak to her when she returned. I left your name and this number, if that's all right?"

"You did good, thanks so much," he replied.

At two–fifteen, Waggner's phone rung and he picked it up with the usual, "Waggner."

"Sir, I have a call for you from Germany."

Waggner felt his breath suddenly being taken away. He paused and then said in a somewhat raspy voice, "Would you put her through, please?"

A woman's voice said, "John?" Waggner thought his heart would burst; his voice caught in his throat.

"Uh, Maria?" came the weak reply.

There was a long sigh on the other end of the phone and then the voice softly replied in a horse whisper, "John Waggner, where have you been, my love?"

CHAPTER THIRTEEN

▼

FLIGHT TO THE PAST

Lufthansa Flight 885
Washington to Frankfurt
Wednesday evening, November 5th, 1997

The plane was full and Waggner was thankful that the NSA had booked a first class ticket for him to Frankfurt. It would make it easier to start off fresh when he arrived at his destination. There was a lot to do when he got there. He thought for a moment that some minion at the NSA or in the Senate might interpret what he was doing as a lark or flight into fantasy for a member of the Senate Staff. No, he didn't think anyone outside the NSA or even Jonathan's firm knew the real reason he was going or even of the trip itself. As far as anyone knew, it was just a trip...one for which he was taking vacation time...the other reason, looking up an old girl

friend at taxpayer's expense, would have made the
tabloids fairly well dance with glee.

After takeoff, the flight settled down to a humming
monotony. About five minutes out, the stewardess asked
if he wanted another drink and explained his selections
for dinner. Waggner asked for a Beefeater's Martini and
settled down to enjoy a novel that Charlie had given
him for his birthday, but he had never gotten around to
read it. A half-hour out, dinner was served which was,
even in first class, not that exciting, but satisfying.
When he had finished eating and settled down with a
brandy, he started to reminisce about the first time he
had been to Germany. Splotches of memory began flitting through his subconsciousness and he dosed in
between them; the memories began to flow into his
dreams as the vibration of the plane lulled him to sleep.

The late afternoon sun cast spotted shadows on the
black pavement of road as it wound through a dense
portion of the Black Forest south of Stuttgart. John
Waggner gunned the engine of the 1968 British Racing
Green MGB. He had bought the sports car two weeks
earlier from a dealer along the Hauptstrasser. He spun
around a sharp corner surrounded by dark, pine-tree
shadows...he wanted to see the license plate number of
the brown sports car ahead of him; he was sure that he'd
seen it...her...before somewhere. It was less than a
minute ago that he had briefly caught sight of the car
and driver through a break in the trees on the hillside.
The car was climbing the hill ahead of him and he knew
the road well enough to know that there were no inter-
sections or homes in this stretch of forest. If he could
only get close enough to see a number, he would be able

to identify the car again, if it was parked some place. The driver was the same one he had seen last week in generally the same vicinity, he was sure of that. He imagined her to be beautiful, but in fact all he had seen was her hair flowing in the wind behind her...long blond hair...it must have come down to the middle of her back. John took the left-hand turn easily...downshifting in the process. The MGB responded as though it were a part of him. For a split second the shadows across the road hid the small sports car parked on the right side of the road ahead of him. Suddenly, it was right there in front of him. Waggner cramped the wheel to the left and swerved hard, cutting his turn even more drastically. The wheels squealed their complaint and the car came within a hair's breath of side swiping the brown sportster. He caught a fleeting glimpse of blond hair in the right front seat as the scene left his vision. The road straightened and John was able to bring the MGB under control and ease it to a stop. In his rear view mirror he saw the Morgan still parked on the side of the road behind him. Gripping the shift knob between his middle and ring finger, he flung the shaft into reverse, turned in his seat, and popped the clutch. The car reacted and accelerated back down the road straight towards the Morgan. At a distance of ten yards, John slowed down and brought the car to rest a few feet ahead of the Morgan. Turning in his seat, he gave a weak smile and addressed the other driver, "*Entschuligund sie mir bitte, Fräulein, ich hatten sie nicht gesehen,*" Then added, "*Sind Sie...*OK?" The latter comment lapsing into English when the expression in German escaped him.

The head of blond hair rose slowly over the top of the windshield as though it were a sunrise on some tropical island and John could see that it encircled the most beautiful set of blue eyes he had ever seen and a ruby-lipped smile that melted his heart and left him speechless.

"Your driving is almost as bad as your German," she said teasingly in nearly perfect English. He recognized the tease and detected an accent, but couldn't really place it, although it held just a hint of British crispness. "Were you following me?" she teased again.

"A little too closely, I'm afraid," John returned. "I'm sorry."

"Apology accepted," she replied. "There's a Gasthaus in the village about a kilometer ahead that serves a delightful wine, if you'd buy me a glass, we'll call it even."

Waggner waved his hand in concurrence; it was the easiest thing to do as the invitation had left him speechless and overwhelmed by this stroke of luck. The Morgan pulled around him and sped off down the road, the MGB was soon in hot pursuit. As Waggner rounded the next curve in the tree-lined road, he could see the Gasthaus ahead of him on the left. The brown Morgan was already parked in front of it and the driver's seat was empty. He pulled up next to the other car, climbed out of the MGB and entered the door of the tavern.

Looking around the room, he saw several booths of heavy wood along the far wall and two long wooden tables in the center of the room. There was one table in the far corner with a carved sign that said "*Stammtisch*"; that would be for the regular customers. He looked to his left where there were several square tables next to the line of windows looking out onto the street. At the far end of the main dining area, was the woman he had just spoken to several minutes before. She was seated at a small table for two. She smiled and he returned the smile walking over to where she sat.

"I didn't introduce myself when I almost ran into you…I guess I didn't know the proper protocol in such a situation," he said. He held out his hand and was about to say his name when she interrupted him.

"I know who you are, Mr. Waggner; Mr. John Waggner from the Intelligence Committee of the United States Senate."

Waggner felt as though his mouth fell open and he was gaping at her in disbelief. Either she hadn't noticed or he wasn't as obvious as he felt.

"You are full of surprises," he replied. "How do you know who I am and what I do?"

"I could keep you guessing all day," she said, "and it might be fun, but I won't." She offered her hand and wearing a giant sized grin, completed the introduction. "My name is Maria, Maria Sergeievna Kochenko and I'm with the Soviet Trade Union whom you will be meeting with tomorrow. I'm the official interpreter for the group."

"Well I'll be damned," he replied.

"I certainly hope not on my account," she laughed.

Waggner sat down as a matronly looking woman in a white apron walked up to the table. "*Guten tag*," she said.

"*Guten tag*," replied Waggner, "*Zwei weisse wein, bitte.*" ordering wine for the both of them. Maria said something in German that sounded like the name of a grape or locale, but he missed it. The woman didn't however, smiled broadly she said *"Ja, gewiss, meine dame."* She turned and left them alone.

After an awkward moment when neither of them spoke, Waggner asked how she knew so much about him, but was interrupted when the woman returned with two large stemmed glasses etched with grapevines and filled with a white wine.

"We are fully briefed before leaving the Soviet Union and once more when we come into a foreign country. Aren't you?"

"Uh…well yes," he stammered. "But obviously not in as much detail. Have you been here long?"

"For almost a month, why do you ask?"

"I have a hard time imagining a Soviet citizen driving a British Morgan, that's all," he replied.

She laughed. "Oh that," she said. She paused and then continued in a lower voice, "I met a man a few weeks ago who insisted that I have my own transportation while I'm here…you know, for my own convenient. I think he was trying to impress me, but he was also very nice. Anyway, he parked the car in front of my hotel and left a note with the desk clerk. There were ownership papers in the console of the car made out in my name. I have had lunch with him several times, but I think he just wants to impress me with his wealth…he is married, of course."

"And what about you?" he asked.

"What do you mean, am I married?"

"Yes, I obviously don't have the same information on you as you do on me."

"No," she replied simply and looked out the window.

"And of course you know all about me."

After a moment, she replied, "A man is either married or he is not. What he tells you is what the real truth is…perhaps not the facts, but the truth."

"That's quite profound," Waggner responded.

She laughed again and said, "Me, profound? Oh, my dear John Waggner, I certainly hope not."

The sun went down, but the two people sitting at the table didn't notice. After a while, they ordered supper and talked throughout the evening. Their mood became quieter and more mellow as the evening wore on. Local people wandered into the Gasthaus and later that night they began singing and enjoying the fellowship of friends as is the custom in Germany. The couple at the corner table joined in and shared the camaraderie of the evening. When it became much later than both of them realized, Waggner suggested that they leave. Outside, Maria opened the door to the Morgan and turned to find Waggner close behind her. She turned and putting her hand behind his neck, kissed him passionately. He returned it with equal ardor.

"I will see you tomorrow, " she said in a determined manner. "We will finish early. See you for dinner?"

"Of course," he replied. "Are you OK driving back to your hotel?"

"Yes, I drive better like this than you do sober," she joked and both of them laughed. "It is thoughtful of you to ask, though; thank you." She climbed into the Morgan, backed onto the road and drove off.

Slowly, Waggner walked over to his MGB. The evening had been magnificent and he had enjoyed talking with a woman more than he had in years. And not just a woman, but a beautiful, cultured and intelligent woman who seemed to enjoy his company equally as much. As he pulled out onto the road towards Stuttgart, he was happier than he had been in a long time.

The next day, Waggner met with his trade group early in the morning in the lobby of the hotel. They left in three cars to go to the meeting with the Soviet trade group. He had not spoken a word to anyone of his meeting the evening before with Maria. He didn't know what to expect when he saw her and decided to let her set the scenario. In about fifteen minutes, they had reached the estate of Baron Karl von Klauss who had generously offered his home as a meeting place for the conference.

The conference was uneventful for the most part and Waggner's apprehension about Maria was unfounded. She played the part of the interpreter with a great display of competence and professionalism. During the proceedings, she addressed him formally and acted as though she didn't know him. Towards the end of the day, there was a break in the discussions and he met Maria in one of the hallways of the estate by accident...or so he thought. She came up to him to formally introduce herself and handed him a note while shaking hands. He palmed the piece of paper, and offered a knowing and relieved smile in return; she returned it quickly, turned and walked back into the conference room. Waggner waited until he was sure no one was watching and looked at the note she had handed him. It said, "Hotel dem Kronigen, Kronig Ludwigs Platz, six o'clock in the lobby." The rest of the day seemed to be a dream world to him. He couldn't wait until it was over and he could think of nothing but Maria and the evening to come.

At five forty–five, he entered the Hotel dem Kronigen. The lobby was elaborately furnished in a nineteenth century decor. Rich dark woods blended warmly with the deep red velvet of the furnishings. He went over to an overstuffed chair at the rear part of the lobby and sat down. In about ten minutes Maria walked down the stairs. She was halfway down when she spotted him and a smile suddenly decorated her face. She looked around as she entered the lobby, and seeing no one else in particular, she went directly over to Waggner and took his hands in hers. "I'm glad to see you, John, is your car outside?"

"Yes."

"Let's go."

Together, they quickly walked outside to where he had parked the MGB. He held the door open for her and she stepped down into the passenger seat. Waggner walked around the car and climbed into the driver's seat. Quickly, he started the car and drove around the corner into Kronig Ludwigs Platz. At the next corner, he turned right and headed down the Hauptstrasse. Then he turned to Maria and said, "Are we safe?"

She laughed and said, "Yes, I'm sure; they aren't worried about me, I have friends."

The evening was all that Waggner could have asked for. Alternately, they either laughed or sat talking earnestly. Eventually they ended up at his hotel room. That night was to rank as one of the most memorable in John Waggner's life.

When they awoke, it was Sunday morning and there was very little noise from the square outside the hotel to disturb them. Waggner was first to waken and opened his eyes to see Maria's face surrounded by her generous blond hair on the pillow next to him. The starched white decken bed covering barely covered her breasts; and there was a smile on her face giving her an angelic countenance. He stared at her for a long time. Eventually, she started to stretch and finally opened her eyes. Upon seeing Waggner, she smiled and reached out her hand to pull his face towards hers. They kissed long and passionately. After the embrace, she finally pulled back slightly and looking into his eyes, sighed in a husky voice, *"Und so, meine leber, wie gehts du?"* (And, my love, how are you?)

"Maria, you have made me the happiest man in the world." It was weak, that he knew, but was all he could offer at the moment.

Maria smiled and kissed him again hard on the lips. They made love once more, prolonging it as long as they could. Then they dozed for a short time in each other's arms.

It was almost nine o'clock when they finally got out of bed. They showered…together…went back to bed to make love again and finally decided to get dressed about nine–thirty. That day, they went for a ride in Maria's Morgan…she even let him drive. They strolled through the zoo, went for a tour at the castle, and walked along the riverbank. That night, they had dinner in a quiet inn and finally retired back to Waggner's room.

The rest of the week was spent having conferences during the daytime and being together at night. When the conference came to an end, they drove the scenic route to Nürnberg together in Maria's car. For the next week, they spent every minute together. Neither wanting to admit that this moment in time would ever end for them.

For Maria, this was what she had worked for and had planned for ever since she left Grozny for Moscow many years before. John Waggner fulfilled her dreams and expectations in life. If that weren't enough, she had actually fallen in love with him as well. The fact that he was married was only a minor impediment to her plans, and would soon be taken care of when John returned to America. They hadn't really talked about it, though. She knew that he wasn't happy in his marriage and simply assumed that he would make arrangements when he returned home. Maria would leave to return to Moscow, but she knew she would soon accompany another group to the West. They would make their plans then.

In the midst of his growing unhappiness at home, the thought of being with Maria was very appealing to John. He didn't know how he would break it to Martha, but was sure he would do so not long after he returned to Washington. He was worried about Charlie though, and how a sixteen–year–old girl would take a family breakup. That thought bothered him immensely.

Finally, it came time for both to resign themselves to the fact that a return to their own countries was imminent; the dream world of these last two weeks had come to its end. Maria was the first to mention it one night as they were walking back to their small hotel along Ostern Tür Strasse. "We'll need to leave for Frankfurt on

Sunday; tomorrow will be our last day here. What would you like to do?"

Waggner couldn't think, he had all but forgotten that his time was almost up and he had to meet the Staff contingent at the Frankfurt Flughaven on Monday morning. "Let's talk about it over breakfast tomorrow morning, Maria...at breakfast."

"Breakfast, we're serving breakfast now, Mr. Waggner. Mr. Waggner." The voice took on a persistent tone. Waggner stirred and opened his eyes, half expecting to see Maria bending over him. Instead it was the stewardess who had served him supper almost five hours before. "We'll be landing in Frankfurt in a little over an hour," she said. He quickly brought himself into the present and began to review the instructions that Maria had given him over the phone. From Frankfurt he would rent a car and drive to Stuttgart and the von Klauss estate. There hadn't been enough time or the opportunity to ask her about her old friend in Moscow. After breakfast, the plane began to lose altitude; it was beginning its approach into Frankfurt Flughaven.

▼

THE BARONESS MARIA SERGEIEVNA KOCHENKO VON KLAUSS

Aeroflot Flight 183
Moscow to Frankfurt
Wednesday, May 17th 1978

The flight had been delayed almost an hour from leaving Moscow's Sheremet'yevo Airport. It had been about a half-hour ride from downtown Moscow to the Airport earlier that morning. After the delay, it was finally good to get into the air even though Maria was still apprehensive. She had never flown before. Maria Sergeievna Kochenko was with a Trade Commission group going to Germany. She was to interpret for the group made up not only of Germans, but also of English and Americans. It had been a number of years since she had graduated from the Moscow State University although she had stayed on with the help of a scholarship to get her advanced degree in foreign languages and was the pride of her instructors. She had been picked up by the Bureau of Interpreters shortly after her graduation. Although she had interpreted in Moscow for over twelve years, this is the first time she had left the Soviet Union.

Maria sat back in her seat and tried to get some rest. It had been a long day and the evening flight to Frankfurt might give her a chance to sleep. She let her thoughts wander. It had been many years now since she had left Andrei; and it did seem so long ago. She had found an apartment close to the University within a week and continued her studies. She had half expected that Andrei would have tried to contact her or even have her arrested, but that didn't happen. As far as Maria knew, Andrei had returned to Grozny. She often thought about Andrei. He had been kind to her.

The plane landed in Frankfurt without incident and they processed through the West German customs easily as they were part of a sponsored group. Following the orientation by the political advisor at the embassy, they were driven to Stuttgart to their hotel. The next few days were spent learning about the people they would meet at the conference. Twice, they were brought to the estate of Baron von Klauss to attend receptions. There she met the Baron. Karl was a tall handsome man of about sixty–five years old who looked at least a decade younger. She could tell that he had quickly developed an interest in her. She saw no harm in allowing him to pursue the relationship.

It was at the end of the group's first week in West Germany when she was surprised by a note from the desk at the hotel that her car was available and parked in front of the hotel. She walked out of the double front door of the hotel and saw a brown British Morgan parked exactly where the desk clerk had described. The key was in the ignition and she fumbled through the glove compartment to find the papers. They were made out to Maria Kochenko. A note was attached from the Baron saying that a beautiful woman should never be without her private transportation.

The Baron von Klauss had been a survivor all of his life. He was one of those people who correctly analyzed the current situation and accurately saw the flow of coming events. He would then prepare for them and end up on the surviving side. Karl von Klauss' first involvement with politics was the summer he graduated from college; he recognized the emergence of a new leader in his Fatherland, Adolph Hitler. He didn't approve of the man and considered him very rough mannered and brusque, but also recognized that his rhetoric was strong and convincing to a people who needed an excuse to feel good about themselves. At twenty–three years old, he was a graduate of Heidelberg University, was heir to his father's title, and possessed a noble bearing that made him a welcome addition to the new order. He was quickly promoted in the Wehrmacht to the rank of Colonel and joined the initial invasion of Poland and then Russia in the first days of the war in 1939. He survived the horrors of Stalingrad and was decorated by the Fuhrer for his bravery. Karl spent very little time in Germany during those years, returning only twice to his father's estate near Stuttgart. During the last days of the war, he joined the conspiracy to assassinate Hitler hoping to secure a better bargaining position with the Allies to end the war and retain some sense of dignity for the German people. The attempt, of course, failed but Karl's part in the conspiracy was never revealed to the Nazi high command. It was, however, acknowledged by the Allies and at the end of the war Karl was allowed to return to his father's estate without the normal internment. Shortly thereafter, his father died and he inherited the title of Baron and the considerable wealth of his family.

The Baron spent his days after the war building up the economy of Western Germany and the fortunes of his family. Although considered by some to be German nobility's most eligible bachelor, he remained single until in 1970 he married a very young actress named Gretchen Strauss. Gretchen sadly died in childbirth only a week prior to their tenth wedding anniversary. In the late spring of 1978, Karl had met Maria Kochenko, a beautiful blond Russian interpreter who was part of a Soviet delegation that was using the baronial estates for an international conference. After Gretchen's death, Karl became suddenly aware that he had no heirs and emotionally needed to find another partner in life as well. Maria had returned to Germany on several occasions and each time was escorted by the Baron. Although he was decades older than she, they were finally married in 1991. The Baron died three years later and Maria retained the title and privileges of her marriage, if not the family fortune which would eventually go to Karl's cousin. Maria was content with the conditions of her situation and became a German citizen. Karl had left her a substantial trust which was more than adequate for her needs. She continued to live at the baronial estate.

The estate itself occupied over a hundred acres on the outskirts of Stuttgart. The house was a three-story building on the order of a French manor house. The courtyard which extended along the western side of the structure was of cobblestone pavement surrounded by beds of flowers. The gardens occupied the efforts of two full time gardeners. The lands were overseen by a forest-meister who looked to the woodland and the game, which was plentiful. The stables housed a half dozen horses and a winery processed the product of nearly forty acres of a Muller Turgau vineyard.

Inside, the manor was spacious, of nineteenth century motif and boasted of several extensive libraries and sitting rooms which provided adequate opportunity for small and large international contingents to ply the trade of compromise and inter-communication. On the second floor were sixteen private bedrooms for guests as well as a private wing for the baronial family. The third floor was occupied by the staff who administered and ran the estate.

Maria was content with the house and in her new-found position; she traveled abroad extensively and entertained at the estate as her husband had done before his death. She maintained the contacts of her husband although with the exception of the vineyard, she was precluded from any financial affairs affecting the von Klauss family business.

The von Klauss estate 25 kilometers South of Stuttgart,
Germany
Thursday, November 6th, 1995

The telephone call two nights ago from John Waggner was one of the few times that Maria had been truly surprised. Somehow, though, she had always believed that John would contact her if he were free and had some idea that she also was free. Their time together, although brief, had been passionate and intense. She had finally understood why he broke off their relationship. Secretly she was very jealous of the mutual love that existed between John and his daughter. It was a special love that they could never have…but she also knew that it was a different kind of love. On the telephone, she had told him that she would wait at the estate and asked him to drive there to meet her.

It was nearly eight o'clock in the evening when John finally arrived at the estate. At a window in the front study, Maria held the curtain aside as she peered out at the road leading up to the manor; the head lights of a car stopped at the gate and then continue up the road that led into the courtyard. She watched as the car stopped opposite the main door and a man of medium build and height climbed out of the BMW sedan. A far cry from the British MGB sportster, she thought. She seemed to remember him as being somewhat taller, but maybe it was the angle from the window that made him appear shorter, or maybe it was her memory of this lovely man that had made him larger than he really was. She dropped the curtain and walked down towards the entrance hall and the main doorway.

As she approached the hallway, she heard the bell and saw her head maid open the door.

"*Guten Abend,*" the man said, "*Ich heisse Waggner, John Waggner.*"

A woman's voice interrupted the exchange with, "There are no introductions necessary here, John Waggner, I would have known you anyplace." Maria glided down the hallway towards the newly arrived guest. The maid quickly picked up Waggner's two-suiter bag and disappeared up the stairway with it, leaving the visitor with her mistress.

Upon reaching Waggner, Maria placed her hand behind his neck and bent his head down to her lips and kissed him long and warmly. He put his arm around her waist and drew her closer to him.

The dinner before the open fire in the manor's private wing had been very welcome and restful after the many hours of flying and driving, but Waggner still felt exhausted. The wine had soothed him somewhat, however, and raised his spirits. The two of them were lying together on pillows set in front of the fire. Being so close to Maria was in itself intoxicating and finally at almost midnight, the combination began to overcome him. "Maria," he said in a soft voice, "this has been one of the most enjoyable evenings I've had in years. Just remembering the times we had together again is like reliving them. But, we should talk about the real reason that I'm here."

"And what is the 'real' reason that you're here?" she answered in a tone that had a deeper question than what appeared on the surface. Waggner understood her perfectly and reflected several moments before answering.

"I know of two very good and 'real' reasons why I came to see you. The first reason is perhaps the excuse I had to come and the second is the curiosity and pleasure of being with you again."

"Curiosity?" she inquired.

"Bad choice of words, perhaps...too cold, but somewhat accurate in a way. When I learned that you were now the Baroness, it really didn't come as a shock. I remember how attentive he was even then. He was a good man."

"That he was, John Waggner, but he wasn't you." The comment was meant to be both a gentle slap and an invitation; he took it that way.

"I'm sorry, Maria, but you did understand finally. I sensed it from your letters."

"Yes, I suppose I did understand, but I didn't like it," she replied. "Anyway, you're here, we're together again, so let's pretend that we were never apart."

"I don't think I'm going to be up to an evening with you, my dear," he quipped.

"Let me take charge of that," she said seductively. "I have my ways."

The next morning after breakfast, Waggner and Maria walked down the dirt road behind the manor house to the stables where two horses had been saddled and were waiting for them. The weather was somewhat chilly and their jackets felt good as they rode together down the pathway which crossed the meadow behind the manor house. Across the field there was a path which led into a wooded area. Tall conifers rose high above them as the horses plodded quietly through the silent forest. About thirty minutes out, they came to the top of a rise that overlooked the entire estate. A clearing was set up which included a place to tether the horses and a wooden bench with a back to it. The two dismounted and sat together looking over the view before them. Finally, Waggner spoke.

"Maria, you mentioned years ago of a time that you spent in Moscow with a person from your city in Chesnya…Grozny, I believe."

"That would be Andrei, and he was my cousin, but old enough to be my uncle," she replied. "What's the interest in Andrei?"

"There was something that you mentioned at the time, something about 'Rasputin;' that name has come up again just recently in connection with some documents. Do you remember anything else about it?"

Maria was quiet for a few moments and then asked quietly, "Do you really think this has anything to do with Andrei?

"I don't know for sure, all I know is that the name 'Rasputin' appeared on the documents and a number of people are being killed who are…were Soviet citizens living in the United States."

"Andrei couldn't do anything like that…you don't know him, it made him sick when he had to…" Her voice dropped off.

"Had to what?" he asked.

"Had to kill someone," she replied.

"How? With a signal?" he asked again.

"Yes, then you know."

"We know part of it, but not everything. There were apparently 181 deep agents planted in the United States sometime in the sixties and early seventies. All of them were implanted with a microchip which was designed to locate them…or to kill them if necessary," he explained.

"Yes, that was Andrei's creation. He was so proud of what he had done until he had to implement the second phase of it…it almost destroyed him. That's when I left him. I never saw him again."

"What does Andrei look like and what's his last name?" he asked.

"His last name is Kilyaikin, his patronymic name is Mikailovitch; his father was my father's brother and shared my patronymic name, Sergeiovich or Sergeievna. We were close when I was a little girl and I fell in love with him…that's why I went to live with him in Moscow when I left home. After a while, I suppose I grew up and realized that it was more infatuation with an older man, than love. When he came home to tell me that he was forced to kill someone…two people, I used it as an excuse to leave him and found an apartment which I shared with another student at the University."

"You say two people; when was this?"

"In 1960, early…January or February, I think. Why?"

"There may be a tie in with part of the documents," he replied. "Did he say anything more about his system or the people?"

"Only that they were a couple with a teenage son. They had apparently defected," she said. "Do you think that Andrei is killing people now in the States?"

"I don't know, Maria, I honestly don't know…someone is. Do you have a picture of Andrei?"

"Why, yes," she replied. "I don't know why I've saved it after all these years, but I suppose it was out of loyalty; he was kind to me."

"May I see it?" he asked.

"Of course, it's in the chest in the parlor. Tonight after supper I'll get it for you."

After returning to the manor house, Waggner and Maria spent the rest of the day driving her replacement Morgan, a modern copy of the original. Touring through the German countryside brought back the fondest of memories of their encounter so many years ago. Later that evening, they were enjoying an after-dinner wine while lounging in front of the fire in the parlor. The supper that evening was one of the finest that Waggner could recall. It was Maria who brought up the subject of Kilyaikin's picture. She suddenly rose from where she had been reclining on pillows in front of the fire.

"The picture you wanted is over here in the chest," she said. "I hardly ever open it anymore; it holds memories I just don't need right now." She stood up and walked over to a large ornate chest against the far wall of the room. It was heavily carved and apparently quite old with a large brass hasp on the front. The top was raised in the form of a hump. Maria lifted the lid and pushed aside a tray. Reaching into the bottom of the chest she extracted a smaller box. She closed the lid to the chest and walked back to where Waggner was still reclining on the pillows in front of the fire. She sat down again crossing her legs as she did so and opened the box. Inside were a number of photographs that were now yellowish brown with age. Sorting through them, she stopped at one and stared at it for a moment; slowly she handed it to Waggner. "This is Andrei," she said quietly.

Waggner looked at the photograph; it was perhaps forty years old. The man's face was long and hollow. He had a haunting look in his eyes; his eyebrows were thick and his hair, black and beginning to gray, was thick, long, uncombed and wild. There was a wry smile on his face as though he were forcing the look exclusively for the camera and at the prodding of the photographer. He was wearing a long black coat with a scarf around his neck. In the background there was snow on the ground; he held a fur hat in his hand.

"The picture was taken a couple of months before I left him. You can see that there's still a lot of snow in Moscow," she said, bringing her head close to his, trying to see the picture from the same angle that he did.

"Do you mind if I borrow it?" he asked. "I'll send it back to you."

"Would you bring it back to me?" she asked in return.

"If you'd like that," he replied.

Waggner leaned over and placed the picture in the inside pocket of his jacket that was draped over the arm of a chair. He then turned back to face Maria. There was a tear slowly making its way down her right cheek. He furrowed his brow and with his finger stopped the tear in its downward path and scooping it up brought it to his lips. "John, don't leave me," she said plaintively. "Please don't leave me again."

"Would I do that again, if it were not your will?" he asked.

She smiled and melted into his arms.

Early the next morning, Waggner left the manor house and climbed into the BMW that he had parked there two nights before. He drove through the gate and turned onto the road that led to Stuttgart. It was almost twenty minutes later when he drove into the courtyard of the US Consulate in Stuttgart. The Charge de faire, Andrew Pickerly was expecting him and he was quickly ushered into the private office. "Can you fax a picture for me to the NSA?" asked Waggner.

"Of course, does it need encoding?"

"I don't believe so, but let me write a note to accompany it," said Waggner scribbling out a message on a pad of paper, then ripping it off he handed it to Pickerly. "I'll also call to make sure that they're expecting it."

"Easily done," replied the Charge de faire. "Is there anything else I can do for you?"

"No, I think this will do, thanks."

"Don't mention it," said Pickerly, taking the picture and sheet of paper that Waggner handed him. He left the room and Waggner sat back to wait until the man returned.

In about five minutes, Pickerly returned with the photograph in hand. "Done, here's your picture back. It was received at oh…three–oh–five Washington time at NSA and was to be delivered to a Colonel Henderson as soon as he arrived and a copy was sent to Charlie Waggner at Jonathan Banks, Inc. as your note indicated. Relative of yours?"

"Yes, my daughter. Thanks," said Waggner as he got up to go. He turned and said, "If there's any message or inquiry about me, I'll be at the von Klauss estate outside the city."

"I know where it is; I'll see you get the message," replied the Charge de faire.

Waggner thanked him again and then shook hands. After leaving the Consulate, he drove back to the estate.

Mission accomplished, he thought. Now to spend some quality time with Maria. He smiled to himself and felt some sort of weight lifted from his shoulders. Charlie would understand if he didn't hurry home. Besides, she had the Morgan and now he had Maria...at least for awhile.

CHAPTER FIFTEEN

▼

THE PICTURE

Jonathan Banks, Inc.,
Chevy Chase, Maryland
Monday, November 10th 1997

Charlie Waggner arrived early as usual at the firm and went to the portion of the east wing set aside for the Task Force on the top floor. On her desk, she was surprised to find a note that had been faxed to her from her father and a picture. The note read:

Charlie

I have met with Maria again and it has been wonderful; I know you will understand. The picture is of Andrei Kilyaikin who was responsible for creating the project as we suspected; Maria has confirmed that. The picture is twenty years old, so I suspect his hair is white and he has aged a bit, as have we all. She also confirmed that there were two people, a couple, who were assassinated in

February of 1960 which may reinforce the Deiter con-
nection we spoke about. See what you can come up with.
I will remain here another few weeks or so and will let
you know when I will return. I love you; Dad.

Charlie leaned back in her chair and looked at the
picture of Andrei Kilyaikin. He seemed to have a compassionate face, despite the gaunt look and that seemed
to contradict the idea that he was assassinating people.
Who or what was Kilyaikin, anyway? She pondered over
the question for awhile and then decided that she
should share the picture with Jack Deiter. From what
her father had said, Deiter's parents might have been
involved in this somehow and it looked like they may
have been deep agents themselves. It would be delicate,
but Jack Deiter looked like he was the type of person
that could take it. On hearing a noise, Charlie looked
up to see Rose coming through the door. "Morning,
Rose," she said cheerfully.

"Hi, Charlie, anything new?"

"Yes, matter of fact and I'm glad that you got here
first," Charlie replied.

"First? First before whom?" Rose asked.

"Before Jack."

"Oh, what's going on?"

"Did you see the translated list of names yet?"

"No, why? Something's going on, I can sense it."

"Two of the names on the list are John and Constance
Deiter. By some coincidence, that's also the names of
Jack's parents. And I've just received confirmation that
the dates of his parent's deaths coincide with the deaths
of two of the deep agents," explained Charlie.

"Oh, my God!" exclaimed Rose sitting down in a chair opposite Charlie. "Does Jack know yet?"

"No, it just came in. I thought that maybe you should be the one to break it to him, You two seem to be close."

"I appreciate that, Charlie, I'm just going to have to think about what I'm going to say. He hasn't spoken of his parents in a long time. I'll pick the time."

"Thanks, Rose, I feel better," Charlie sighed and seemed to relax.

"I don't think the others need to know about this yet, give me a chance to tell Jack before they find out."

"You got it," said Charlie. "Sean may notice the name similarity, though."

Rose went over to her desk and sorted through the incoming traffic in her box. She turned to Charlie and asked. "Heard from your Dad yet?"

"Yes, I'm afraid he's found an old flame and won't be back for awhile," she said trying to hide a smirk and failing miserably.

"Good for him," replied Rose. "Good for him."

The door opened and both women turned to see Jack Deiter come in.

"Get lost in the parking lot?" teased Rose, getting up from her chair and crossing over to where Deiter was.

"No, just talking with Sean; he's doing some research downstairs."

The two women exchange anxious glances. "Charlie's got a picture for you," said Rose interrupting the sudden silence.

Charlie came over to where the other two were standing with the photograph in her hand. "This guy is

Andrei Kilyaikin, the brains behind the microchips," explained Charlie as she handed the picture to Deiter.

Deiter looked at the photograph for a few moments and then raised his eyebrows. "We've got a problem, Houston," said Deiter. "We've got a problem."

Both women turned towards him with puzzled expressions on their faces.

"This is our man in the alley," he said. "A number of years older and with eyelids, but, I swear this is the same guy."

"Do you think your contact with the NYPD could confirm that?" Rose asked.

"Good idea, I'll fax him a copy. I'm sure, but it's always good to get another opinion."

Charlie sat back in her chair and looked at Deiter. "If what you're saying is true, that means that the killing is over and the killer is dead," She paused, "No wait. That's only partly true. Someone killed him for whatever was in the cane, so we're still looking for a killer who may have the list of agents and the means to locate them…the killing could still go on.

"That's right, Charlie," he said softly. "That's right."

At one–thirty that afternoon, the phone in the Task Force room jolted Deiter who was in deep concentration over a list of stroke victims provided by Bank's researchers. Deiter answered it. "Deiter."

"Jack, you struck pay dirt. I just got your fax and I'd say that our John Doe from the alley is none other than Andrei Kilyaikin," said NYPD Detective Ken Polk.

"That's what I thought," replied Deiter. "Got any suggestions on where we go from here?"

"It all depends," said the detective, "we still have a homicide and still have a killer on the loose. It may hinge on what the killer wanted with whatever he found in the cane. I'll run a check to see if I can find where Kilyaikin was staying and let you know if I come up with anything."

"Thanks, Ken," Deiter said hanging up the phone.

It was late morning of the next day when Deiter received a call back from Detective Polk. The NYPD had located a room rented to an Andrei Kilyaikin on 13th Street in lower Manhattan. They asked for and received a court order to enter it and had found information which indicated Kilyaikin also had an apartment in Washington that he was apparently renting. Polk gave Deiter an address at 1297 Wisconsin Avenue NE; Apartment 415. Deiter immediately called the FBI to get a court order to enter the apartment. Rose had left to do some shopping and he contacted her through her beeper and left the message to have her meet him at the apartment building lobby at four–thirty that afternoon.

At exactly four–twenty, Deiter walked into the apartment building on Wisconsin Avenue. He waited a few minutes and was finally joined by Rose McGuire. "What's going on?" she asked. "I had Charlie drive me over here."

"Kilyaikin had an apartment here; Polk called me this morning. There may be something up there that can blow this thing wide open. There doesn't seem to be a good reason for him to have an apartment in two cities at the same time."

Deiter went over to the desk where the clerk, a middle-aged man of Indian origin was busily pawing through a set of registration cards while seated behind the counter. "Excuse me," Deiter said holding up his badge, "My name is Deiter, FBI; This is my associate McGuire from the National Security Agency; I have a search warrant for Apartment 415, would you please show us to the room or give us the key."

The clerk looked up at the badge over his reading glasses. After carefully reading the identification and examining the badge, he asked in a heavy Indian accent, "Do you have the warrant?"

Deiter reached into his left inside breast pocket and withdrew a folded piece of paper. He unfolded it and thrust it before the clerk. "This satisfy you?" he inquired.

The clerk nodded and turned around to the bank of boxes behind him. Selecting a key from one of the boxes, he made his way around the end of the counter and headed for the elevator. "Follow me, I'll show you the room," he lilted.

The elevator door opened on the fourth floor and a man barged through the doorway as it was opening, bumping into the desk clerk in the process. Deiter came face to face with him and placed his hands on the man's shoulders. For a moment the two looked straight at each other, then Deiter asked, "In a hurry? Mind if we get out first?" Deiter's steely eyes stared directly into the wide staring eyes of the stranger. The man diverted his eyes and moved into the corner of the elevator. The clerk slunk around the corner of the door and headed down the hallway. Rose looked back over her shoulder as she walked into the hallway and saw that Deiter was still staring at the man. Deiter then stepped backward and allowed the door to close in front of him. "I wonder what that was all about," she whispered to Deiter.

"Beats the hell out'ta me," he replied. Both of them turned and walked down the hallway towards where the clerk was standing impatiently outside a door.

The clerk unlocked the door and went in followed by Deiter and Rose. The apartment was in fact a suite with two bedrooms, a living room and a kitchen. When the desk clerk had left, and they had the freedom of the suite, Deiter suggested that they split up and take separate rooms to search. Rose went to the door of the bedroom on the left, while Deiter took the one on the right. Rose opened the door to the room and walked in. There didn't seem to be anything out of the ordinary except that it didn't have the feel that it was lived in. Suddenly she heard Deiter exclaim, "Rose, in here."

Rose darted from the bedroom, across the living room and into the room that Deiter had entered. He was standing in front of a display of electronic equipment and a computer console.

"My God, the transmitter," she exclaimed.

"That's my guess," he responded. "If there was any question that this was a Russian program, my guess is that this squelches it. This has to be an independent operation otherwise they would be transmitting from Russia."

Rose and Deiter looked at each other and Deiter was first to say it, "The guy in the elevator…I wonder if he's got anything to do with this?" He walked over to the telephone and called the desk. "The man that bumped into you in the elevator," Deiter asked the clerk, "do you know him?"

"I have seen him before, but I do not know his name," replied the clerk.

"Is he registered here?"

"I do not believe so, Sir, but he has been visiting here for the past week."

"Is he in the lobby?"

"No, when I returned to the desk, he was no where to be seen," lilted the Indian clerk.

"Thanks, if you see him, I want to know immediately."

"Yes, Sir, of course, Sir," the clerk replied. Deiter hung up the phone and turned his attention to the electronic equipment that Rose was examining.

"Well?" he asked, "Anything?"

"All of this stuff is US made. Somehow, I was expecting Soviet equipment, but all of it's brand new and the latest on the market," Rose said studying the identification plates on the backs of the stacked electronic components.

"This looks like a transmitter," said Deiter switching on the equipment. He took out his pen and wrote down the frequency that had appeared digitally on the screen. "I'll check this frequency against the lists to see if there's a match,"

"We should have a team look this stuff over and brush it," Rose remarked.

"Wow, right back in the saddle as if you'd never left," Deiter observed.

She smiled at him, partly in appreciation of his wit and partly for his compliment.

"There's not much we can do here, but we have a choice…leave it as is and have it watched or run a team in here and dismantle it."

"If this equipment is being used to kill people, I don't see how we can let this maniac use it again," replied Rose.

"I suppose you're right," Deiter responded, "but I would love to catch this guy."

"Why not do both?"

The idea appealed to Deiter. "Of course, we can keep an eye on who wants to come in here and at the same time, have a couple of guys just look over the equipment to see if there's something we can use. I'll set it up." Deiter walked into the living room, picked up the phone and in three minutes he had set up the operation. He then joined Rose who was reviewing some of the files that she had brought up on the computer screen.

Some three hours later, Deiter began to feel somewhat hungry. "How about some dinner?" he asked Rose.

"Sounds good to me, where?"

"Maybe there's someplace around here, we can ask the desk clerk on our way out," Deiter offered. Rose nodded, took a last look at the room, and both of them left and locked the door behind them.

They took the elevator to the lobby and walked over to the small counter that served as an office for the desk clerk. Deiter looked around the lobby for any sight of the man in the elevator, but saw only a tall man with an unkempt mustache that didn't match his gray hair seated in the chair on the other side of the lobby reading a newspaper. He wore thick horn-rimmed glasses and a rumpled brown suit. Deiter thought it odd that he hadn't noticed him before. Maybe he wasn't there before. He shrugged it off and asked the clerk about someplace they could get something to eat that was within walking distance.

The clerk was glad to suggest a restaurant just a half a block away and offered to call ahead. Deiter thanked him, but said that it was still early and didn't think it would be necessary. The clerk agreed. Rose and Deiter left the apartment building and turned left up the street. They could see the sign for the restaurant up the block ahead of them.

Deiter suddenly slowed his walk, then stopped and turned to look into the store window as if he had seen something that had attracted his attention. "I think we're being followed," he said in a whisper.

"Did you get a look at him?" she asked.

"Only a glimpse, but it sure looked like the guy in the elevator." They waited for a moment and then Deiter shrugged. "Seeing things, I guess, let's go."

They opened the door to McHenry's Irish Pub and walked in. The place tried hard to gain the flavor of a true Irish Pub and if you overlooked the obvious, it succeeded. Deiter and Rose waited only a few seconds inside the entrance when a petite young girl came up to them and asked in a rolling Irish brogue, "Are ya here fa dinner or fa drrinks?"

"For dinner, please," Deiter responded. She showed them to a booth in the back of the restaurant, took their order for two Guinness's and left them alone.

The door to the restaurant opened and a figure slid through the door and walked quickly up to the bar. He was fairly tall and wore a green jacket with brown unpressed pants. His collar was turned up. No one

seemed to notice him, even the bartender. He looked
over the early dinner crowd and seemed to spot who he
was searching for in the back booth. He moved away
from the bar and caught the elbow of the hostess who
had just seated Deiter and Rose. "I'd like a booth…that
one," he said gruffly pointing to the one next to the
newly arrived couple.

"Will ya be alone, now, or will there be somebody
joinin ya?" she asked.

"Alone, and I want that booth," he replied, his eyes
closing to a slit. The tone of his voice convinced her that
she didn't want to have an argument with this man and
she picked up a menu and started back towards the
booth. He followed her closely, carefully keeping the
hostess between himself and the booth with the couple
in it. When they arrived at the table, he quickly slid in
with his back to them where he could overhear their
conversation. The hostess left and he shrugged off his
jacket and tried to look a part of the scene. While glancing over the menu, he looked up and noticed a tall man
in a brown suit walk quickly from the doorway of the
restaurant to the bar, selecting a seat so as to be able to
see the rear booth. He could see that the man remained
quite intent on the man and woman in the booth
behind him. He made a mental note of the man and
returned his concentration to the conversation of the
couple behind him. He could only pick up parts of
phrases; the acoustics in the restaurant were not con-
ducive to eavesdropping.

By this time, Rose and Deiter had been served their
Guinness's and were in serious conversation. "Now we
know what Kilyaikin was doing in this country and how

he was doing it," Deiter was saying, reviewing the case once more in an attempt to make sense of the situation so far. "What we don't know is who, if anyone, sent him or if he was a loner." At the name of "Kilyaikin" the man in the booth suddenly became alert and concentrated his entire effort on listening to the couple. "We don't know if he was intent on killing all of the people on the list or just some of them, either."

"It still would be interesting to know if the basis of all this activity was money or politics," mused Rose.

"My bet's on the money. Do you think that Kilyaikin thought this up all by himself, or did he have help from someone...like the Russian Mafia?" questioned Deiter.

"My guess is that he had help. The Mafia has connections in this country and it's not likely that he did. From what John Waggner got from Maria, it looked as though he was a loyal party man and not one likely to be trading away Communist agents for the money."

"Um...I agree."

"Jack, what about the transmitter? Shouldn't we disable it? It could cost more lives; it certainly cost Kilyaikin his in the long run."

"That brings us back to the question of who killed him...it certainly wasn't done by the transmitter, but I suspect that whoever did kill him wanted to know as much as they could about the transmitter...and the list."

"We're due for another meeting tomorrow morning at the firm. Why don't we flush it out there and see if anyone in the group can get a handle on it?"

"Good idea, Rose, I'll call Charlie and set it up," replied Deiter reaching for the cell phone in his inside coat pocket. After a couple of tries, he groaned and slid out of the booth. "These things don't work inside of restaurants some times," he complained. "I'll step outside." As he rounded the bar, he noticed the man he had seen in the hotel lobby sitting at the bar. He turned around to see if Rose was watching. She wasn't, but he did see a man sitting in the booth behind Rose whom he hadn't noticed before. He appeared to be of medium height and build. In the dim light of the restaurant he seemed to have light colored hair, possibly gray or blond. He looked a lot like the man that bumped into them in the elevator. The man appeared to be studying the menu a bit too intently.

In less than five minutes, Deiter had reached Charlie and set up the meeting with the agenda that he and Rose had discussed. It was to be at nine Wednesday morning. As he reentered the restaurant, he noticed that the booth behind Rose was now empty. The man at the bar was getting his coat on and seemed ready to leave…his glass, still half-full sat in front of him. As Deiter slid back into the booth opposite Rose, he asked, "Did you notice the man behind you get up?"

"No, I felt someone get up, but I didn't turn around."

"I think it was our friend from the elevator."

"Did he go out by you?"

"No, I would have noticed."

Deiter motioned to the waitress. When she finished with the table across the dining room, she came over to where they sat. "Arrrya ready ta order?" she lilted.

"Yes, but first…did you notice the man sitting behind us in this booth?" Deiter asked indicating the booth next to them.

"Indeed, and a strrange one he was too. Mean lookin for sucha honsome fella," she went on. "Insisted on this very booth, he did. Looks like he left in a hurry. Didn't even leave a tip…didn't order eitha. Musta slipped out the back by the powder rooms," she added with a shrug.

Rose and Deiter quickly ordered dinner and asked for another Guinness.

"Do you suppose he was listening?" Rose asked.

"I'd bet on it." Deiter looked up briefly as the man at the bar disappeared out the door. "Why do I get the feeling we'll see those two again?"

"Do you think it has anything to do with Aldridge Mason?" asked Rose.

"Could be one of them, but I doubt if both of them would be working for Mason," Deiter replied.

"That reminds me of something that happened earlier today," Rose quietly interjected.

"What's that?"

"Do you recall much about your parents, Jack?"

"I was eighteen when they died; I remember my childhood and growing up with both of them. They were good parents and I loved them very much. The shock of losing them both at the same time was kinda hard to take. I'm glad in a way that the appointment to the Naval Academy came up so suddenly, it helped to take my mind off their deaths. Funny how that happened," he mused. He then looked up at her with a puzzled expression on his face. "What brought this up? You said something happened earlier today."

"The translated list of names. The ones that Charlie was working on. The names of John and Constance Deiter were on the list."

"Oh, my God," Deiter whispered to himself. A wry smile suddenly began to spread over his melancholy expression and he sighed. "The thought just struck me. I should have had a long talk with my Uncle Bill before he died, I think he may have known a lot about this."

"Uncle Bill?" Rose asked.

"Um...yeah, sorry...that's what I called him anyway, he was a close friend of my parents. I think they did some work together, but I was never let in on it. William Colby; he was Director of the CIA when..."

"Oh, THAT Uncle Bill," Rose interrupted. "You're full of surprises, aren't you? You never told me about that."

"After my parents died, he looked after me during the funeral and the estate settlement. I always suspected that it was him that wangled my appointment to Annapolis." Deiter paused. "If they were deep agents, they must have been double agents. I do remember they took a trip to Russia not long before they died. I always thought it was either on business or a vacation, but...."

"They died from strokes, didn't they?" asked Rose.

Deiter nodded. "My guess now is that it was the fine handiwork of Dr. Kilyaikin," Deiter leaned back into his seat and raised his pint of Guinness. "I guess I don't quite feel as sorry for the old man in the alley now," he added.

Following dinner, Deiter and Rose walked down the side street to where he had parked the Jaguar just off Wisconsin Avenue. The night air was cool, but lacked the wind of the past few weeks, so the night was pleasant. They climbed into the Jag and Deiter started it and shifted into gear. As they were pulling out of the parking

space, Deiter noticed a red Mustang quickly pull into
traffic behind him. As they crossed Memorial Bridge,
the Mustang stayed a comfortable distance behind
them, keeping several cars between them. He berated
himself for being too suspicious. They were the hunters
after all, not the hunted.

CHAPTER SIXTEEN

▼

MASON'S SEARCH

The Law Offices of Symond, Hennessee and Smith
Upper Saddle River, New Jersey
Tuesday, November 11th 1997

It had been almost a week since Aldridge Mason had made the telephone calls that set in motion the search for Rose. He had been anxious all week, but resisted making any calls to inquire about the status of his source's success. At 2:15 PM the secretary buzzed Mason's line…he reached over and pushed the response button on his console. "Yes?" he asked.

"A Mr. Kinder on line three, sir," she said.

"I'll speak to him. Hold all other calls," he responded. Mason switched over to the line that was now glowing on the console and said, "What do you have?"

"She's in the Washington area; that I know for sure," was the reply on the other end of the line. "She's with someone named Deiter, a John Deiter with the FBI…I got that from a friend of mine in the Bureau. He has something to do with counter espionage, I'd guess."

"I don't pay you to guess," warned Mason.

"I'm down here now. I looked up where he lives in Alexandria, Virginia."

"What's the address?" demanded Mason. There was a pause on the phone.

"I'd advise against anything overt," cautioned the PI.

"What do you mean?" asked Mason.

"Something is going on and I don't think it's just 'hanky-panky' either," he explained.

"Oh, and what do you think it is?" Mason asked with a sarcastic emphasis on the "think."

"I've been in this game for a long time, you know, and I just have a feel that something bigger's happening then just two people shacking up."

"Go on; what makes you feel that way?"

"I'm getting…..'put-off' answers from people, people who normally say it like it is."

"I think you're getting too sensitive for this type of business. Now, let me tell you this…I want you to follow those two and find out what the hell they're up to, and when you find out, you'll tell me and then I'll teach not only her, but him as well, that neither of them'll play games at my expense. Get me that information, and get it fast!" Mason threatened as he slammed down the phone. He sat there seething, his chest rising and falling heavily; his eyes closed as he fought to gain control. His face had become red and his knuckles white as they grasped the arms of his chair. He was feeling his heaviness now…the years of rejecting exercise. Slowly, the red color faded from his face and his hands relaxed; his breathing became less severe and he appeared to relax.

Kinder would locate them and find out what was going on...and then he would go down there to confront them personally. Deiter; who was he and what was going on between he and Rose? He had to find out more about the man, had to find his weakest point, his deepest secret, his worst scar; every man had one. Then he would have the weapon he needed to force him away from Rose and force Rose back to him. Mason reached for the telephone, pulled out the desk shelf above his right side drawer and ran his finger down a list of telephone numbers. His finger stopped next to one name and Mason began to punch in the numbers. The phone rang three times and then was picked up. "FBI, Jenkins."

"Jake, this is Aldridge Mason."

"I haven't forgotten, Aldridge. It's just that I haven't heard anything about a missing woman that matched Rose's description."

"I have a name; works for the FBI...maybe you know him."

"Who is it, Aldridge, and what's the connection?"

"I don't know the connection yet, but the name is Deiter, John Deiter." Mason could hear the man's breath inhale on the other end of the phone.

"Deiter? Are you sure?"

"Yes, I'm sure, damn it; who the hell is he?"

"Aldridge, what is it that you've got up your sleeve?"

The question caught Mason off guard. "Nothing...just want to find Rose," he replied.

"I'll check around, Aldridge, but this may be something that may be too sensitive to release," cautioned the FBI man.

"I don't want anything going public, I just want to know who the hell Deiter is?" demanded Mason. He felt himself losing control again and closed his eyes.

"Aldridge, can I get back to you? I...uhh...I have a meeting just now." The phone went dead and Mason slammed down the receiver. Who the fuck was Deiter and what was he doing with Rose? The color deepened in Mason's face again and his jaw clenched.

Jake Jenkins hadn't liked the feeling he had talking with Aldridge Mason. He had heard some pretty vicious stories about Mason although his relationship had been amiable enough. They had worked together on a case and Jenkins found him to be very intelligent and a hard worker. By all accounts, Mason could be very vindictive. He had heard that he had an on-going affair with someone on his staff and had seen him with a tall redhead at an exclusive supper club on Pennsylvania Avenue in Washington earlier in the year. Jenkins had been down there for a special course. He guessed that it was Rose McGuire...the person that Mason wanted to find. Now this thing about the FBI's chief agent for espionage and counterintelligence...Geez, what the hell was he to do. He decided that his allegiance was certainly to the Bureau and not to Mason. He picked up the telephone and dialed in two numbers and then three more. He waited, and when the operator at the J. Edgar Hoover Building in Washington answered, he said, "I'm looking for the office of John Deiter," The operator answered in the affirmative and Jenkins waited as she rang the extension. It rang four times before it was picked up.

"John Deiter's office, may I help you?" It obviously was the secretary.

"Yes, this is Jason Jenkins from the New York Office; I'd like to speak with Mr. Deiter."

"I'm sorry, Mr. Jenkins, but Mr. Deiter is on special assignment just now. Could someone else help you?"

Jenkins cursed under his breath. "Yes, but I have to either speak with Mr. Deiter or get a message to him."

"I'll connect you with Mr. Stroeman who is filling in just now," the secretary said. Jenkins heard the phone ring again and a man's deep voice answered. "Stroeman."

"I'm Jason Jenkins from New York. I'm trying to get in touch with John Deiter," Jenkins said.

"He's away for a few months, can I help?"

"I know he's away, but it may involve something that he's working on right now," explained Jenkins. "Would you tell him that a certain Aldridge Mason is trying to find out information about him and.... and mention the name Rose McGuire, too. Tell him he can contact me at extension 4122 at the New York Office if it's something that's of an interest to him."

At the mention of Rose McGuire's name, Ken Stroeman's ears perked up. "Did you say Rose McGuire?"

"Yes, and this may be important."

"I'll let him know, and yes, I do think it's important. Thanks, Jenkins." Stroeman placed his finger on the receiver handle and then released it again. He punched in the number of the Task Force at Bank's firm. The phone rang three times and a woman's voice answered.

"This is Ken Stroeman from the FBI, I need to talk to Jack Deiter."

"This is Rose McGuire, Jack just stepped out for a few minutes; he'll be back soon, can I have him call you?"

Stroeman froze for a moment and then continued, "Ms. McGuire, this may affect you also."

"Oh," Rose replied, "how's that?"

"I know that Jack trusts you, so I guess it's all right to tell you. There's been an informal inquiry about Jack and........and you by an Aldridge Mason."

Now it was Rose's turn to freeze. She hadn't thought of Mason for almost a week. "Does he know where I am?" she asked.

"I don't know," he replied. "A Jason Jenkins from the New York office called here looking for Jack and mentioned that some guy named Mason was trying to find information about you two. If you could pass on to Jack that Jenkins can be reached at extension 4122 in New York, he may have more for you."

"Thanks, I'll be sure to pass it on to Jack; and.....well, just thanks." Rose hung up the phone and sat there thinking for awhile. What was Mason doing? What was he planning? She thought she knew the answers and shivered. Rose picked up the phone, hesitated for a moment, and then dialed her telephone number in New Jersey. She figured that Mason wouldn't be there at this time of the day and she had to find out what messages might be on her answering service. The phone rang four times and the service answered. She punched her code number into the phone and waited. The first message was Mason; he was going to come over that evening; that would have been Sunday. There was another message from Mason…he seemed upset. Rob had called about some minor problem at college. Her mother left a message. A few more messages about repair to the house, an insurance agent, and the local fire department fund raising effort, followed. The last message was recorded earlier that day and was again from Aldridge Mason.

"I will find out where you are, Rose. I don't appreciate what you're doing and quite honestly, don't understand it. Is there anything that I haven't given you? I really think that you're being very selfish and foolish. I don't know who this guy, Deiter, is and I frankly don't care. You know that you have to come back and so do I. You need to stop this now before it goes any further." The message stopped abruptly. Rose slowly replaced the receiver oblivious of everything else and leaned back in her chair as a pair of hands closed around her neck. Rose jumped up and in the process her head hit Jack Deiter in the mouth as he was kissing the top of her head.

"Ow," he cried. "What the hell was that for?" His hand went up to touch his cut and bleeding lip.

"Oh, my God," said Rose turning around. "I'm sorry Jack, I'm so sorry."

Deiter wiped a drop of blood from his lip and grimaced as he tried to smile at the expression on Rose's face. "What's the matter, Rose?" he asked, his handkerchief now out and swabbing the left corner of his mouth.

"Two things…no one thing," she replied.

"Make up your mind before I bleed to death."

Rose threw her arms around Deiter which made his efforts at stemming the flow of blood from his lip even more difficult. "I'm sorry, I love you, Jack, don't leave me!" she exclaimed.

Deiter tried to laugh, but felt it wiser not to at the moment until he found out what the problem was. "Slow down; I'm not going anywhere...not without you anyway."

Rose wilted and let go of Deiter as she sank into the chair. "I just receive a call from Ken Stroeman from your office; he had a call from some guy in the New York office who said that Aldridge Mason is looking for us...and I just called my telephone service at home and got a threatening call from Mason. I'm worried and scared, Jack. I know him and I'm scared," She started to quietly sob, her face now in her hands.

"He can't be that bad, Rose, I've had to deal with much worse...and so have you."

"That was a long time ago and I didn't know any better then," she sobbed. "I didn't know how one man could ruin people's lives...I learned from Mason."

"Well, you just haven't had the companionship then that you've had lately," he replied.

Something in what he said seemed to suddenly bring her out of her depression and she looked up at him. She smiled. "By God, you've got that right; thank you John Remington Deiter the Third, thank you," she said as she kissed him hard on the lips.

"Ow," he cried again.

CHAPTER SEVENTEEN

▼

ANDREI'S MISSION

Aeroflot Flight 220
Moscow to Frankfurt
Saturday, June 15th, 1996

It had been a long train ride from Grozny to Moscow and Andrei had walked the three kilometers from the Belorussia Station to the shuttle bus stop at the Moscow Central Airfield. There he caught the shuttle to Moscow's Sheremet'yevo Airport, thirty kilometers from the city. He went through customs with little bother, the papers he had been given were flawless. After a five-hour wait, the flight to Frankfurt finally departed with Andrei aboard. Upon reaching Frankfurt, he would use the visa he was given to book a flight to New York; no use divulging his final destination while still in Russia. Andrei sat back and tried to get some sleep.

The last few days had been full ones for Andrei; he had convinced the people in Grozny that he would participate in their plan and in return had been given the money and papers he required to leave Russia and travel to the United States. He had also been promised the equipment that he needed would be available when he reached Washington. All he had been given was a telephone number to call when he arrived in New York. If they didn't provide him a place to work from, he would have to find an apartment large enough and private enough to set up the equipment. He saw no problems, though. He fingered the cane with the brass falcon's head and smiled to himself. He didn't relish the thought of killing again, but it would be important to the order...to the new Soviet Union, when it was reestablished. He would only contact those who had betrayed their country...the rest would remain in hiding. This would still provide more than enough money to continue the cause. Andrei slept.

The change of aircraft in Frankfurt was effortless and in two days, he was walking through the international arrival gate of Concourse C at Newark International Airport. He caught a cab to the Marriott Hotel near the airport. It took him only five minutes to check in and another five to get settled into his room to rest. Travel was exhausting to him; it must be his age, he thought.

The next morning Andrei awoke, showered and called Room Service to order a large breakfast. It wasn't a natural thing for him to do; one part of him kept thinking about the cost, but he knew that the cost to him was nothing. He had been given more than enough money to take care of the expenses of his mission. Over coffee, he had turned on the television and was watching some the morning news. English was still difficult despite the many years of classes. As he listened, it became easier. He knew that he had to relax and let the words flow to him; he mustn't fight it. Yes, now he was beginning to understand easier. It was good to listen to the language; it made understanding easier. Forget the Russian words and characters; he let the English words and phrases soak into his mind. He began to think in English; this was good; he needed to do this.

Suddenly, his mind switched to his mission and Andrei stood up and walked over to where his suitcase was sitting on the unused bed. He took a small penknife from his pocket and slit open the back inside fabric of his suitcase. Pulling the fabric apart, he withdrew several pieces of paper he had previously hidden there. He checked the instructions on the first piece of paper once more although he had already memorized them. In the instructions was a telephone number that would inform his contact that he had arrived. He knew that no one would search his personal documents on air travel within the United States, they were only interested in weapons. It would be safe having the documents on him. He picked up his cane and unscrewed the brass falcon's head handle. Inside there was a cavity he had hollowed out to accommodate the papers; he rolled them tightly and slid them into the opening. Screwing the brass head of the cane back onto the shaft, he tossed the cane onto the bed. He then sat back to watch more of the newscast; he was beginning to understand the English more fully.

At exactly ten o'clock, he dialed the telephone number written on the first piece of paper. After four rings, a voice message instructed him to leave a message after the beep. Andrei said "Have arrived, my telephone number is 201–985–4000, Room 6251. I await your call." He hung up the phone and went back to watching the news channel on television.

It was almost an hour later when his telephone rang. Andrei answered it. "Yes?"

"Did you have a good flight?"

"Yes, it was all right."

"We have prepared you a suitable place here."

"Where?"

"Tomorrow you will fly to Washington National Airport and take a taxi from the airport to the Crystal Gateway Marriott Hotel in Crystal City...it is close by the airport; we will contact you again there." The phone went dead and Andrei hung up the receiver. He leaned back and tried to concentrate on the newscast. He knew that this was the way these people made contact to protect themselves and he should have been more comfortable with the procedure, but he wasn't. He picked up the phone again and dialed the number for the airlines listed on the hotel index of telephone numbers. After a brief conversation with the agent, he booked a flight to Washington National Airport at 10:35 on the next morning. He went back to listening to his English language programs.

Washington National Airport
Washington, DC
June 15th, 1997

Andrei walked through the sliding door of the terminal at Washington National Airport and onto the sidewalk outside. The bright sun hurt his eyes. He looked to the left end of the terminal and spotted a line of yellow cabs waiting; they seemed to be poised to pounce on the first available hapless tourist. He raised his arm and signaled the hovering queue of taxis. The first one pulled out and came to a stop next to him. Andrei shoved his suitcase into the rear seat and wedged himself in beside it. To the driver he said, "Crystal City Gateway Marriott," The driver nodded, bent down to look in his outside mirror, and pulled out into traffic. In five minutes, the taxi was at the front entrance to the Marriott Hotel and a bell clerk opened the taxi door for Andrei.

"Do you need help with your luggage, sir?" the bell clerk asked.

"No thank you, I can manage," Andrei replied.

After registering, Andrei picked up his suitcase and took the elevator to the eighth floor and walked a short way down the hallway to Room 812. He quickly surveyed the room; it was nicely furnished with a large king-sized bed, a sofa and the ever-present large-screen television set. Shear curtains hung over the window, bordered by deep green velvet drapes. The carpet was plush and soft under his feet. He was not used to such luxuries and his Communist Party training left him somewhat ill at ease in such surroundings. He placed the suitcase on the bed, walked over to the telephone and punched in the telephone number he had used the day

before. It rang four times and the same answering service message greeted him. Andrei responded with, "I have
just arrived; my telephone number is..." he paused and
looked for the number on the phone dial "....is
703–920–3230, extension 4812." He hung up the
phone, took off his suit jacket and threw it on the bed
with the suitcase, loosened his tie and sat on the sofa.
Picking up the TV remote, he clicked on the television,
surfed through the channels and then decided on an
interesting looking soap opera. He put the remote down
and sat back for his English lesson.

At 6:15 that evening, Andrei ordered dinner from
room service. It was delivered at seven o'clock. He had
purchased a bottle of vodka on his way through Newark
Airport at the Duty Free counter and he pored himself a
tumbler glass full to drink with his meal. He quickly finished eating and sat back to listen to a news panel discussion on the television. Andrei was beginning to get
anxious when suddenly at ten o'clock the phone rang.
He picked up the receiver and said, "Yes?"

"We are glad that you have arrived. Tomorrow morning you must pack your luggage and leave it in your
room, but do not check out of your hotel; at precisely
nine o'clock walk out of the front door of the hotel and
turn right. Walk up the street for one block and we will
pick you up. There will be two people in the front seat
of the car, a man and a woman. Open the back door and
get into the back seat." The phone went dead and he
hung up the receiver.

It was nearly nine o'clock the next morning and
Andrei stared through the front window of the hotel
watching the rain splash on the pavement and run down

the gutter on both sides of the street. Passengers were dashing from cars with coats over their heads to seek the safety of the overhang extending from the second story of the hotel entrance. Andrei looked at his watch again and noticed that it was one minute before nine o'clock. He was glad he had thought to bring a trench coat at the last minute. He had returned to his room to retrieve it after he had first come down to the lobby and saw the rain. He stepped up to the revolving doors, pushed them open and walked out into the dreary daylight. As he started walking up the sidewalk, he looked behind him to see if he could spot a car that might be his contact. He saw nothing and pulled up the collar to his coat. Holding it gripped together tightly with his left hand, he held his cane in his right hand to assist him. Andrei walked quickly, hoping that he could cover the distance up the block before he became soaked. The rain landed on his shoulders and flowed down his back in rivulets. Within a minute, he had covered the distance and spotted a dark colored sedan with two people in the front seat parked just around the corner on the other side of the street. He headed for it.

He could hardly see through the front window, but could make out that the passenger had long hair so concluded that it was a woman. He walked past the front door and opening the rear door, slid into the car quickly closing the door behind him. The car suddenly lurched forward startling him; he had not noticed that the car engine was even running. As soon as the car had turned onto the highway and heading North on Route 1, the woman turned and smiling at him said,

"Zdravstv$te! Prostite, v9 doktor Kili$ken?"
(Hello! Excuse me, are you Dr. Kilyaikin?)

"Da Q Ki;i$ken," *(Yes, I am Kilyaikin.)* Andrei replied.

"That must be the last time you speak in Russian unless we are in the privacy of the safe house," the woman replied. "My name is Carol Walker and this is Carl Anderson," she added motioning to the driver. The driver nodded, but said nothing. Andrei doubted that these were their real names and didn't even attempt to try to remember them. "We have been instructed to bring you to the place from where you will operate. The equipment that you have ordered has been delivered. It will be up to you to get it into operating condition, however, we know nothing of what it is or why you need it. Carl will return to the hotel and pick up your luggage and check you out of your room. He will drop your luggage off at the apartment. After that, you will not see us or hear from us again. Please give me your hotel room key. Do you have any questions?"

Andrei sat in the rear seat with his cane between his knees with both hands clasped on the brass falcon's head handle. "No," he responded indifferently, "that will be fine." He tried to look disinterested, peering out the car window at the heavy rain cascading down on the streets.

In about twenty minutes, the car pulled up in front of a four-story brick apartment building on Wisconsin Avenue in Washington. The woman handed Andrei a key and an envelope. He grunted a qualified thank you, opened the door and quickly walked to the doorway of the building. As he reached the door of the apartment building, he could see the car disappear around the corner. It was quiet now except for the rain. He put the key into the door, unlocked it and stepped inside to the lobby area. He looked at the key again and noticed that it was stamped with the number 415. He took the elevator to the fourth floor and walked down the hallway to the apartment numbered 415. He tried the key in the door and it turned smoothly. He tried the door handle and let himself into the room. The apartment was completely furnished, but seemed to have nothing of a personal nature in it; just furniture, bland pictures on the wall and sufficient rugs on the floor to make it look lived in. He took off his trench coat and draped it over a bench that was placed opposite the doorway. Down a hallway on the left was a kitchen; he walked into it and opened the refrigerator. It appeared to be fully stocked as were the cabinets. In the drawers he found eating and cooking utensils The upper cupboards included plates, glasses and a large bottle of vodka. They seemed to have thought of almost everything to make him comfortable. He shook the water from his hair with his hands and walked back down the apartment hallway. On the right, he found a bedroom furnished similarly to the rest of the apartment with a single bed and a chest of drawers. At the end of the hallway, he found a second room that had the door closed. He opened the door and stepped inside. This room was completely empty except for several stacks of cardboard boxes in the center of it. Andrei quickly concluded that this was the equipment he had ordered; he didn't bother checking it just then for he knew it would be keeping him busy enough for the next several days.

Andrei remembered the envelope that the woman had given him and reached into his pocket to draw it out. He tore it open and unfolded the paper that was within it. It contained a single telephone number. This, he supposed would be his only contact, should he need it…he doubted he ever would.

CHAPTER EIGHTEEN

▼

FIRST CONTACT

Dale City, Virginia
Monday, September 16th 1996

It had been years since Hank Dobson had even heard Russian spoken; to pick up a ringing telephone and suddenly hear it again came as a frightening shock to him. What the voice on the phone had said was even more frightening.

"Tovari] Domnitski, vremq ne xd&t, mil($ mo$!" *(Comrade Domnitzski, time is running out, my dear fellow!)*

"Pusti menq!" *(Let me go!)* whispered Dobson hoarsely, "Pusti menq!"

Boris Alexandrovitch Domnitzski had always dreamed of someday escaping to the West. He had been successful in school and had looked forward to a mechanical engineering job with a design group in

Leningrad. Eventually, he had hoped to find a position that would bring him into contact with Americans or Brits who shared his line of work, maybe even to travel to the West. He knew that he was too ambitious, too sure of his own abilities to remain under the brutish system that had strangled all innovation in his beloved Russia. But, it had only been a dream before Colonel Alexandre Maskhadov of the KGB had contacted him. Maskhadov had offered him an opportunity to become a deep agent for the Soviet Union in the United States. Boris knew that if he didn't agree, he would have to wait many years for another chance to go to the United States, many years of meeting just the right people, making just the right contacts, saying just the right thing. One slip and a lifetime of effort would be wasted, or worse. Going along with the system at that time had been the only possibility, a chance to see his dreams become a reality. Once in the United States, he could drop out of sight and he did; he had been trained by the best. Boris Alexandrovitch had managed to elude the espionage control net and gave up his deep cover identity assuming the new identity of Hank Dobson. Hank Dobson still remembered how it was though, and who he was then, but to some extent...that old life now seemed to belong to someone else.

Dale City is a commuter town along the Interstate that provided the North-South lifeline to the Nation's Capital and a relatively short drive to the center of world power. Living close to a densely populated area is a lot safer than being a stranger in a small rural town in the Midwestern states. No one asks questions that may prove embarrassing in a place like Dale City. Living in his condominium at Prospect Farms, he was relatively inconspicuous. He worked for a small engineering design firm that had its office only five minutes away. He had been well accepted at his work and outside of an off-and-on office romance over the past few years, he had pretty much kept to himself. The condo allowed him to come and go as he wanted to and there wasn't the bother of having to keep up the outside of the building which might expose him to the curiosity of his neighbors. His life was totally uneventful and he lived in the relative freedom of obscurity...until today.

"There is information I must have from you," the voice on the phone continued in English, "then you will be left in peace. All I want is the information that you once memorized."

"What information?"

"The numbers."

"Are you KGB?"

"There is no more KGB and no more Soviet Union, either."

"Then what do you want with the numbers?"

"That is my business; after, you will hear from us no more."

"Who are you?" Dobson asked in a whisper.

"You do not need to know who I am Comrade, but we will have to meet, it is not safe to reveal information over the telephone."

"Where?" asked Dobson.

"I will be at the Springfield Mall just off Interstate 395, south of the beltway; do you know where it is?"

"Yes, but it's too large a place...how would I know you?"

"I will find you. At exactly seven o'clock tonight purchase something at the MacDonald's Restaurant there and sit down at one of the tables just outside the door. I will join you after I have assured myself that you are alone and have not been followed."

"Who would follow me?" Dobson asked.

The phone went dead without an answer to his question.

Andrei Mikailovitch sat back in the overstuffed chair in the living room of his apartment on Wisconsin Avenue and smiled. That contact seemed to have gone all right. He would meet with the defector later and learn the code number he needed. He guessed that the man would probably recognize him as someone he had met or seen before, but not be able to identify exactly who he was and where they had met. That was good. His name was never given to the "clients" at the house in Grozny and none of them knew what his responsibilities were.

This one, this Domnitzski, was not to be trusted. He was a loner with no attachments to cause him to be silent. If he became worried, he may notify the authorities; Andrei couldn't let that happen. He would have to be eliminated. Some of the agents may be loyal enough and would not expose him. Those who had betrayed the cause; they must be destroyed as well. Andrei thought about the first time that he had done that…destroyed someone…the couple with the child. At the time, it was devastating to him. He had always felt that if Maria had been there for him when he needed her, he would have not become so embittered. He still didn't like the idea of killing, but he was now a soldier in the cause, not a civilian anymore. In his mind,

Andrei went through the ones that he had to eliminate. It was almost twenty years ago when the traitor Dimitri Polyakov had fingered some of the best agents that the Soviet Union had recruited. It was too late for them to be of further use and it was essential to eliminate the threat that they could have been. Unfortunately, the code numbers had died with them and Andrei would not be able to retrieve the bank accounts that had been set up for them. When Polyakov was finally caught and subsequently executed by the Soviet Union in 1988, he had done great harm to the system of deep agents in the United States. He had also been a threat to Project Rasputin. Had the implanted chips been discovered by the United States, they might have been able to unravel the code and destroy the entire system of espionage by the Soviet Union. The project to control the deep agents could have been the means to destroy the entire operation. Andrei knew what his "reward" would have been in that event. It was little wonder that Polyakov had been shot for his treason.

At six–forty–seven that evening, Dobson parked his car in the MacDonald's lot in the Springfield Mall. He went inside and ordered coffee from the counter. He was served and held the cup in his left hand as he swung open the door leading to the outside tables. He walked through the doorway and saw that there were several empty round tables just outside the doorway. He pulled out the bench that had been slid under the table furthest away from the door and sat down. Placing the cup of coffee on the table, he pealed off the lid and drank of the hot, black liquid. He looked around, but could see no one except a woman and a small boy at one of the tables. She was laughing at the way the boy had smeared ice cream around his mouth as he relished the dessert.

Dobson waited for almost ten minutes before a man exited the doorway, looked around, and came towards his table. In the half-light of the Autumn evening, he could see that the man had a full head of white hair with eyebrows to match. He was, of course, elderly, but his face was gaunter than what age would account for. The man walked with the use of a cane, favoring his right leg. In his left hand, the man carried a cup of what appeared to be ice cream. "May I join you?" he asked of Dobson.

"Certainly," Dobson replied.

"I can not get use to ice cream tasting so good," the man responded as he sat his cup down on the table. He pulled out another bench and seated himself on the opposite side of the table. He placed his cane between his knees and with both hand covering the handle, sat studying Dobson.

"Have we met?" asked Dobson.

"It is not important," the man replied indifferently. "Is your memory of facts and numbers still as sharp as it used to be?"

"Yes."

"Good, what numbers do you remember?"

"If I tell you, then what?"

"Well then, this meeting never took place and you will never hear of me or Boris Alexandrovitch Domnitzski ever again," The white-haired man spooned out a bite of ice cream.

Dobson's head drooped perceptively. He slowly muttered six numbers "One–eight–seven–eight–six–six," and then looked up at the other man.

"One, eight, seven, eight, six, six," responded the older man. "Thank you, Comrade."

Leaning on his cane, Andrei Kilyaikin pushed himself up from the table and nodding at the seated man, then turned and walked away. Dobson looked back towards the doorway of the restaurant to see whether anyone else might have been within hearing range or was watching them...he saw no one. When he turned his head back again he found that the white-haired man with the cane had disappeared. Slowly, Dobson picked up his cup of coffee and finding a waste receptacle opened the swinging door on top and deposited the remainder of his coffee and cup inside. He walked briskly to his car, climbed in and drove out of the parking lot towards Interstate 295 and Dale City. Was it all at an end as this man had said? Hank Dobson hoped so, but he still had a terrible feeling of dread that caused the hairs on the back of his neck to stand on end.

Back at his apartment, Andrei peered at the list of names and numbers until he came to the name he wanted, Billy McPherson. In front of the name was the number 344. Turning to the second page of numbers, his finger moved down the page to the third row of number sets; his finger moved right to the fourth group of numbers and down to the fourth number listed. On a pad of lined paper he wrote out the number 912345013. On the third page of numbers he once again chose the third row, fourth column and the fourth set of numbers. On the lined pad he wrote the set of numbers 436231; he followed that set of numbers by the six that he had received from the man Domnitzski/McPherson/Dobson. He wrote 187866. Satisfied that he had done that correctly, Andrei picked up a book with a soft blue cover. He scanned the numbers at the top of the pages until he found the ones beginning with nine; he located the one matching the first set of numbers...the Alexandria Savings Bank, 34 Fern Street, Alexandria, Virginia. Andrei smiled; tomorrow he would pay the bank a visit. Under the name of Billy McPherson, he would register his signature to that account and collect the bankbook. It had been a good week's work tracking down the man and getting the numbers. If all worked out, he would then send a coded message for the satellites to eliminate Domnitzski and complete the process. He slept well that night.

CHAPTER NINETEEN

▼

YURI HAPONCHEK

New York City
Thursday, October 16th 1997

Andrei leaned back in the overstuffed chair, closed his eyes and removed his glasses. Ten days ago, he had rented this flat on West 13th Street to be closer to this particular contact and one other in the New York area. It wasn't much, but it was furnished completely and was private; he could come and go as he wanted. It also came with an off-street parking place for his car...a rarity in the City. Most importantly to him, his name would not show up on hotel listings of guests...it was too easy to be spotted by the authorities. Owners of apartment buildings were different and sometimes hid their change in tenants from the authorities. He had been reviewing some of the information that he had collected on the remaining agents on his "selected" list. He was getting used to this process now. He had made contact six times now and had been successful each time. The agents had given up their coded numbers to him and he had easily made the bank account transfers. He had found out early on that it was easier to change the name and social security number on the account to a common one that he could easily use than to remove the money from the bank. Banks do not appreciate giving up multimillion-dollar accounts and make it difficult to do so. It was just as simple to leave the money in the account under his ownership.

Contacting this particular agent was to be somewhat different from the rest, however. Andrei had known of this man, Yuri Ivanovitch Haponchek, from his superiors in Moscow and he knew that Haponchek had accomplished several covert missions for the Central Committee. Andrei had hoped that he would be of value to him now as well. He needed a confidant to help him; he was getting too old to keep this pace up for long. He felt that of all the agents, he might be able to trust Haponchek to do what was right for the Party and not be enticed to jump ship with the chance of landing a fortune.

It wasn't until after the third time that he had activated the locator signal that Andrei had finally located Yuri Haponchek living in a place called Sparta in Northwestern New Jersey and had driven there twice in the last few days. He had observed the house on a quiet street near Lake Mohawk that the man occupied with his wife and young son. The name on a letter delivered to the address was Rudolph and Barbara Kurtz; it checked with the list of agent's names. Andrei used his

cell phone briefly and the operator provided the telephone number that Andrei needed. At eight–thirty that
evening, when Andrei reasoned that Haponchek should
be home, he dialed the number. The phone rang three
times before it was answered by a male voice. "Yes?"

"V(zdesb odn$ Tovari]?" *(Are you alone,
Comrade Haponchek?)*

"Who is this? Are you trying to be funny?"

"Net, (uri Ivanovnc, teperb ne vremq
]ut$tbk." *(No, Yuri Ivanovitch, now is not the time for
joking.)*

"I don't understand anything you're saying."

"You understand very well Mr. Kurtz, very well
indeed," said Andrei switching to English. "There are
those who have a need of your services."

"We should really speak in person," replied Yuri
Haponchek.

"I fully agree, I will meet you tomorrow night at
seven o'clock at a small restaurant called *Figero's* on East
28th Street between 4th and 5th Avenue in the Village.
The dinner is on me, my friend; this is business; you
will recognize me. I will be carrying a cane with a brass
falcon head handle," Yuri Haponchek grunted an assent
and hung up the phone.

Figero's is one of a number of New York City restaurants that are small and cater to some of the more fash-
ion-conscious inhabitants of the City. Dining in the
"Village" seems to have an attraction with certain people. But to Andrei, however, it was the simple fact that
the dining area at seven o'clock in the evening could be
very private and secluded. The regular customers didn't
begin showing up until at least eight–thirty. He was

seated at a table for two in the front left corner of the restaurant where he could observe the doorway and entrance. He knew what Haponchek looked like, so had the advantage. He wanted to assure himself that the man had not been followed. Andrei sat at the table with his cane between his legs, his hands over the handle of the cane, hiding it from view. He had been there for about fifteen minutes and a glass of white wine sat now half full on the table before him.

At five minutes after seven, a middle aged man with blondish looking white hair, dressed in baggy slacks and a plaid shirt with a knit tie stepped through the doorway and stood in the entrance way. He was about six foot one and a little over 285 pounds. His face was pale and somewhat puffy with pale blue eyes set wide apart and thin lips; he narrowed his eyes and looked around; his head tilted slightly back as though looking down his nose. Andrei recognized him from his time at the house in Grozny to be the man Haponchek; Andrei let him stand there for nearly a minute, judging that the man would be more ill at ease and not so arrogant if he was caused to wait. From their brief conversation on the telephone, Andrei sensed an arrogance that bothered him. Finally, seeing no one outside and no indication that the man had a contact also seated in the restaurant, Andrei lifted his right hand from the handle of the cane and lifted the cane slightly in recognition of the other man. He nodded his head as Haponchek looked in his direction. Without a smile of recognition, Haponchek walked towards Andrei's table, pulled out the empty chair and seated himself.

"Would you care for a glass of wine, Mr. Kurtz?" Andrei asked motioning towards his own glass. "The *Santa Margherita Pinot Grigio 1995* is excellent."

"I thought this was business," retorted Haponchek. "I don't drink alcohol and don't trust those who do."

Andrei sighed visibly. "Then you miss some of the finer pleasures of this life," he responded, "That is such a shame," Andrei lifted his glass towards the other man and said, "Na Zdroviq, Tovari]!" *(To your health, Comrad)*.

"What I drink is my business; what is yours, how did you find me, and who the hell are you?"

"All in good time, Mr. Kurtz, all in good time," Andrei replied setting his glass down slowly.

Andrei was beginning to feel a bit uneasy and shifted slightly in his chair; he leaned back and cocked his head back to one side, narrowing his eyes in the process as though silently and critically appraising the other man. He began to remember now some of the evaluations he had read of Haponchek as an agent. He was, above all, considered to be an excellent agent, even though he was thought to be somewhat paranoid, schizophrenic or possibly even sociopathic. He was known to be ruthless, clever, completely indifferent to emotion or compassion…possibly even evil, and yet very innovative. He was credited with the reputation of following orders and has what was judged to be a perfect cover. He enjoys a special calling as an assassin. Apparently, he was loyal to the cause in every way. He never did hide the fact that he was prone to despise the weakness of those who had the misfortune of being appointed over him, considering himself to be far superior to them…he abhorred individual authority, but fairly worshipped institutional authority. He was a total controller and becomes furious when challenged. Haponchek had been called on at least twice before to eliminate a particularly bothersome danger to the program and had done so with obviously great relish. As Andrei surveyed the man, he noticed that the scar on his cheek just in front of his right ear was beginning to turn bright red.

"How is your wife, Barbara I believe, and your son, Mr. Kurtz; well I expect?" inquired Andrei slowly.

"You didn't answer my question," Haponchek replied, his eyes closing into slits.

"Nor you mine," replied Andrei with a one-sided smile. The smile suddenly faded from Andrei's face and his tone became low and menacing. "I am from the Central Committee, Comrade," he continued, spitting out the last word as though it were curse. "We have work to do. My name is Dr. Kilyaikin."

"Where is my regular contact?" interrupted Haponchek.

Andrei waited for a few seconds and continued in a voice of resignation. "All that I have been informed about you is apparently true, Comrade, your usefulness to the Party is apparently at an end," Andrei made as if to rise from the table, looking out of the corner of his eye for a change to come to the other man's face. He was rewarded by a hand being placed on his arm. He looked up into a much friendlier face. Andrei marveled at the man's ability to change moods.

"No, wait, I didn't mean to insult you, Doctor,"

"I am not sure you are the person for the assignment; my report will reflect that," Andrei said quietly and resuming his attempt to rise.

Haponchek's eyes narrowed. "Who exactly do you report to?"

"There is still a government in Moscow, unless you have forgotten."

Haponchek relaxed. "What is it you wish me to do?"

Andrei sat back in his chair and looked at the other man for a moment. "Very well then," he continued. "We are to accomplish a cleansing mission. There are a number of your comrades who have not acted "responsibly;" they have escaped their controls. We must locate them and remove the threat to the whole organization."

"How are we going to find them if they aren't under control?"

"It will be shown to you, soon. I need for you to do some traveling for me and confirm the location of certain of these individuals. After you have acquired certain information, I will initiate the elimination procedure."

Haponchek looked amused. "You? I'm the expert at that, why not me?" he said with a shrug to accompany the disappointed look on his face.

"My way is clean and quite natural," Andrei replied. "I need you to do the leg work for me."

"Very well, when do we start?"

Andrei smiled. "Right away. Please, join me for dinner; afterwards we will go to my apartment and you will be fully informed."

The meal was enjoyable, but the company lacked something, thought Andrei as he rode the fifteen blocks in Haponchek's car to his apartment.

CHAPTER TWENTY

▼

BETRAYAL

New York City
Friday, October 17th 1997

As Yuri Haponchek turned right into the traffic on 5th Avenue and started driving in the direction of downtown and Kilyaikin's apartment, he began to evaluate the man sitting next to him in the passenger seat. It had just started to rain and he switched on the windshield wipers. He'd been told by this man that he was going to participate in an operation to eliminate some of his fellow deep agents. That wasn't too much out of the ordinary. Something appeared wrong, though. Why wasn't he just contacted through his control? That was odd. This man obviously knew a lot about the Soviet Union's system of deep agents; there was also something very familiar about him. Yuri was sure he had seen him someplace before...but where? He knew it would come to him in time. The second problem was the insistence on the man's part to do the actual elimination of the errant agents. How was he going to do that if they were under the protection program of the US Government? Also, he should have been the one to do the eliminations; it was his specialty. Yuri decided that he could not trust this man, but he would wait until he learned more...he would play the man's game for now.

Kilyaikin suddenly pointed to an empty parking space and instructed the driver to park. "I have been quick to learn that in Manhattan, you take whatever opportunity you can to park," he explained. The two men climbed out and Yuri locked the car. Both men walked quickly down the sidewalk towards Andrei's apartment. Although the rain had now turned into a light mist, Andrei still felt a chill that caused his leg to hurt. Each time it hurt, he remembered Maria. He put more dependence then usual on his cane. In a few minutes they had reached the doorway of his apartment. Andrei placed his key in the lock and opened the outer door. Once safely inside with the outer door locked, he reinserted his key in the lock of the inner door and allowed his companion to enter. Andrei made sure the inner door had locked and motioned Yuri to follow him as he slowly climbed the stairs to the fourth floor. His leg was really beginning to bother him now, he would have to take a couple of the pills that the doctor in Grozny had given him before he had left Russia.

Once inside the apartment, Andrei initially started to relax. Going to the kitchen cabinet, he brought out a bottle of vodka and absentmindedly placed two glasses on the table. "I hope that one of those isn't for me," exclaimed Haponchek with a perturbed expression on his face.

"I'm sorry," replied Andrei. "I forgot that you abstain; I hope that you'll not preclude me from enjoying some spirits, though?" he asked.

"Do as you like," responded the other. "Now, you were going to enlighten me about this operation."

"Yes, I was, wasn't I" The chill returned to Andrei's leg and ran up the middle of his back.

During the next hour, Andrei described the need to contact the people on the list and extract a number from them which responded to a bank account. Yuri quickly understood the meaning and significance of the numbers. He had used his number on several occasions when he had been ordered to eliminate a particularly nasty situation. He had some idea how much money was involved as well. His own account, he knew had been over a million dollars. After each operation, the Soviet Union had switched the money to another account and he was given another six-digit number to memorize. "Why get the number, why not just eliminate the agent?" Yuri asked.

"You wish for the Party to throw away millions of dollars?" retorted Andrei with a quizzical expression on his face. "Don't you think that frivolous?" he added. "We're talking nearly a half billion dollars here."

Yuri smiled; he was beginning to grasp the enormity of what was happening. "I don't understand how the money is transferred."

"That is none of your concern; it belongs to the Party," replied Andrei.

"The Party or the government? There is a much bigger difference now. I'm sure you're aware of that."

Andrei hesitated. The question was accusatory in nature and questioned his authority. He was about to answer when Yuri interrupted. "I'm sorry, I guess I get too suspicious sometimes," Yuri laughed and slapped Andrei on the back. "We are all in the cause for the same reason. Do go on."

The chill remained in Andrei's lower back despite the glass of vodka he had consumed. He explained that there was a way in which all agents could be located. He was not explicit, but did explain that he would provide a specific address for Yuri to locate and observe. If the subject could not be identified, Yuri must request another "reading" whatever that meant. Finally, Andrei could see by Yuri's questions that he must explain more about the operation. In the next hour and a half Andrei explained the origin and extent of Project Rasputin. When he had finished and it seemed that he'd answered all of Yuri's questions, he turned to study the man's face.

"I have one more question," said Yuri slowly and deliberately.

"Yes," replied Andrei wearily.

"Where is the equipment to transmit the signals?"

"You don't need to know that information and it would be better if you didn't for security reasons."

Yuri smiled again. He suspected that the information he wanted was not going to be readily available to him from Kilyaikin.

"Doctor, you obviously have further information that I would like to know. I don't think that you are capable of performing the mission that you were sent to accomplish.

Perhaps you should enlighten me as to everything,"
Andrei felt the chill more intensely now.

"You should go now, I am tired and will contact you
again when your services are needed," Andrei said, rising
from the chair with the help of his cane.

The smash of Haponchek's fist slammed against
Andrei's face catching him by surprise and he fell against
the table lamp, knocking it to the floor. His cane also
clattered helplessly to the floor and slid across the room.
Blow after blow landed against his head and his chest;
finally a knee slammed into his groin. Andrei gasped
and sprawled out upon the floor. A bright light clouded
his vision and then darkness overcame his consciousness
and with it the pain.

When Andrei finally awoke, his face and his groin
ached. A bright light made it difficult for him to see and
he tried to move his head to the side to escape the light.
His motion was met by a slap to his face. In the semi-
darkness, he could make out a face...Haponchek. He
struggled to rise, but his arms and legs were immobi-
lized with straps of some kind; he was strapped to the
kitchen table, face up. A feeling of panic suddenly
engulfed him, his eyes closed and he felt a sob persist-
ently climb up into his throat. When one acknowledges
the end of life, it is a reality that transcends everything
else. Andrei knew as though it was an instinct that the
end of his life was about to come and that this situation
could end in no other way. Memories returned to him
segment by segment, reviewing his life as though it was
a motion picture. He thought of the movies he had seen
with Maria in Moscow. He couldn't remember any of
the names, he just remembered Maria beside him in the

cinema. Maria; where was she? Andrei felt a sadness encompass him, a complete and total sadness.

The hours and days that followed were out of a nightmare. The relationship between the torturer and the victim is a subject that psychologists have discussed for years. It is an intimate one beyond simple explanation. There is an intimacy that is both spiritual and sexual. Andrei prayed for death time and again. Andrei, who espoused the communist line of atheism was praying continually now to a god he said did not exist to save him from the pain he could not endure.

Yuri Haponchek actually was enjoying himself. He had tied the man to the table using the sheets as bonding. A short walk to the nearby shopping area located a store where he purchased a roll of duct tape, a sharp scalpel-like carving knife and several additional blades. His training had provided him with the knowledge of the art of torture. There also, he found a lamp with a high intensity bulb and several tubes of acrylic glue...the kind called "Super Glue," That would be all he needed. Now it was up to him to provide the atmosphere of horror that would be effective enough to extract the information he needed. In the end he would simply terminate the subject.

During the next two days, Andrei knew what hell would be like. The knife cut slowly and deeply into the sensitive flesh on his face. The nerve endings screamed at him. He felt his blood run in warm rivulets down his neck and puddle against his shoulders. When the glue was dripped into the cut, his body ached with intense pain. The blood stopped flowing and his inquisitor would speak to him again, asking the same questions.

The light burned holes into his eyes as he tried again and again in vain to shut them...his eyelids had been the first cuts made by his torturer. Andrei knew excruciating pain beyond his imagination. It threatened to make his entire being crumble. He wanted to cry out for help, but he quickly learned that the pain only became worse when he attempted it. He knew he would die, but he must also outsmart his executioner. He must keep faith with the Party so that it would survive. He didn't know why, but he felt that the principles of the Party were more important now than life itself. The identification of the agents who were Party faithful must be protected at all costs. In the end, he would tell his inquisitor about the partial list on papers inside his cane; he would tell him about the apartment in Washington and about the equipment that he would find and how to use it to destroy those people selected to be eliminated because they had been unfaithful to the Party. That would be acceptable, even in his death. The others, the loyal ones must be protected. He would never reveal their existence or provide the instrument of their deaths...even at the expense of his own.

Haponchek was impressed with the courage of his victim. It had been four days now that he had been questioning him, and he still resisted. He had offered him only a little water in response to information, but no food. As he inflicted cut after cut; exposing the man's eyes continually to the extreme light, there was still resistance. On the second day, blindness set in and Andrei suffered the recurring pain in perpetual darkness.

The confession about the cane had come as a finale to the interminable inquisition. Yuri now had the address of the apartment which contained the electronic equipment; he possessed the information on how to operate the system, and he had the names and codes of the people who would provide him the rest of the information. The amount of wealth that he quickly calculated made him giddy with anticipation. There was one last act he must do; eliminate Kilyaikin, a relatively simple task. He would then dispose of the body in an alley somewhere in the City. Yuri picked up the blade he had used so effectively in extracting the information he wanted by torture and stood over the man. A recognition suddenly appeared on the man's face that this was the final moment. Suddenly, Andrei felt a constriction in his throat; it was a feeling of violent indigestion. He hadn't eaten in four days, so he rejected that it was caused by that...then he understood what it meant. In the end, he would cheat his inquisitor twice. He gasped for breath once more and then went limp. His heart had finally given up the struggle. Andrei Mikailovitch was dead.

Haponchek shrugged, he had been deprived of the privilege of causing immediate death in this case, but there would be others. He prepared for cleaning up the carnage he had caused.

From the bedchamber of the Baroness von Klauss, there came a scream. Maria awoke in a sudden sweat and sat up in her bed clutching her knees, afraid to move. She had seen Andrei in her dream, and she knew that the man she had once adored was no longer among the living. Maria cried uncontrollably.

CHAPTER TWENTY—ONE

▼

STIRRING THE POT

Jonathan Banks, Inc.
Chevy Chase, Maryland
Wednesday, November 12th 1997

At just nine o'clock, Jonathan Banks entered the conference room. He smiled at the people seated around the large oblong table as he walked to his seat at the head of the table. "Good morning everybody; Shirley McHendrie couldn't make it this morning; she's having breakfast with the President and sends her regrets. What have we got so far?" Seated around the table in a clockwise direction were Charlie Waggner on Banks' left followed by Sean Stevenson, Rose McGuire, Jack Deiter, and COL Hank Henderson.

Jack Deiter was first to speak and briefed the group on what had transpired since they last met formally. He told them of Kilyaikin's identification by the Baroness von Klauss, the picture that John Waggner had faxed and the full rundown on Project Rasputin. He ended up with an account of finding the transmitter and the encounter with the two men at the restaurant. He didn't say anything about the attempt by Aldridge Mason to locate Rose. He figured that it was an "in-house" FBI matter and also more of a personal matter. He glanced over at Rose and received a thankful smile in return.

"Anything further on the codes?" asked Banks.

Charlie responded by showing a series of overhead projections with the translated pages found on the microdots. She explained that the code was, in fact, somewhat simply and was only English written on a Russian typewriter. "Sometimes, the safest place to hide something is right out in the open," she remarked. Before showing the last page containing the cover names of the deep agents, she looked over at Rose for confirmation that Jack Deiter had been told about his parents. Rose nodded her head in silent confirmation. Charlie had earlier told each of the others privately.

Charlie put the transparency with the translation of the list of names on the overhead projector. "We've run a check against the names provided by both the NSA and the FBI of agents they know to have defected. We're also running down all reported stroke victims to die in the last forty years nationwide. The NIH has been really helpful in generating the information, but as you might suspect, it's a very long list," Charlie explained. "This list," she added indicating the overhead projection, "has annotations after certain names. We suspect that these may have been agents who were...uh, removed from participation in the program."

"That's okay, Charlie," Deiter interjected. "I've come to grips with it a long time ago. I'm glad, now at least, for closure. It also explains a lot. My parents were good people, even though the didn't make very good spies. I now know why they had such a close friendship with William Colby and I'm grateful to him and to the CIA for what they tried to do." There was a release of tension around the table. "So, does anyone think that we're at an end to these murders, or are we going to see more?" he asked.

Sean was the first to respond. "I have a strong sense that the killer we're looking for is on that list of names. Kilyaikin must have made contact with him…either to get the code numbers or to enlist his help; those are the only two options possible."

"I agree," interjected Rose. "I suspect that we can eliminate those with a symbol after their name for starters. That lowers the number by only a few, though."

"If we use the locating transmitter, we may be able to establish how many are now in this area. We could narrow the scope a lot," added Sean. "Hank, can some of your people operate the equipment Rose and Jack found?"

Hank Henderson shrugged his opinion that they could. "I suppose so, but it'll take time."

Banks stood up and walked over to the projection screen. Five sets of eyes followed him. He studied the list for a minute, his arms folded with his hand propped under his chin; he tilted his head to the right. "We have 175 possibilities left. Eliminate the females from the list and it looks to be about 130 left. I don't mean to exclude the ladies, I just feel we're dealing with a man here…especially if one of the two men that Rose and Jack encountered is the killer."

Hank interrupted. "If we can locate two an hour…hypothetically it would take us 65 hours working round-the-clock…about three days. With any luck, we could locate ones in this area early on and investigate them first."

"While it's important to find out his name, locating him is our goal," replied Sean. He may have found other agents already and they're now in danger."

"He won't be using the transmitters in Kilyaikin's apartment though…he'd have to find another one," Deiter remarked. "We don't know what his capabilities are or how much he learned from Kilyaikin before he killed him."

"COL Henderson," Banks interrupted, "if you would get your people…as many as you can spare…on it and locate all the contacts in the Washington area…I hope he's still here…Charlie and Sean will try to determine if we have anyone else on the list who may have been killed or are missing. That will cut down the list and can be done concurrently. Banks looked over at Sean. "I wish I was as certain as you that the killer has to be on that list. We still don't know who sponsored Kilyaikin, if indeed someone did. We could be dealing with a rather well organized and ruthless Russian Mafia. Just keep that in mind and be careful. Let's go."

Henderson packed up his brief case and left the room. Charlie and Sean moved to the end of the table to plan how their search could be done quickly and effectively. Banks received a signal from his beeper, looked down at it and quickly left the room.

Rose and Deiter looked at each other. "And then there were only two," said Deiter smiling. "Whatcha want'ta do?"

"Remember the red Mustang.....the one you spotted following us?" replied Rose, "Why don't we cruise around Alexandria and the Wisconsin Avenue area to see if we can spot it. Maybe your office can get a registration address on all red Mustangs in the area at the same time."

"OK, that ought to keep us busy for awhile."

It was almost noon when Deiter eased the Jaguar around the circle and headed down King Street towards Old Town Alexandria. Rose was sitting next to him and was quickly glancing down side streets as the car moved down the street. "Slow down," she admonished him. "I'm going to miss it,"

"A red car ought to show up easily," returned Deiter.

As their car crested the hill and headed down the next to the last block on the street, Rose suddenly exclaimed, "There...on the right!"

"Oh, oh," whispered Deiter, "What do we have here?" In the next block, a tall man in a brown suit was just crossing the street opposite a parked red Mustang. "That's our friend from the lobby and the restaurant."

Deiter quickly pulled the car into a parking space. As they watched, the man went into a bookstore. A few minutes later he came out followed by the man who they had accosted in the elevator in Kilyaikin's apartment building. "My dear, thanks to your suggestion, we have hit pay dirt...way to go," Rose smiled back. The two men crossed the street and into a restaurant.

In about five minutes, the second man came out of the restaurant and crossed over to where the red Mustang was parked. "Okay, who do we follow, this guy or wait for the other one?"

"We have a bird in the bush here," replied Rose.

"I'll buy that; you get the license number when he pulls out…I'll give him a little start and then pull out after him."

As the car pulled into traffic, Rose said, "Those are Jersey plates!!"

"My, my," replied Deiter, "Old home week for you; wonder if we have old Kilyaikin's buddy or a friend of your old flame, Mason? Did ya get his number?"

"You bet," Rose murmured while scribbling on a piece of paper she had pulled out of her purse.

Deiter let the Mustang turn left at the end of King Street before he pulled out. As he turned left to follow the car, he could see that it was making another left turn to head back up towards the Masonic Memorial. He continued to follow it at a comfortable distance. The car eventually ended up heading South on Interstate 395. Following the car without being noticed on the open highway was a bit more tricky, but the FBI agent was successful. At the Springfield exit the Mustang's turn signals came on and it turned into the exit; Deiter followed. Finally, the car slowed and turned in at the Sander's Motel. Deiter slowed down and slid into a parking space just outside the motel entrance. He could see the Mustang parked in a space about halfway down the line of cars parked in front of motel rooms. Deiter picked up the cell phone and punched in numbers. In less than a minute he had set up surveillance of the motel, the Mustang and its driver. They decided to wait until the surveillance team arrived before leaving.

Deiter looked at his watch. It had taken about an hour for the first surveillance team to show up at the motel and now it was almost two o'clock. "I wonder if our friend's finished eating back at the restaurant?"

"I'd bet on it, but why don't we go see anyway. Maybe the waitress can tell us something about him." Deiter swung the Jag around and headed towards the on-ramp to 395 North and Alexandria.

As Rose and Deiter entered the restaurant, it only had three tables occupied…none of them by the man in the brown suit. Deiter spotted the waitress and walked over to her.

"Would you like a table for two?" she asked.

"No thank you, but I do have a question for you."

"Sure, what?" she responded.

"About an hour to hour and a half ago, there was a man here wearing a brown suit; do you remember him?"

She paused and then said, "Oh yes, he was seated over there by the window. He went out for a few minutes and then returned with another guy."

"Right, that's him," said Rose.

"That other guy was kind of queer. I set him a place and then he just disappeared when I went into the kitchen. I served the other guy and he left….oh, about twenty minutes ago."

"Did you notice anything else?"

The waitress looked at Deiter askance. Deiter shrugged and pulled out his FBI credentials to show her. Her face brightened and she added with a smile, "Lousy tipper. As I was bringing him his lunch, he was telling the other guy that he had to clear something with his client.....yes, I'm sure he used the word 'client.'"

"Thanks, that may be very helpful," replied Deiter. "If you remember anything more or if you see him again, will you please call me and leave a message if I'm not there," he added handing her his card.

"Sure," she replied.

They left the restaurant and started walking back up the street; both of them were silent. As they climbed into the Jag, Rose was first to mention what they both were thinking. "My guess is that Mason has hired a detective to find me," she said softly.

"Could be. I wonder what the connection here is with the other guy? He may be the killer."

The ringing of the cell phone interrupted what he was to say next. Deiter answered it.

"Deiter...Yeah, Sean...okay, I'm heading there now...about twenty minutes, I'd guess...okay."

"What was that?"

"Sean says they've uncovered a few agents in the Washington area. None of them are in the motel location, however. There are several more on the East Coast; he wants us back at the firm." Deiter pulled the Jag out into traffic on King Street and headed up the hill towards the entrance to the beltway and Maryland.

"What do you think about Jonathan's comment on the Russian Mafia?" Rose asked.

"Interesting point. Kilyaikin could have been recruited by them to collect the bank assets," Deiter replied.

"The history on him doesn't reflect that he's either a criminal or greedy. He was just a loyal Communist...even if the Soviet Union's not there anymore."

"That may be part of the problem...or solution, whichever way one looks at it."

"How's that?"

"Maybe Kilyaikin was doing it for the Mafia because he needed them...but welshed out on his part of the bargain and they killed him."

"And," Rose interjected, "just maybe they tortured him to get the information on how to do the job themselves."

"Sounds reasonable. And if that's so, then we're a long way from finding the killer."

Rose and Deiter walked into the Task Force Center to find Sean and Charlie there as well. On the way there, Deiter had alerted his office at the FBI to check anything they might have on the Russian Mafia in the United States. "Sean, can the NSA run a scan on everything they have on elements of the Russian Mafia, internal...you know, Stateside?"

"Sure, Charlie and I were just discussing it."

"There may be something to what Jonathan was referring to this morning," remarked Charlie. "If it was the Russian Mafia and not one of the agents, we have a whole different problem."

"That's the way I'm beginning to see it," replied Deiter. "It may not be as simple as we figured."

"I'll stir up the pot a bit," said Sean, scratching his beard, "Let's see what comes to the top."

Charlie looked over at Sean and a smile curved on her lips. " Yeah, I'll bet you really could," she added. She was starting to realize that there was real depth to this man and was beginning to feel a new closeness to him as well.

Sean picked up the phone and for the next twenty minutes made a number of calls, mostly in Russian. Finally he leaned back in his chair and sighed. "That should do it," he said. "I've let every part of the Russian community aware that there's something going on; I should hear back soon." It was almost four o'clock; Sean looked at his watch and turned to ask Charlie, "Want to have dinner tonight?"

"Sure, are you buying or me?"

"Dutch?"

Charlie shrugged and replied, "OK by me, let's go," Both of them put their papers into their brief cases and moved to leave the room. As they got to the door, Charlie looked up at Sean and grinned. He was holding the door open and as she went by he almost kissed her...almost. She knew it and her grin grew wider. This could be something great, she thought. Sean was somewhat bewildered in his thoughts, but very happy; this was an extraordinary person he was with right now...yeah, really extraordinary.

CHAPTER TWENTY–TWO

▼

CONSPIRACY

The Yachtsman
Alexandria, Virginia
Wednesday, November 12th 1997

Although Mort Kinder had worked for Aldridge Mason on several assignments, he didn't particularly like the man. He had done some work for him during Mason's nasty divorce, and that had not been a particularly pleasant relationship. Mason could be vindictive to the point of being cruel. The flip side was that he tended to pay well. Now it was this thing with Rose McGuire, again. Kinder was sitting at a single table in *The Yachtsman* restaurant on lower King Street in Old Town Alexandria, Virginia. It was located just around the corner and a block from the town house of the FBI agent, Deiter, whom he had been following. He had seen both of them, that is Rose McGuire and Deiter, going in the town house the previously evening. His conversation with Mason left no doubt in his mind what the man wanted. Kinder's business was to gather dirt on whoever the client wanted. Sometimes, this had a positive feel; when a person was being deceived or hurt. What he did then was justified and for the good of all. He wasn't sure what Mason wanted this time and it worried him. The woman was single and so was the man. What was the problem? Jealousy on the part of Mason? Kinder decided that jealousy was a good part of it. Not that he felt that Mason could ever love anyone except himself; it was more a sense of possession. Mason, he guessed, didn't like to lose his possessions. OK, he would do what Mason wanted and then get out of there. What might Mason do afterwards, though? That could be a problem. Kinder decided to document everything including taping any conversations with Mason.

Earlier in the week, he had followed Deiter to a building on Wisconsin Avenue in the District; there, Deiter was joined by the McGuire woman. Within half an hour, both of them left and walked down the street to a restaurant. Kinder had followed them to the restaurant and sat at the bar watching them. When Deiter had left to make a call, he noticed a man sitting in the booth next to them suddenly get up without ordering and leave through the back door next to where the rest rooms were located. That seemed strange. At that point, he didn't want to be suspicious, so quickly left to wait outside in his own car until they came out. When they did, he watched them as they walked to where Deiter's car was parked. As the car pulled out into traffic, he followed at a discreet distance, but noticed in his rearview mirror that a red Mustang that had been parked up the street pull up behind him and then fell back. The driver looked like the man who was sitting in the booth behind the couple, but he couldn't be sure. He followed the man and woman across the Memorial Bridge and down Route 1 and into Old Town Alexandria. That's when he had discovered that both of them were staying at Deiter's town house on Prince Street.

Kinder absently looked out the window of the restaurant just then and saw a red Mustang pull into a space across the street. Suddenly, he remembered that strange feeling he had experienced while tailing the couple home; he had felt as though he was the one being tailed rather than the other way around. Later on, after he had watched Deiter and the woman go into the house on Prince Street, he drove once more around the block and had seen the red Mustang again parked up the street from Deiter's house. Kinder didn't like coincidences, in fact he didn't believe in them. As he watched from his seat next to the window of the restaurant, he saw a relatively tall man with blondish looking hair and a somewhat pasty or pudgy appearance climb out of the car and go into the book store across the street. Quickly, he told the waitress that he had to leave for a moment, but that he would return in a few minutes. He crossed the street and entered the bookstore.

The man was arguing with the proprietor of the store when Kinder opened the door to the shop. When the man saw Kinder, he stopped talking. Kinder made his way to a row of books on poetry and started examining the titles. The man turned and approached Kinder.

"Don't we know each other?" the man said.

"I don't think so," replied Kinder.

The man lowered his voice and whispered, "I believe we have a mutual acquaintance on Prince Street?"

Now Kinder was assured of his suspicions. "That may be possible."

"Perhaps we should talk."

"Perhaps so," replied Kinder. "Uh...I've already ordered lunch across the street, would you care to join me?"

Both men crossed the street and entered the restaurant. The waitress brought another setting and when she had left them alone Kinder said, "What's there to say about the man and woman on Prince Street?"

"I know that you were following them," the man replied.

"And so were you."

"We might share information on them," offered the man.

Kinder paused and then said, "Let me introduce myself, I'm Mort Kinder; I'm a PI from the New York area," Kinder offered his hand and the other man took it.

"My name is Rudy Kurtz," replied Haponchek giving his cover name.

Kinder looked at the other man quizzically, "I have a license to do what I do, what's your excuse?"

"The man, Deiter," he lied, "uh....was involved with my sister."

"I see, and your sister was...hurt?"

"We're a close family. She thinks that he's still interested in her...and I believe he's lying...I know he's lying," explained Haponchek. He was looking down and quickly glanced up to see if his story was being believed.

"I'd do anything to find out more about their relationship and to destroy his credibility with my sister."

"Perhaps we can work together," said Kinder, "My client would like to separate them as well." Kinder paused. "I suppose that you know that he's an FBI special agent." It was more of a question than a statement.

"That's not what he told her," replied Haponchek quickly. He suddenly realized what was happening. He was correct in assuming that the two of them were in Kilyaikin's apartment on Wisconsin Avenue. He didn't know about the FBI connection, however. He must find out what the woman's role was. "Who's the woman?"

"Her name is Rose McGuire. She works for my client, but apparently she has run off with the man Deiter. My client wants her back."

Yuri Haponchek smiled to himself, never letting on to the other man. "I think I can help you," he offered.

"That's something that I'd have to clear with my client," Kinder replied quickly as the waitress approached them.

"Do you want to order something?" she asked the newly arrived customer. Haponchek shook his head and she turned and walked away.

Haponchek fished in his pocket and produced a card. Taking out a pen, he wrote his name and room number on it. The card was from the Sander's Motel in Springfield. "You can contact me here," he said shoving the card across the table towards Kinder. Kinder thanked him and shook hands as the man got up to leave.

"I'll be in touch as soon as I talk with my client," Kinder said as the waitress was bringing him his lunch.

Haponchek left the restaurant and Kinder pondered on the credibility of this man as he started to eat. He would report it to Mason and let him decide.

It was nearly six o'clock in the evening when Kinder dialed Mason's private telephone number. Aldridge Mason was sitting at his desk reviewing a brief that he had prepared for Friday's court session. Most of the rest of the staff had left and he was just finishing up his work. Mason answered the phone. "Mason."

"Kinder. I know where they are, but not what they're doing, yet."

"I know what they're doing, I need to know where," demanded Mason.

"Old Town Alexandria, 125 Prince Street. That's Deiter's house. There's a new wrinkle."

"What's that?"

"I ran into a man who has a bone to pick with Deiter as well, he wants to help...something about his sister and Deiter; he could be useful."

"What's his name?"

"Rudolph Kurtz," replied Kinder reading the name from the motel card.

"I'll be coming down tomorrow; I have to clear my calendar and get reservations so it may be later in the day. I'll contact you when I get in. Set up a meeting with this man tomorrow night...someplace neutral and quiet."

"OK," Kinder said as he responded to only a dial tone. He wished he were working for someone with a better personality. Kinder shook his head and hung up the phone.

Sander's Motel
Springfield, Virginia
Thursday, November 13th, 1997

It was nine o'clock in the morning and Yuri Haponchek smiled as he received instructions on the phone from Kinder. They were to meet at eight–thirty that evening at the same restaurant where they had talked together the day before...the client would be there. He hung up the phone and sat back. He needed to finish his plan. Somehow, the FBI agent and his woman must be thrown off his trail...if in fact they were even on it. He must regain access to the transmitter for at least one more operation. This man's client could be of assistance. Why was he so intent on getting back an employee? Maybe there was more to their relationship than that. Of course, she must be his mistress and apparently had flown the coop. He liked how this might play out. Oh, yes, jealousy...a man who will travel several hundred miles to get back a woman. What else might he be willing to do...murder perhaps? This was sounding better and better as Haponchek thought out the scenario. The client and the PI were chasing the woman and the woman (he supposed) and the FBI man were chasing either him or Kilyaikin...or both. Did they know about Kilyaikin? Had the body yet been identified? Yuri didn't know how it could have been identified. Yet what was the FBI doing in Kilyaikin's apartment? He had to move carefully.

The Yachtsman
Alexandria, Virginia
Thursday, November 13th 1997

The maitre 'd had just seated Aldridge Mason at a back table of *The Yachtsman*, when he was joined by Mort Kinder. It was eight o'clock sharp. "I told him we'd meet him at eight–thirty; we'll have some time before he gets here," explained Kinder.

"Fill me in," demanded Mason.

Kinder was about to speak when the waitress interrupted them. "Care for something to drink?" she asked.

Mason sighed and grabbed the wine list, looked it over quickly and then slid it back behind the condiments. "Just bring me a Dewers on the rocks," he said impatiently.

"Same for me," said Kinder as the waitress looked over at him. She smiled and left them alone.

"So?" asked Mason.

Kinder brought Mason up to date as far as all the activities were concerned with Deiter and the woman. "I think that this guy Kurtz can be useful to us. He has a thing about Deiter."

"Maybe so," Mason observed cautiously.

"I'd recommend you not use your real name; let me do the introduction," warned Kinder.

"Fine by me, nobody needs to know I'm here."

They had just ordered their second drink when Yuri Haponchek stepped through the doorway and looked around. He spotted Kinder and made his way to the back of the restaurant towards the two men.

"Good evening gentlemen," Yuri said in a low voice.

"Good evening, Mr. Kurtz; I'd like to introduce Mr. Flynn." The two men shook hands briefly and Yuri sat down at one of the free chairs at the table.

"I believe we have a similar dislike in common," observed Yuri.

"I have neither likes nor dislikes, I just get what I want," responded Mason, without humor, his eyes narrowing to slits.

"I appreciate that and I hope that what you want is satisfied. Maybe I can be of assistance."

"Oh?" Mason asked sarcastically, sitting back in his chair.

Yuri eyes flashed at the intended insult, but he caught himself before saying anything.

"Gentlemen, please, we can all work together," interjected Kinder.

Mason turned to Kinder. "Perhaps Mr. Kurtz and I should speak alone," he suggested. Kinder finished his drink in one gulp and stood up.

"Contact me if you need me," he responded to Mason.

After the Private Investigator had left, Mason's eyes followed the PI until he disappeared through the front door of the restaurant. He turned back to Kurtz who now wore a surprised expression on his face and a sardonic smile. "Mr. Kurtz, would you be willing to assuage your anger and at the same time do me a favor...a favor for which I will be quite willing to pay you handsomely?" asked Mason.

"What do you want?" asked Yuri.

"I don't want the man Deiter to be a nuisance to me anymore," Mason replied looking down into his drink.

He lifted his head slowly and looked into the other man's eyes; his own closing to a squint. "Whatever that may take, but it must be permanent and it must look like he simply disappeared."

Yuri sat back and tilted his head, looking at Mason. "I like to know who I am dealing with, Mr....Flynn," he replied and added, "If that's your name."

"You don't need to know. You'll find my money to be cash and untraceable."

Yuri shrugged. "How can I contact you if I need to?"

Mason thought for a moment. "I'm registered at the Embassy Suites in Washington under the name of Aldridge Mason."

"And how much money are we discussing?"

"Ten thousand dollars...five now and the rest later. I'll leave it at a predetermined location suitable to both of us."

"Done," said Yuri.

Mason reached into his inside coat pocket and withdrew an envelope which he slid across the table towards the other man.

"I'll leave you to your meal," concluded Yuri standing up to leave. "I'll be in touch with you for the remainder at the conclusion of our deal."

"Send Mr. Kinder back in here; I believe you'll find him waiting outside."

Yuri nodded and left the restaurant.

The waitress came over to Mason to inquire about ordering dinner just as Kinder reentered the restaurant. Kinder took his seat and the two men ordered. Mason reflected to himself the possibilities of what had just happened. He didn't want Kinder to know that any transaction had been made between them. If Deiter simply disappeared, he could convince Rose that she had been deserted and she was better off back with him. It sounded good to Mason. That man should not have interfered; it was his own fault. Mason was convinced that he knew Rose very well indeed.

CHAPTER TWENTY-THREE

▼

CAPTURED

125 Prince Street
Alexandria, Virginia
Friday, November 14th 1997

The light was just beginning to seep into Deiter's bedroom as Rose rolled over to see him straightening his tie before his dresser mirror. He turned around at the noise and smiled at her. "I have to go in early to check over some things with Ken Stroeman. Even though I'm on this case, I still have section work that goes on. Ken needs my okay on some personnel things. I should be back at Banks' building by..," he looked at his watch. "oh, say ten o'clock," He went over to where she was lying on the bed. "I couldn't bear to wake you when I got up, you were sleeping so beautifully."

"That's okay," she purred. "I'll get something to eat and meet you there." She reached her arms up to encircle his neck and brought his head down to meet her lips. "Umm, will that hold you?"

Deiter returned the kiss and smiled broadly as he turned to go. "No, not really, but it's all we have time for. See ya 'bout ten."

Rose stretched her arms out and closed her eyes. Things had been good since Jack Deiter had come back into her life. The whole business with Mason now seemed so sordid. She wondered why and how she could have ever done it. Her brow wrinkled at the thought of Mason. What was he up to? She could bet it was not good. Her thoughts then switched to the case. The list of people including Jack's parents...she wondered about that. Right now, the people from Hank Henderson's office should be busy locating the agents on the list. She suddenly had a yearning to visit the apartment and find out how they were doing. Maybe they would have something that she could bring back to Jack. She could drive into the city and check it out...she wasn't doing anything else that day. Last weekend, Jack had driven her up to New Jersey and picked up her car so she could be mobile again. Rose wondered what Aldridge Mason would have made of her car suddenly disappearing...would he report it stolen? She jumped out of bed and headed for the shower. Twenty minutes later she was behind the wheel of her car heading for Washington and the apartment on Wisconsin Avenue.

Rose found a parking place around the corner from the apartment building and walked into the building at eight–fifteen that morning. The traffic had been horrendous, but finding the parking space was a pure blessing and made her morning. The Indian desk clerk was busily sorting through what appeared to be a collection of bills, perhaps the monthly rental bills, she guessed. "You remember me?" she asked. "I was with the Federal team."

He looked up and smiled broadly. "I'm so glad to see you," he said, "I was wondering who I should give the rent bill to this month."

Rose smiled knowingly and put out her hand. "I'll take it, is someone up there now?"

"Oh no, they left almost an hour ago. They said they were finished."

"Really?" That didn't take them long, she observed to herself. "Do you have a key then, I was counting on them being there."

"Yes, certainly," he replied in his heavy Indian accent. He turned around and visually searched through the nest of boxes until he came to the right one and picked a key out of the box. He then stopped and turned back to the box. "Oh, there is a letter here for the occupant. It did not come in the mail so it must have been dropped off by someone."

"Oh, really?" Rose mentally slapped herself. She sounded like she was repeating herself. "I'll make sure it's delivered," she said holding out her hand for both the key and envelope.

The clerk paused and then handed both to her. "I suppose it is all right."

Rose headed for the elevator and as the door closed behind her, she tore open the envelope. Inside was a single sheet of paper with a telephone number on it. The elevator stopped and she walked out into the hallway and down to Kilyaikin's apartment. When she closed the

door behind her, she checked all of the rooms and confirmed to herself that the team had left and that she was
alone. In the living room, she plopped herself into an
overstuffed chair next to the telephone. She held the
sheet of paper in front of her and had started to dial the
number when she stopped. She sighed and hung up the
phone; it wouldn't be smart for her to make the call after
all. The message was obviously meant for Kilyaikin and
she didn't sound anything like him. She picked up the
telephone and dialed the Task Force communications
room. After two rings a male voice answered. "Yes?"

"Sean, is that you? It's Rose."

"Going to be late this morning?" he teased.

"No, I'm over here at Kilyaikin's apartment. The team
from NSA must have finished because there's no one
here. When I arrived, the clerk downstairs gave me an
envelope that he said was hand delivered. All it contains
is a telephone number...it looks local."

"That's all?"

"Yeah, I think it was meant for Kilyaikin. I was going
to call, but I think a male voice might be better. This
may be his contact. Be prepared to speak Russian."

"Good thinking; what is it?"

Rose repeated the number to Sean and he responded,
"I'll make the call. What's your number there. When I
get something, I'll give you a call...oh, how long are you
going to be there?"

Rose gave him the number listed on the telephone
and added, "About a half hour. I'm suppose to meet Jack
at ten back at your place."

"OK, if I don't get anything in a half hour, I'll wait
for you here."

"Got it, thanks. Oh, the desk clerk gave me the monthly rent bill too, do you want to take care of it?"

Sean laughed and looked up at Charlie, "Give it to Charlie, she takes care of details like that," Charlie returned his look with a quizzical look on her face.

Rose hung up the phone and went into the room filled with electronic equipment. She sat down at the computer and turned it on. She knew that the team had probably scanned everything on it, but they might not understand Russian as well as she did and while she had the time she might as well check it out. For almost a half-hour, she scanned the files that she assumed Kilyaikin had set up. Names and addresses were listed as well as a separate file for expenses he had obviously incurred in his travels. There were airline flights around the country, hotel bills, restaurant bills, even tips. Kilyaikin must have been a stickler for details. She smiled to herself to think he might need to give his "employer" an expense voucher. She doubted that. She heard the outside door open, but assumed it to be the desk clerk or the NSA people returning.

Yuri Haponchek slid the key into the door of Kilyaikin's apartment. He hadn't been there for the last couple of days, ever since he had come face-to-face with the FBI agent and the woman. Right now he needed to spend a couple of hours on the transmitter and computer. He had been successful in locating two more agents, but he knew he could probably have time to locate a few more before it became too dangerous. He opened the door and quickly moved inside. As he started to close the door, he heard sounds coming from the equipment room. He eased the door shut and quickly walked to the doorway of the room. What he saw surprised him. The surprise quickly turned to delight. A scheme immediately developed in his mind and he considered it to be a brilliant turn of events. The shocking mass of red hair in front of the computer could belong to no other than the McGuire woman. He could hardly contain himself on his good fortune.

"Be with you in a minute," Rose said over her shoulder.

"Longer than that, Sweetheart," came the reply.

The sudden pain in her head gave way to a bright light and then darkness as Rose's head slumped onto the keyboard of the computer. A rivulet of blood was hidden as it made its way through the thick red hair.

Haponchek knew that he had done well when he rented the apartment down the hallway from Kilyaikin's. It had been another spark of his genius. The woman wasn't light and he struggled as he lifted her up from the computer table and made his way out into the living room. He set her down on the sofa and went to open the door to his apartment down the hallway. Returning, he picked up the unconscious woman and went to the open door. Looking both ways, he entered the hallway and then quickly carried her out of the door, down the hallway and into his apartment. He sighed in relief as he turned towards the open door and closed it behind him. Quickly he placed her on the couch and went back to clean up any trace of his activity in Kilyaikin's room. He returned smiling and was satisfied with his actions. Where to hide something you don't want found except under the noses of those searching? He picked up the still unconscious woman and carried her to the bedroom. Laying her on the bed, he picked up a pillow and pulled off its case. It wasn't easy to tear the case into strips, but with the help of a small pocketknife, he was able to get five strips out of it. He tied the woman's wrists and ankles to the bedposts, stuffed half of a strip of cloth in her mouth, and tied the rest of it around her head covering her mouth. When he had finished, he stood at the end of the bed and looked at her. She was just beginning to regain consciousness.

Rose opened her eyes and immediately panicked as she realized that her arms and legs were tied to the bed. She tried to yell, but could only create a moaning sound. Her head hurt. At the end of the bed was the man she had seen in the elevator. He was smiling at her.

"Oh, don't worry, my dear, you are much too valuable for me to defile you," he said with a sardonic smile on his face. "I have plans for you, thanks to your FBI boyfriend. I'll bet you really fell for his line." Yuri turned and left the bedroom closing the door behind him. He had two telephone calls to make; one to Mason and one to the FBI.

Flynn or Mason had said that he was staying at the Embassy Suites in Washington. He picked up the telephone and dialed 411 and the operator gave him the number of the hotel. He held down the receiver button, lifted it again and punched in the number he had just been given. An operator answered. "The room of Mr. Aldridge Mason," he said waiting for the operator to transfer him.

"Yes?" growled Aldridge Mason into the phone.

"Mason? I have the woman."

"What? Where?"

"All in good time. Here's what I want of you…and you must play the part."

"I don't take orders!" shouted Mason.

"You will if you still want her alive. It's your choice."

Mason was silent. He didn't like the way this was going, he was losing control. He had been standing next to the bed and he sat down as he said reluctantly, "What do you want?"

"That's better. Forget the story I gave you and your PI. I want Deiter dead all right, and getting rid of his girlfriend wouldn't be any more difficult," replied Yuri. He paused and then added for Mason's benefit, "I may even have fun with her in the process,"

"I will not have her hurt."

"Do you really think you're in a position to dictate terms?"

Mason was silent again.

"Just think, you'll be a hero and rescue the woman and then you'll take her home with you. I'm quite sure that should satisfy your needs. What I want in return is for you to kill the man Deiter. I don't think that should bother you too much after he ran off with your woman. At exactly six–thirty tonight, you will come to 1297 Wisconsin Avenue. Do not go to the desk. Enter the elevator and go to the fourth floor, Apartment 415. The door will be unlocked. Deiter will come there at exactly six–forty–five. When he enters, you must shoot him. He will not be expecting it. You will find a revolver with a silencer under the sofa in the apartment," Yuri let the information soak in for a few moments.

After he was sure that Mason had absorbed what he had said, he continued. "Afterwards, you will take the body to the elevator and to the basement. There is a room just outside of the elevator and you will put the body in there…leave the revolver there too. I'll take care of the rest. When you've done that, and only after you've disposed of the body, go to Apartment Number 421, you will find the woman there; she will be tied up and very thankful to you for finding her, but she will be unharmed only if you follow my instructions."

"How'll that story play with the police?" Mason asked.

"Very well, you'll not be connected at all. You will say that you came looking for your friend and received a telephone message to go to the apartment where she was being held. Deiter will have disappeared with the money or killed by someone avenging Kilyaikin's death and the loss of a great deal of money."

"Who?" asked Mason.

"It's not important; they'll understand and believe you." Yuri hung up the phone.

Yuri was content with his plan. He could make Deiter disappear and make it appear that the missing money was taken by the FBI agent. Also, if the body were ever found, there was always the assertion that revenge would be the motive for killing the FBI agent. He smiled. The plan seemed to Yuri to be just one more creation of his wonderful genius. He wondered what the Chechen underworld would do when they finally realize that Kilyaikin was dead and their investment had gone sour. They had no way of connecting him to anything, of course. By then, the money would be his and the equipment destroyed. A perfect plan. He went back to

Kilyaikin's apartment...there was still some more work
to do before setting the final chapter in motion.

CHAPTER TWENTY—FOUR

▼

RANSOMED

Jonathan Banks, Inc.,
Chevy Chase, Maryland
Friday, November 14th 1997

Sean keyed in the number that Rose had given him and waited for the phone to ring. It rang four times and an answering machine finally responded. "I received your message," he replied after the beep, gave the number at the Task Force, and hung up the receiver. He sat back wondering how the number would be receive at the other end. It was almost ten o'clock when the phone rang. Sean picked up the receiver and spoke somewhat away from the mouthpiece. "Yes?"

"I'm glad you responded," came the reply.

"What is it?" asked Sean tentatively.

"We have heard rumors that all is not as it should be."

"I don't understand."

"We have heard rumors of your demise."

Sean managed a laugh, "Well, I hope that rumor's now dispelled."

There was a pause at the other end of the line. "Would you give me your name; this number is not familiar?"

"I'm Doctor Andrei Kilyaikin, that you should know. Are you the one I spoke with before? I've installed a second line; one line is insufficient for my work; the computer requires a separate line," Sean bluffed.

"I was worried for a moment; how's the project going?"

"Well for now," Sean grimaced to himself. He didn't know how much longer he could keep up the charade, nor did he really know if he should. It made sense to him now that these people were Kilyaikin's contacts. He also realized that they didn't know Kilyaikin well enough to instantly recognize his voice. He wondered what would happen if he came right out and said that Kilyaikin was dead, what effect would that have on finding the killer? Would they be able to flush the killer out...would they suspect who it might be? Sean decided to let the others make that decision; until then, he would simply play the game.

"Do you need any assistance?" the voice asked.

"I will contact you if I do, is this number still good?"

"For the time being; are you sure everything is all right."

"Da poxal$sta, (*Yes, certainly,*) I will contact you when I have something more," Sean wanted to get off the line before he made a blunder; he thought a little Russian might be more convincing. He also wanted to check the source of the number he had just called; he kicked himself for not doing it earlier. The line suddenly went dead.

Sean wondered if the inquiries he had placed in the Russian community had precipitated the message to Kilyaikin. Had he indeed struck a nerve? He decided to call Rose at Kilyaikin's apartment. He punched in the number she had given him and waited while it rang. There was no answer. He looked at his watch...nine–thirty; Rose may have already left to return to the center. He decided to wait for her. In the meantime, he would contact the telephone company to find out who the number was listed under.

At ten–thirty, Deiter entered the Task Force communications center. Sean and Charlie were there, but he noticed that Rose wasn't. "Sean, has Rose been in yet?" he asked.

"No, but I talked with her at about nine o'clock; she gave me a number that someone had left in a message to Kilyaikin at the apartment. She wanted me to call it and find out what I could; than she said she was to meet you here at ten. She isn't at the apartment anymore; I called at nine–thirty and nobody answered. She may have gotten caught up in traffic."

"She went to the apartment? Why?" Deiter asked. He didn't like it. He'd felt guilty about leaving her that morning, but he didn't expect that she'd go over to the apartment. With a killer on the loose and Mason sniffing around...well, it just worried him, but he didn't say anything to the others. After all, they didn't know that part of the story.

Sean described what had happened when he made the call to the telephone number Rose had given him and Charlie added that Rose was bringing the bill for the apartment's rent back with her. Deiter waited impatiently another hour and then stood up and started out the door. "Call me on my cell phone if she comes in," he said over his shoulder.

It took fifteen minutes to get to the apartment. Deiter spotted Rose's car still parked around the corner as he circled the block looking for a parking space. That wasn't a good sign. He parked in a restricted parking lot next to the apartment building and hurried into the lobby. The desk clerk was just getting up from his seat behind the counter as Deiter passed him. Deiter hit the elevator button and at the same time turned towards the clerk. "Did the lady who was with me a few days ago come in here today?" he asked. "You know, the one with the dark red hair."

"Yes sir, I gave her the key…I suppose she is still there," the clerk replied.

The elevator arrived and Deiter stepped in and pushed the button to the fourth floor. He waited impatiently as the elevator slowly climbed. He headed down the hallway and tried the door at Apartment 415. The door was unlocked and Deiter barged in. No one was in the living room and Deiter quickly crossed the room and heading for the equipment room. The door to the room was shut and he turned the knob slowly and opened it. The room appeared to be empty; on the table with the computer was a copy of the apartment bill where he supposed Rose had left it. Deiter suddenly paled as he saw the red stains on the keyboard. As he stepped forward to touch the dark red liquid, a crushing blow hit the back of his neck and he felt himself drifting into darkness and floating slowly to the floor unable to stop his fall. Yuri stood over him smiling. "Thank you for being so accommodating, Mr. Deiter."

Yuri dragged the unconscious form into a closet and locked the door. He had to finish his work before he was discovered again. He sat down at the transmitter and began the sequence that he had been told by Kilyaikin. He only had five more agents to locate precisely and two to eliminate. He worked quickly. He wanted to finish and be gone when the FBI man regained consciousness. He could have killed him now, but he wanted Flynn or Mason or whatever his name was, to do that. It would be cleaner that way. He might have an opportunity to use the man again...he was sure of that.

Deiter slowly drifted into consciousness surrounded by darkness. He felt a nausea creeping up his throat from the intense pain to the back of his head and neck and he tried to shake it off. Next, he tried to move and found he was cramped inside a confined space of some sort. He listened, but heard no noise that he could identify. His hands felt the walls of his confinement and he judged that he was inside a closet of some sort. He guessed he was still in the apartment. He tried the doorknob, but it was locked from the outside. He slowly stood up, but hit his head on a bar and he winced at the new pain. He pressed his ear to the door, but no noise was coming from the outside room. Deiter felt above him and found the metal bar that ran the full length of the closet. Grabbing the bar with both hands, he leaned back bracing his shoulders against the back wall. For a moment he concentrated hard, letting his breathing slow down and become deep. Suddenly, he lifted his legs up and slammed both feet against the door. The lock burst and the door flew open. The light in the outside room blinded him at first and he put his hand up to his eyes to shield them. He looked around...he was alone. He stumbled into the living room...no one there either; he checked the kitchen and bedroom. Nothing. He slumped into the easy chair next to the telephone and looked at his watch...it was three–thirty. He'd been out for almost four hours. He called the communications center. "Charlie, did Rose come in?" he asked.

"No, Jack, she didn't," Charlie replied. "We have some more information from the NSA guys, though. Where are you?"

"I'm still at the apartment. Something's happened to Rose. Her car's parked outside and there's something that looks like blood on the computer keyboard." He paused, almost too embarrassed to mention his brief encounter with an unknown assailant. "Someone hit me from behind...I've been out since about eleven–thirty and have a splitting headache to show for it."

"Is there something we can do, Jack" Charlie asked.

"I don't know, Charlie, let me think and get my head together. I'm going to nose around here for awhile and see what I can find out about Rose."

"Sean says he's coming over."

"OK, I'll be here."

Deiter hung up the phone and leaned back in the chair and closed his eyes. God, his head hurt. What had happened to Rose? Where was she? He tried not to think of the worst possibility. He wondered if the desk clerk could tell him anything. Pushing himself up from the chair he headed down to the lobby. As he exited the elevator, he saw the desk clerk sitting behind the counter and went over to him. "Did you see anything of the lady with the red hair after she was here earlier this morning?" he asked.

"No sir, as far as I knew she was still in the room...and she still has the key," he reminded Deiter.

"Is there another way out of the building?"

"Oh yes, of course. The elevator goes to the basement. There is a back entrance to the alley in the rear."

"Thanks," Deiter replied as he headed for the elevator. He stepped in and pressed the basement button. When the door opened again, Deiter found himself at the end of a long hallway leading to an outside door at the end. Along the hallway were a number of doors with padlocks on them. In the dim light he could make out numbers on each door. They appeared to be apartment numbers. Deiter guessed that these were storage rooms for each of the apartments. He followed the numbers until he reached Number 415. There wasn't a lock on the door and Deiter opened it and went in. Along the right side of the doorway, he felt a light switch and turned it on. The room was bare. He turned off the light, closed the door behind him and walked to the end of the hallway. The door to the outside had a panic bar latch and Deiter pushed it open and looked out at the alley. Nothing out of the ordinary attracted his attention; it was filled with garbage cans and dumpsters, but nothing to indicate that Rose might have gone out this way. For all he knew, she could still be in the building.

He went back inside and took the elevator back to Kilyaikin's apartment.

Deiter had been back in the apartment only about ten minutes, when Sean arrived. "Find anything?" Sean asked.

"No, not really; there's a back entrance through the basement, though. Someone could go out that way without the clerk seeing them," Deiter replied.

"Possible, but not conclusive."

"Yeah, I know. What did NSA find out?"

"Looks like we have several contacts right here in the Washington area," Sean started to say. He was interrupted by the telephone.

"Yes?" said Deiter into the receiver.

"Jack, it's Charlie. We just got a call from your office. It seems like someone, a man, just called your office and left you a message."

"What'd he say?"

"He said that if you want to see 'the woman,' as he put it, alive you will go to Kilyaikin's apartment...he didn't say that, of course, but he did give the address and apartment number...at six–forty–five tonight, alone. And he did stress 'alone,' Jack. He said you should drop the investigation and turn over any lists you have to him in exchange for Rose. Once he's safely away, he'll tell you where she is."

"He must take us for idiots," Deiter replied. "OK, have my office set up a surveillance team on the apartment building; Sean and I'll stay here in the apartment."

Deiter hung up the phone and joined Sean who had already started a search of the apartment for anything they might have overlooked. Deiter explained what

Charlie had told him about the call to the FBI and then on impulse went into the equipment room. The reddish-brown stain on the computer keyboard drew his attention and left him with a feeling of dread. Next to the keyboard was an envelope and the bill from the apartment building. He picked up the envelope and opened it. Inside was a single sheet of paper with a telephone number on it. Next, he went over to the stack of electronic equipment that included the transmitter. He turned it on and pulled out a notebook from his inside coat pocket. When the digital numbers indicating the frequency came up on the screen, he jotted them down. He was interrupted by a call from Sean in the living room. "Hey, Jack, c'mear."

Deiter moved quickly to the doorway and leaned into the other room. "Yeah, what?"

"Look what I found under the sofa!" Sean exclaimed.

Deiter moved over to where Sean was kneeling beside the sofa with his head on the floor. Leaning down, Deiter followed Sean's gaze. About midway under the piece of furniture was a black revolver sporting a long heavy silencer.

"Do you ever remember seeing this before?" Sean asked.

"Never looked under there before," came the reply.

Deiter took out his handkerchief and reached for the weapon. He pulled it from underneath the sofa and sat down examining it. "Wow, what a cannon...looks like it was meant to do somebody real harm," observed Sean.

"I wonder why our guys didn't find it before?" asked Deiter absently.

"Maybe because it wasn't here before," replied Sean.

Deiter nodded his agreement. "My guess is that my friendly mugger put it there, but why?"

"What was the message you said the guy left you? You were supposed to come here at exactly six–forty–five. Why so exact and why here?"

"Maybe because that's where the gun is? But who was suppose to meet me here with the gun? The guy on the phone?" Deiter responded.

"I doubt it…he'd probably would carry his own gun."

"Well, whoever it was won't be using these," Deiter said as he emptied all six rounds into his hand. He then reset the cylinder and returned the weapon to its place under the sofa. "If somebody wanted me to be here at six–forty–five, then maybe someone else was suppose to be here a few minutes before hand to pick up the gun," He looked up at Sean. "The guy went out of his way to bate me. I hate to be paranoid, but my guess is the I was suppose to be the victim here. I really don't think I had that effect on people," he mused.

"Oh, I almost forgot to tell you that I talked to the NSA team chief that worked on the transmitter," Sean remarked. "They started out using the machine in the other room, but soon figured out that they could do better with their own equipment and left. That's why Rose didn't see anybody when she arrived."

"What'd they find out?" Deiter asked.

"Five contacts in the Washington area. One had to have been right here in this building according to the coordinates displayed on the equipment. That was another reason they wanted to get out and use their own equipment. No use scaring the guy off."

Deiter grimaced. Rose must have walked right into the killer…isn't that just wonderful?

"Sean, I'll be right back. I need to get something from my car," Deiter said. He took the elevator to the basement and walked down the hallway and out into the alley. Before closing the door, he picked up a piece of cardboard lying next to the door and slid it into the opening so that he could let himself back in without going around to the front door. Satisfied, he turned and walked down the alley towards where he had parked the Jaguar. He needed some protective equipment. When Deiter reached the Jag, he pressed his keyless entry button and the boot lid opened as he walked up to it. He slid his hand up under the hinge and pulled a lever which caused the floor to slide back revealing a series of weapons each housed in its own cutout space. He looked around to assure himself that no one was watching him and pulled out two Ceska Zbrojovka 100 semi-automatic pistols in clip-on holsters which he slid onto the back of his belt under his suit coat. He picked up two boxes of.40 caliber S &W ammunition, a couple of small high intensity flashlights, two Thomas-developed lightweight protective vests, a small hand-held night vision device, and a pair of small portable radio transmitters. He rolled them up in the vests and tucked them under his arm. He wasn't going to be caught by that guy twice in one day. He locked the Jaguar and returned to the apartment through the alley door.

"I got the frequencies that the NSA team had come up with for the contact they figured was in the apartment building," offered Sean as soon as Deiter had closed the door to the apartment. "The name listed against them in Kilyaikin's files was that of a Yuri Haponchek with the cover name of Rudolph Kurtz. The possible combination of numbers for bank accounts against names that Charlie came up with gave a possible match. The bank numbers identified a branch of PNC bank in Sparta, New Jersey and the telephone directory says a Rudolph Kurtz lives there as well."

"Well, that's in the right area if it's the same guy that killed Kilyaikin in New York," replied Deiter. "Can you get a lock on him using the stuff in the other room?"

"I don't know, but I'll give it a try…we've got time and we might get lucky," Sean walked into the equipment room and started experimenting with the transmitter's computer.

Deiter looked at his watch…almost five o'clock…a little over an hour and a half to wait. He laid out the two CZ 100 semiautomatics, the night vision device, flashlights and the two protective vests. At least Sean and he would be armed and covered. Absently, he wondered what special training deep agents like Sean went through that could prepare them for this. He guessed by the look of Sean that the guy could take care of himself without much of a problem. For the hour, he sat in the living room and tried to game plan in his mind what the evening might hold for him. Finally at six o'clock, Deiter walked over to doorway to the equipment room and leaned in. "Maybe we'd better get suited up," he suggested.

Sean came into the living room and Deiter handed him a weapon, radio, flashlight, radio and a vest. "At six–fifteen," he said quietly, but so it still sounded like an order. "I'll take the stairway to the basement and go out the back door. You wait here and see who shows. They may be waiting to make sure I show up alone." He paused and added, "Don't take any chances, Sean, if you take cover in the bedroom, you can see what's going on. If the guy looks under the sofa, you know the guy didn't just wander in here by accident."

Sean smiled at that and replied, "Not to worry, we were taught by masters."

"I'll bet you were; ever use one of these?" he said offering the night vision device to Sean.

"Not just like it, but close enough," responded Sean.

"I figure you can leave the lights off and let him locate the gun under the sofa with the light from the street."

Sean returned to the transmitter while Deiter sat back to wait. He thought about Rose. Where was she? He still felt guilty about leaving her this morning. He never could imagine that something like this would happen. That guy, what was his name, Yuri Haponchek? He'd pay for this. If only she was all right.

At six–fifteen, Deiter went to the doorway to the equipment room. "I'm going now. I'll show up in about twenty–five minutes, but I'll be close enough to help if you need it. You can call me on the frequency that I set on the radio. I've got a team watching from outside." He turned and went out the doorway and down the stairwell to the basement. As he passed the basement elevator door, he noticed that the door to the room next to the elevator was open. He could have sworn that there was a lock on it when he was there earlier. He looked at the number; it was 421.

CHAPTER TWENTY–FIVE

▼

RETRIBUTION

Kilyaikin's Apartment Building
Washington, DC
Friday, November 14th 1997

Sean looked at his watch. It was just six–thirty. At this time of year in Washington, the darkness settles in early. He had left the lights turned off and had pulled the plugs from the sockets on the wall. He didn't want anything except the ambient light from the street lights outside the window to illuminate the living room. The night vision device that Jack Deiter had given him worked amazingly well and he was accustoming himself to it as he sat on the bed with the bedroom door open a crack so he could observe the main door to the apartment. A minute later, there was the sound of someone opening the apartment door. Sean quickly moved to the crack in the doorway and focused on the apartment door. He turned the night vision device to the left and focused on the sofa. Yes, he could follow any movement easily.

Aldridge Mason came out of the elevator door and walked slowly down the hallway reading the numbers on the apartments as he passed them. He stopped at number 415 and tried the doorknob. The door was unlocked and he opened it. There was no light in the apartment and no indication that anyone was there. Mason looked both ways in the hallway and assuring himself that the hadn't been seen, slipped inside the apartment and closed the door behind him. Well, he thought to himself, he was there and about to do something that he had never before done in his life. He was sweating profusely and his hands shook. He started to search for the light switch, but thought better of it. He couldn't take the chance that someone was watching the window, waiting for a light. His eyes became accustomed to the darkness and he could make out the furniture in the main room. The sofa was in the center of the room facing the window. The light from the window was sufficient to see the interior of the room and he quickly walked over to the sofa and bent over to fish underneath it, groaning as he did so. On the second swipe of his arm, his hand touched a cold hard and heavy object, a gun. He quickly grasped it and pulled it out from underneath the sofa and sat down in the overstuffed chair next to it. Although he couldn't see the gun very well in the semi-dark room, he quickly determined by feel that it had a silencer on the barrel and that it was a revolver. He waited silently in the darkness.

In about ten minutes, he heard sounds outside the apartment door. He checked his position once more, comfortable that he would not be silhouetted against the window and unseen by anyone coming in from the hallway. As the doorknob turned, he used both thumbs to draw back the hammer on the revolver. It clicked...once...twice. He lifted the heavy revolver and pointed its large muzzle at the darkness where he judged the doorway to be. His breath was coming in quick gasps now and his eyes stung with the perspiration. He took his left hand off of the revolver quickly and wiped the sweat from behind his glasses. As the door opened, he waited for a form to be backlighted in the light from the hallway. Light flowed into the room....he waited. He could now see the large silencer on the end of his weapon shaking in the light of the open door. He could see only the top portion of the doorway, the lower third being blocked from view by the sofa. Seconds seemed like hours to Aldridge. He heard a loud thump, like something or someone crashing onto the floor on the other side of the sofa, and then the bedroom door slammed shut.

Sean, peering thought the open slit of the bedroom door heard the noise as well. The night vision device he had been using told him something else as well. He slammed the door and dove under the bed.

Deiter was entering the lobby of the apartment building and had just nodded to the desk clerk when he heard the explosion. In three seconds it was followed by the staccato of an automatic weapon firing. He headed for the stairwell...now was not the time to get into an elevator. His CZ 100 was in his hand as he bounded through the door and clamored up the steps. He was only somewhat winded as he came to the fourth floor. He waited for a moment outside the doorway and listened. Nothing. He slowly opened the door a crack. No response. He opened it wider and peered around the corner. He was met by smoke and a blast of heat from a fire that had started. There was no noise of activity nor sign of anyone in the hallway. He moved down the hallway and made his way through the smoke. At the door to Kilyaikin's apartment, he paused and then brought the semiautomatic around the door edge and pointed it inside. He didn't need to, the inside of the apartment was decimated. A light had somehow stayed lit from the hallway and he could see the devastation inside. He rounded the corner of the doorway and made his way into the living room. He knew that Sean was suppose to be in the bedroom to the left. "Sean, Sean," he shouted. "Are you OK?"

"Jack, in here," a disembodied voice called out.

Deiter walked through what remained of the living room and then turned left into the bedroom. He wasn't encouraged by what he saw. The room was in shambles. "Sean!" he yelled.

"Here," came the answer under the rubble in the middle of the room. He went to what remained of the bed and pulled some of the rubble away. He yelled again and got an answer. Finally he lifted the bed frame and Sean came slithering out from underneath.

"Nice to see you took my advice," Deiter said.

"Yeah, not bad. Did you expect this?"

Deiter laughed, "Hey sorry, guy, I can't foresee everything."

The two men moved into the other room and started to search the rubble. "Someone was in here. He came in and got the gun from under the sofa," Sean begun.

"Did you recognize him?" asked Deiter.

"Nah, it was a man, that's all."

Under the rubble on the left side of the room a foot protruding from the mixture of plaster and concrete. They begun to dig around it and finally uncovered most of the body of an older man about sixty. They looked at each other and simultaneously both asked, "Haponchek?" Somehow neither of them believed it.

Deiter rolled the corpse over and reached into the inside pocket of the man's suit coat. He found a wallet and pulled it out. Flipping the wallet open he looked at a New Jersey driver's license and gasped. "Aldridge Mason! What the hell?"

CHAPTER TWENTY-SIX

▼

RESCUED

Kilyaikin's Apartment Building
Washington, DC
Friday evening, November 14th 1997

Sean pulled himself up and turned to look at the partially destroyed doorway to the equipment room. He bolted for the door and stood framed in the doorway as Deiter looked up at him. "What's the matter?" Deiter asked.

"The transmitter...its been destroyed."

Somewhere outside in the street, a siren sounded followed by another and another. Flashing red lights flickered through the open hole that had once been the window of Kilyaikin's apartment. A cold breeze swept through the opening in the wall and kicked up ashes and debris around the smoldering ruins bringing some of the still hot embers to a flickering flame. Deiter had retrieved the fire extinguisher from the hallway and had used it on the most serious flames in the apartment. He looked up as the desk clerk put his head around the corner.

"What am I going to do?" the clerk asked no one in particular.

"Here, put out the rest of the fires...I take it you called the fire and police?" he asked the clerk while handing him the extinguisher.

The man nodded and took the fire extinguisher from Deiter. "Who is that?" he asked staring wide-eyed at the body on the floor.

"Don't worry, we'll take care of him," Deiter replied. That didn't seem to really satisfy the clerk, however.

Deiter joined Sean in what was left of the equipment room. "Anything worth salvaging?" he asked.

"Not really, I think we can use the NSA equipment if we need to. This stuff was good, but not half the caliber of what they have." Both men went back into the living room and at the same time two policemen and a fireman came through the door.

"Anybody hurt?" the first policeman asked.

Deiter walked over and flashed his ID at the cop. "Deiter, FBI. He's Stevenson of the NSA. That guy's a lawyer from New Jersey," he said nonchalantly indicating first Sean and then the body of Mason. Deiter handed the cop Mason's wallet. "The guy on the floor had a gun that's someplace under all the rubble, we'll need it for our investigation."

Several other firemen showed up at the doorway and began inspecting the hall for any undiscovered fires. Another policeman came into the room and after a short briefing by the first one joined them in sifting through the rubble. The first cop bent down and picked up the revolver. "I think this is what you were looking for," he remarked turning towards Deiter. The policemen took a plastic bag out of his inside coat pocked and deposited the gun in it.

In the excitement, Deiter had all but forgotten about Rose. He mentally kicked himself and suddenly felt desperately depressed. He looked over at Sean and could tell by his expression that the thought came to him at the same time. Sean was first to vocalize it. "What do we do about Rose now?"

"I don't know," Deiter muttered. He looked around once more and took Sean by the arm as he headed for the door. "Come on, let's get out of here," he said brushing past the bewildered desk clerk. They had gone halfway down the hallway towards the elevator when they heard a voice behind them. "Mister, Mister, wait!" Deiter shrugged. He didn't want to talk with the desk clerk anymore tonight; he was just too exhausted. He kept on walking, but the voice was persistent. "Mister!" Deiter and Sean stopped and turned around,

"What?" said Deiter exasperated.

"The first time you were here you asked me to tell you if the man we ran into in the elevator returned."

"Yes?" Deiter replied uninterestedly.

"He did."

"When?"

"The next day," answered the clerk.

"And?"

"Why, I thought it may have been important. He rented an apartment down the hallway from the one you have been interested in."

"What number?" shouted Deiter turning to grab the clerk by the coat lapels.

"Number 421," the clerk quivered.

"Oh my God," shouted Deiter thinking of the newly unlocked basement storeroom. "That's where Rose is."

Suddenly, the whole plan seemed to make sense to Deiter. Haponchek had convinced Mason to shoot him and then Mason would "rescue" Rose. He didn't wait to understand the rest of it, he sprinted back down the hallway towards apartment 421, the memory of that unlocked door in the basement now very vivid in his mind.

Deiter stopped at the apartment marked 421. Turning to the desk clerk still standing where they had left him down the hallway, he shouted, "Do you have a key?"

"Yes, yes, right away," the clerk responded hurrying down towards the room. "Do not kick in the door, I have it, I have it."

The clerk produced a key and unlocked the door. Deiter drew his semiautomatic and pushed open the door. Sean unholstered his weapon as well and crouched leaning against the right edge of the door while holding the gun in both hands between his knees. The apartment seemed empty. Deiter moved in slowly; Sean was right behind him. Both of them were holding their weapons at the ready. A noise came from one of the bedrooms; it seemed to be a moaning sound. Deiter went to the closed door and put his ear to it. Sean covered him at the edge of the doorway and nodded. Deiter tried the doorknob, it was unlocked. He slowly turned it and when the latch had clicked open, he kicked it with all his strength. The door flung open and he was met with total blackness in the interior. He slid his left hand down the edge of the doorway and found the light switch. The overhead light revealed the figure of Rose tied to the four corners of the bed. At the sight of Deiter, she closed her eyes and slumped back onto the bed. Sean moved quickly to the bathroom door and swung his weapon around the corner; finding nobody he returned to the scene in the bedroom.

"You're a sight for sore eyes," Deiter said sitting on the edge of the bed grinning broadly. He quickly untied Rose's hands from the bedposts and then worked on the knot from her gag which was behind her head. Finally it came free. Rose spit out the gag that was in her mouth and flung both of her arms around Deiter.

"Jack, I knew you'd come, I knew it," she wept.

"Are you OK?" he asked when their lips finally parted.

"No, God damn it, I gotta pee; I've been tied up for hours!" Trying his best not to laugh out loud or even smile, Deiter quickly untied her feet and she bolted for the bathroom door pushing Sean out of the way with, "Sorry, Sean, gotta go."

Sean leaned against the doorway to the living room and smiled at Deiter. "You rescue the damsel in distress and she runs out on you."

"Hey, whatcha gonna do?" Deiter shrugged laughingly.

When Rose returned, she once again embraced Deiter. After a moment she suddenly pushed him away and said, "What about the explosion and shooting I heard?"

"Someone threw a bomb into the apartment."

"Why? Was anybody hurt?"

Deiter paused for a moment and then slowly said, "Rose, Mason was in the room...he's dead."

"Oh my God. Why?"

"Apparently he came to kill me...I'll fill you in later; now let's take care of you."

Deiter supported Rose as they went into the hallway and headed for the elevator. Deiter moved quickly by the firemen and police; he didn't think they needed to know about the kidnapping of Rose at this time. He needed time to think.

The elevator opened onto the lobby and Deiter, Rose and Sean moved quickly towards the doorway. They were met there by Charlie coming in the front entrance. "What's going on?" she asked throwing her arms around Rose. "Rose, thank God your safe."

"It's OK now," returned Deiter.

Charlie whispered into Rose's ear, "Are you sure you're all right, Rose?"

"Yes, just tired and a little bit stiff from being tied up all this time; it's OK, really, Charlie, thanks."

"I'll take Rose home," said Deiter, rushing Rose out of the door and down the street towards where the Jaguar was parked. "We'll see you tomorrow morning sometime," he called over his shoulder.

Charlie looked at Sean and said, "Any more damage you can do tonight?'

"How about supper?"

Charlie grinned and grabbed his arm. "Love too. How'd you get so dirty?"

"It's a long story, I'll tell you over dinner."

A crowd of people had been drawn by the explosion and emergency vehicles and were lined up behind a yellow tape across the street. Sean and Charlie ignored them and strolled across the street and up Wisconsin Avenue for about a block to where Charlie had left the brown Morgan. As they climbed into the sports car, it began to rain. Charlie started the Morgan, switched on the windshield wipers and pulled out into traffic heading North. She was glad that she had thought to put up the ragtop on the car. Neither of them noticed the car that suddenly pulled in behind them following closely.

CHAPTER TWENTY—SEVEN

▼

RETREAT AND COUNTERATTACK

Kilyaikin's Apartment Building
Washington, DC
Friday evening, November 14th 1997

Yuri had waited in the alley for about twenty minutes before the sound of an explosion ricocheted off the buildings and into the alley. He bolted around the corner and skidded to a sudden stop. In the middle of the block on Wisconsin Avenue he saw a gaping hole in the second story of the apartment building. There were four men running from across the street; one was heading in his direction, one down the street, and the other two headed for the front entrance to the building. He knew his plan had just changed. Yuri turned and ran down the block and into a hotel lobby at the corner. He took the elevator to the fifth floor and then walked down to the basement garage. He didn't think he had been seen, but he had to be sure. He waited for another ten minutes and walked out of the garage entrance and back onto Wisconsin Avenue. The flashing lights from police cars and other emergency vehicles crowded both sides of the wide street down the block. A large square, bulky truck was parked near the entrance of the apartment building and Yuri guessed that it was the bomb squad. He decided to find out what had happened and casually strolled down in the direction of the activity. Knowing is much better than remaining ignorant and guessing, he thought to himself. A crowd of people had gathered by now and Yuri blended in with them. A yellow and black tape had been stretched and taped onto temporary three-foot plastic cone-shaped poles to keep the crowd away from the scene.

"What happened?" he asked an elderly man who was standing close to the yellow tape.

"Looks like a bomb went off!" the man exclaimed.

"Anybody hurt?" Yuri asked.

"They brought a few people out, but they were all walking, but a cop told me that one guy was killed outright...made a hell of a mess of the building."

Yuri stayed there awhile watching the scene develop. Mostly, uniformed police and firemen were going into the building. A few people were being ushered from the building to waiting ambulances although none of them seemed badly hurt. Suddenly, Yuri stiffened. A shock of red hair caught his attention as a woman walked quickly out of the main entrance. She was being supported by the FBI agent...his arm tightly around her waist. Two others were with them; a woman with short blond hair and a man with a beard. He watched as the agent and the McGuire woman turned left and walked rapidly down the street. The other two waited briefly while talking to each other and then started to amble across the street in his direction. Yuri backed away slowly and blended into the shadows of the building across the street.

He watched as the couple walked up the street; when they were safely ahead of him, he started to follow. They stopped beside a small sports car and started to get in. Yuri was at the corner of the street at which he had parked his car earlier and he broke into a sprint towards it. Climbing behind the steering wheel, he started the car and sped to the intersection just in time to see the sports car pull out and head up the street. Yuri stepped on the accelerator and squealed around the corner in hot pursuit. It started to rain heavily now and Yuri had a difficult time keeping the small car in view. After going about five blocks, the sports car turned right and then left and parked about fifty feet from a restaurant. Yuri slowed down and finally parked about half a block behind them and watched as the couple sprinted through the rain and into the restaurant. He waited about ten minutes; satisfied that they would be now in the middle of dinner, he stepped out of his car and opened the trunk. Rummaging through a cardboard box, he selected a small compact package containing C4 explosive with a centrifugal fuse. He slipped the detonator that had been taped to the side of the package into a hole on top. The tape he transferred to the top to hold the cap in place. As the rain beat down on him, he walked quickly to the brown Morgan, looked around him to confirm that he was not being observed, and crouched down beside the right rear tire. He felt underneath the car and smiled to himself as he felt the car's gas tank. He leaned down and placed the package up against the inside of the wheel next to the underside of the gas tank. The magnet secured it and he pushed a switch on the side of the package. Now, the device would detonate as the wheel begins to turn. Yuri was drenched by the rain; the water flowing down the gutter next to the car looked like a small river. He quickly walked back to his own car, opened the driver's door and got in, thankful to be out of the rain. He smiled again as he started the car and pulled away from the curb. That will take care of those two problems...now he needed to find a place to think out his next moves.

It would be impossible for Yuri to ever use Kilyaikin's apartment or the locating transmitter again and the apartment where he had left the woman was equally dangerous. He needed a new base of operations. The hotel that he had walked through earlier may have a room for him; being so close to the bombing scene, they never would think of looking there. He headed back down Wisconsin Avenue and pulled up in front of the hotel on the corner. From the trunk, he grabbed a small suitcase that contained a full change of clothes, shoes and a jacket. In fifteen minutes he had secured a room and convinced the clerk that his car had broken down and he had been caught in the rain. He also explained that the rest of his baggage had been lost by the airlines and would be delivered sometime later. Ten minutes later he was safely ensconced in a room on the ninth floor. As he pulled off his wet clothing, Yuri looked at his watch...almost nine o'clock. He suddenly felt hungry; he

hadn't had time to eat today. He picked up the telephone
and ordered room service.

After his supper had been delivered, Yuri relaxed for
the first time in several hours. He ran through his mind
again the events that had transpired during the day.
Earlier that evening, he had unlocked the door to the
basement storage room and returned to the apartment
one last time to confirm that the woman was still
securely tied up and assured himself that nothing else
was left behind to connect him to the affair. The
woman, of course, would even now be describing him to
the authorities. With Deiter out of the way and Mason
in control of the woman, he would have been safe. Now
things had changed. He had to be careful. He had no
doubt who was responsible for setting off the bomb. He
knew all too well the Russian underworld and its tenta-
cles into the Western world. Kilyaikin had told him that
he was bankrolled by them and somehow they found
out that something had happened to their investment.
The pipe bomb was typical. What had happened to
Mason? Was he the dead man? Yuri thought that it was a
good possibility. Did they think that Mason was him?
He smiled. Mason had performed well, after all. If the
woman had not been in Kilyaikin's apartment, then
Mason wouldn't have been so easily...if ever...con-
vinced to kill the FBI agent and he would have had to
do it himself. Now what should he do? He could, he
thought, always go back to New Jersey; somehow he felt
that option wasn't very likely.

Something was troubling Yuri. How had the FBI
found out about Kilyaikin and how did they find the
apartment on Wisconsin Avenue and the transmitter?

Did they even know what it was that they had found? If so, how? As far as he knew, only Kilyaikin and he were aware of it...oh yes, the Russian Mafia, too. They wouldn't have contacted the authorities, so who did or how did they find out? Yuri shook his head. He had collected several bank accounts all ready. His and the ones that Kilyaikin had done. He estimated that perhaps he now had three or four million dollars among all of the accounts. He could simply go back home and take up where he had left off, or he could start a whole new existence. He certainly knew how to do that well. The options were always open to someone who was willing to take them and not be held back by sentiment or loyalty; or family, he added to himself. It would have been easy to walk away except for one thing. He had somehow been outsmarted by the FBI agent. Deiter had rescued the woman and they were now looking for him. How did he ever find her? The thought infuriated him.

Yuri started to pace the length of his room. Each time he came to the window, he looked out. Below, he could still see activity around the building on Wisconsin Avenue although it appeared to be diminishing. Soon only one police car and a single fire engine remained. He looked at his watch...nine–thirty. He would wait until ten o'clock before going back to his car.

Yuri resumed his analysis and his pacing. If the authorities knew about Kilyaikin and the transmitter, he guessed they somehow knew about the microchips transplanted in the agents. That thought was very sobering to him and with his hand he felt the back of his neck. If they knew about this, then they could find him. He needed to have it removed. While he was in control and had the list, it didn't matter. Now that someone else may have the list, he was in danger. He didn't like that; in fact he didn't like anything that wasn't under his control. He stopped. The equipment was destroyed, though…or so he surmised from the extent of the damage done by the bomb. The Russian Mafia wouldn't have wanted it to fall into the hands of the authorities, so they had to make sure it was destroyed. They, at least were efficient and thorough. Nevertheless, he had to have the microchip removed, just to be on the safe side. The revelation to him by Kilyaikin that he had been located by using of the device became a constant concern to him; it robbed him of his ability to disappear or change identities.

First, however, he had to attend to the immediate details. Only the private investigator, the FBI agent, and the woman could positively identify him…and, of course, the desk clerk at the apartment. He would eliminate them in reverse order. Tonight, later, he thought…the clerk; the others would have to wait. Their two companions of the agent most probably would have been eliminated already.

The dinner wasn't anything to brag about, but both Sean and Charlie agreed that the company couldn't have been better. It was almost eleven o'clock when they left the warm comfort of the restaurant and headed out into the windblown sheets of rain that were incessantly falling on the street. The gutter looked like a river and the water had risen up to the floorboard of the low riding sports car. The two made a dash through the rain and pounced on the small car, opening the doors and jumping into the small space allowed for the occupants.

When both doors were closed, they looked at each other and laughed. Two drowning rats could not have looked more disheveled or soaked.

Charlie searched her purse for the key and having finally found it, slid it into the ignition and cranked the antique motor vehicle into life. She was amazed that it started so easily. Lucas was not known for weatherproofing their ignition systems. She shifted the transmission into first gear and squinted into the rear view mirror to check on the traffic behind her. Not seeing anything, she pulled slowly away from the curb. It sounded like a gunshot or a rear tire blowout. Sean was the first to recognize the significance of the sound and the smell of burning cordite. "Get out!" he yelled and pushed open his door and dove from the car as it was still moving. Charlie did the same.

As the car slowly rolled away from them, Sean could see the large cloud of gray-blue smoke coming from under the right rear tire and rise into the rain-filled air. The car came to a rolling stop, the engine having succumbed to a lack of fuel and the breaking influence of the clutch. There was only silence now and the incessant rain.

"What the hell was that?" screamed Charlie.

"I think, thank God, it was a dud," responded Sean. He stood up and moved closer to the now stalled car. Bending down, he looked under the right rear of the car and then felt with his hand under the chassis near the right rear tire. When he stood up, he held a device the size of a baseball in his hand. A wire drooped from it; attached were the remains of a blasting cap. Apparently, it had slipped from the hole in the main charge because of the torrent of water flowing around the car.

Charlie reached down and brought the device in Sean's hand up to the light. "Oh my God," she exclaimed. "We could have been killed!"

"I think that was the main idea," returned Sean.

CHAPTER TWENTY—EIGHT

▼

SEARCH FOR HAPONCHEK

Jonathan Banks, Inc.
Chevy Chase, Maryland
Saturday, November 15th 1997

"You look a lot cleaner now...and dryer," Charlie Waggner said smilingly as she met Sean coming into the task force communications center. It was almost ten o'clock in the morning and she had been sorting through some of the information that the NSA crew had turned up on the probable locations of agents. She had also been collating the information against lists of recently reported deaths due to stroke. "Where have you been?"

"Getting my good suit cleaned and fixed. This business is beginning to get rough on my clothes."

"Glad to see you take care of them," she teased. "You were a mess last night." She then added excitedly,

"Look, Sean, I've got some mismatches here that are interesting." She pulled at his hand, forcing him to sit at the conference table. "Here are three agents listed on Kilyaikin's files that didn't respond to the NSA's interrogation," She showed him the list she had compiled. "The names have been run against these deaths; so far we have two out of the three."

"OK, so you're saying that because they didn't respond, they're dead?"

"Absolutely, they were programmed to answer...I mean the chips were programmed to answer," she responded. "The only reason why a chip wouldn't respond is if it didn't have any power supply...like the person was dead. Oh yes, or in your case...you discovered it and had it removed."

"I'll buy that," he responded. "What's going on in that head of yours?"

"I think that our killer only has a partial list. Kilyaikin was a loyal Communist; he wouldn't kill the really loyal deep agents...despite the fact the Soviet Union isn't around anymore. He would have gone after the renegades first, hoping, I'd guess, that eventually the old regime would return and pick up the pieces. This guy, Haponchek could have been one of the dropouts or he could have been someone who was suppose to help Kilyaikin and then double crossed him...and killed him."

"Which way was it?" Sean asked. "You know, I don't believe that the bomb in the apartment was thrown by this guy Haponchek; I think it was the Chechen Mafia and I'll tell you why." Charlie lifted her eyebrow in doubt, but waited as he continued. "I made some calls

to contacts we've made who've access to the large contingent of Russians in this country. Some of them are
Chechens and a lot have joined their organized crime
syndicates. If my theory's right, my telephone calls set
off a train of events that ended in the bombing. If the
Mafia was responsible for bankrolling Kilyaikin, and I
really do doubt that it was a governmentally inspired or
financed plot; then when they learned that Kilyaikin
had been either captured or killed, they wanted to cover
their tracks and get rid of the evidence. I don't think my
trying to play Kilyaikin on the telephone fooled them at
all. The killer also knew of the apartment and the equipment, but my guess is that he wasn't connected with the
other group; he was the one who tortured and killed
Kilyaikin. The timing of the bombing was simply coin-
cidental; they had seen Mason go into the room and
didn't know who he was...for all they knew, he could
have been with the FBI...so they decided it was time to
blow it."

"That's just about what they said," remarked Deiter
who had just walked into the communications center
with Rose. "Our surveillance team covered all the
entrances as soon as the bomb went off and caught the
two who did it. I think it was such a surprise to them,
they spilled their guts...anyway as much as they knew of
it. Rose and I stopped by the Hoover Building on our
way here."

"Then who put the bomb in my car," asked Charlie,
"if it wasn't the Mafia?"

"My guess is that it was Haponchek," replied Sean.
"He was probably waiting outside the apartment and

when he saw us with Rose and Jack, he decided to get rid of us first."

"I'm glad both of you are here," said Rose, "I need to tell you about the man in the apartment last night," Rose sat down at the conference table next to Charlie. "Aldridge Mason is...was, a very personal acquaintance of mine," she began. "I guess over the years, it got out of hand, though. Aldridge, in all honesty, gave me a lot...but it went at a price. Recently, it had seemed more like he owned me...and he acted like it...I suppose I did too. When I came down here with Jack, Aldridge apparently went looking for me...and eventually found me. Our guess is that he somehow made a deal with Haponchek that would have gotten Jack killed and me convinced that Mason had saved me,"

Charlie took Rose's hands in hers and said, "It's all over now, Rose. That part of your life's over."

"That part, Charlie, maybe," interrupted Deiter, "but not Haponchek...not yet at least. For some reason, he wants me and Rose, too, dead. There's a little bit more about Mason, though. A Private Investigator named Kinder called the FBI to clear himself as far as the Mason deal is concerned. Kinder had been hired by Mason to find Rose. He told us all about meeting a guy named Kurtz and how Mason and Kurtz apparently made some secret deal. Kinder was the guy that Rose and I spotted with Haponchek the other day. As far as I can see, he's clean...he just got caught up in the whole thing while trying to do a legit job. He said that Mason had some kind of hang-up about Rose,"

"I never knew how much," Rose said shaking her head. "Sometimes the creeps that infest this world.

Quite honestly, I think he did love me in his own way; but it also had a lot to do with possession. I'd like to believe that there was something else too." She took a deep breath and let it out with a physical expression of one getting rid of an unhappy feeling. She then slapped both hands on the table and looked up as though she were a new person. "So, what do we do now?" she exclaimed, smiling.

"I've got the NSA team trying to locate Haponchek again," observed Sean. "I think we had better do it fast before he gets a chance to have that chip taken out…we'd never find him then."

"That's a good point," Deiter responded. "He hasn't displayed the attitude that I'd like to see roaming around the countryside…he's dangerous. Besides, he may still be able to get his hands on some of that money. There's something else that we were told this morning; the desk clerk at the apartment was shot last night just after midnight. The safe was riffled so the cops are calling it a burglary…I don't think so. The only witnesses that can positively identify Haponchek are Rose and I, now that the clerk's dead."

"Don't forget the private investigator…you said that he met with Haponchek."

"Oh, my God," exclaimed Deiter, I'm sure he suspected something was going on, but he has to be told that he's at risk," Deiter plopped into a chair next to a telephone and picked up the receiver. He hit "9" and then his office number at the Hoover Building. "Deiter here. Get me Ken Stroeman," he barked into the phone.

After a pause, he heard a male voice respond, "Stroeman."

"Ken, I want you to get a hold of that PI that called in…Kinder. Tell him that he's now a material witness and that we suspect that Haponchek will try to kill him. Ask him if he needs any protection and if not, tell him to get back to New Jersey and disappear for awhile…until we contact his office and tell him it's OK to resume his normal life."

"Sure, uh…" Stroeman hesitated. "You and Ms McGuire going to be OK?"

"Yeah, don't worry. I don't think he'll be able to get to us. We have the NSA trying to locate him now."

"I'll take care of Kinder.

"Thanks, Ken." Deiter hung up the phone and sighed loudly as he leaned back in the chair. He looked over at Rose seated at the end of the conference table and smiled. She lifted her left eyebrow at him as though asking a question. Deiter smiled again and shook his head and then nodded silently mouthing, "It's OK."

The phone at the other end of the room rang twice and Sean answered it.

"Yes?" He hesitated and then said, "Thanks," and hung up the phone. He turned to Deiter and said, "The NSA's in full operation now with the satellites. They've started trying to track Haponchek."

"Good," Deiter responded. He then turned to Rose and said, more in the form of a question, "Let's get out of here for awhile?" Rose nodded and started to gather up her purse and glasses. "Call me on my cell phone if anything happens," he said to Sean as he pulled himself up from the chair.

"Sure, you two need a break; get out of here."

"I understand that the two of you had a little excitement too," Deiter quipped.

As the Jaguar rolled down the entrance road away from Jonathan Banks' firm, Deiter turned to Rose and suggested, "Why don't we spent the rest of the day touring the museum circuit? Afterwards we can stop for drinks and dinner and go home."

"Sounds absolutely wonderful, Jack...you lead," she responded leaning over to kiss him on the cheek.

CHAPTER TWENTY–NINE

▼

LOCATED

Jack Deiter's home
Alexandria, Virginia
Saturday night, November 15th 1997

It had been a beautiful day and a beautiful evening for both Jack Deiter and Rose McGuire. After six hours roaming casually through the halls of three museums, they had returned to Alexandria and *The Yachtsman* for dinner. They had parked the Jag outside Deiter's house on Prince Street and had walked the two blocks to the restaurant. The occurrences of the last few days seemed to disappear as they enjoyed each other's company. They didn't immediately walk home that night, preferring instead to walk up King Street and window shop. The night was cool, but very pleasant for a mid-November night in Northern Virginia. It almost seemed like early fall. The slight chill was pleasant because it gave Deiter an excuse to put his arm around Rose while they walked…not that he really needed an excuse, though. It was almost ten o'clock when they arrived at the elegant wooden entrance and flickering brass lanterns of Deiter's townhouse on Prince street. Once inside, he fixed both of them a small cordial and turned on the Boze sound system's CD player. Immediately, the gentle strains of Chopin's *Nocturne in F minor, Op. 55, No. 1* filled the darkened living room. Deiter turned on the gas logs in the fireplace and both of them fell lounging on pillows in front of it. The liqueur and the flickering fire contributed to their own internal passionate fire as they laid there in each other's arms; the chill of the night walk was soon forgotten as they made love. Sam wandered in from some far reaches of the house and started to curl up next to the fire, but then thought better of it considering the activity and retired to the seclusion of the study. Silently, Deiter congratulated himself on owning a cat of distinction and discretion.

At five minutes of two, the telephone brought Deiter immediately to consciousness. They had gone to bed at midnight, both falling to sleep immediately. Deiter grappled for the persistent bleating of the instrument and finally pulled it from its cradle and grunted into it. "Yeah?"

"Sorry to bother you, Jack, but I think we've got Haponchek," came Sean's tired sounding voice on the other end of the phone.

"What have you got?"

"A location; and its only twenty minutes old."

"Here in Washington?"

"Yeah, at a hotel on Wisconsin Avenue. Do you want to be in on it?"

"Pry me away," he replied looking down at Rose. She had opened one eye and was looking at him suspiciously. "Where are you now?"

"At Banks, we'll wait on you."

Deiter looked at his watch. "Be there in...30 minutes...better yet, what hotel is it? I'll meet you there." Sean gave him the name of the hotel and Deiter returning the phone to its cradle.

"What was that about?" Rose moaned wearily.

"They've got a lock on Haponchek. I'm going to meet Sean and we'll take him," replied Deiter, "You stay here and I'll be back in the morning."

"Be careful," she said reaching out her hand to stroke his cheek.

"Don't worry...I'll lock up and set the alarm on my way out."

Rose turned over and went back to sleep. Deiter quickly showered and shaved. He put on his black turtleneck sweater and black slacks. He then donned a black leather jacket, set the alarm and locked the door behind him as he stepped out into the street. The night was cool and it felt like it was starting to sprinkle. A fog was just beginning to roll into the lower end of Prince Street from the river. Deiter walked quickly to his Jaguar, climbed in and turned the ignition key as he pulled the seat belt around him. He shifted into first gear and gunned the engine heading North for Memorial Bridge and Washington.

Fifteen minutes later, he pulled into a parking space in front of the hotel, a block from Kilyaikin's apartment.

Sean met him just inside the hotel entrance; he had with him the four FBI agents who had been part of the surveillance team. "I found out that our man's on the ninth floor, Room 912. The hotel clerk remembered that he came in about thirty minutes after the explosion last night claiming his luggage had been lost by the airlines. He must have returned to the area after he had planted the bomb in Charlie's car and felt it safer to get off the streets."

"You sure he's up there now."

"An hour ago, he was…nobody goes out at two AM."

"Let's do it, then. Have we got the warrant?"

One of the FBI agents held up a piece of paper in response. All six men moved to the elevator and were joined by the hotel security officer. The elevator door closed behind them and they started slowly upwards. At the ninth floor they walked out into a deserted hallway and turned left. At Room 912, they stopped. All six men drew their weapons and the security officer produced a plastic key card and slowly inserted it into the slot. The red light switched to green and he quietly depressed the handle as though he had done this a hundred times before. The door swung open and the FBI agents moved in with their weapons ready. A light was on over the bed, but the room was empty. The last agent in the room came out of the bathroom, "No one here," he said.

Deiter looked at Sean and asked, "No one goes out at two AM?"

Sean shook his head. "He was here an hour ago."

"Can you get another fix?" asked Deiter.

Sean flopped down into a chair and picked up the telephone. He punched in a set of numbers and waited for an answer. The phone rang three times and was finally picked up. "8426"

"Stevenson here, can you get another fix on our guy?"

"Yes, sir.....wait one," They waited for almost five minutes and then got their answer.

"We have a new location on him now.......Alexandria, Virginia," Sean and Deiter looked at each other with a questioning look on both their faces.

"What the hell is he doing in Virginia at this time of the morning?" Deiter remarked. Then the impact hit him. "Oh, my God," he exclaimed, looking at Sean. "Are you thinking what I'm thinking?"

Sean turned to the telephone again. "Can you get us a twenty meter reading on the location?" He waited for a reply. The time dragged by and then finally he got his answer and closed his eyes. Deiter knew where Haponchek was now before Sean said anything; the fear and dread felt like it would engulf him. He pulled his cell phone out of his coat pocket and punched in his home telephone number. It gave him a busy signal. He was sure now that the killer was in the house with Rose. He also knew he would never get there in time to save her.

CHAPTER THIRTY

▼

NIGHT TERROR

Jack Deiter's home
Alexandria, Virginia
Early Sunday morning, November 16th 1997

Rose didn't know what it was that woke her. She supposed that it had been a car noise in the street outside. She opened her eyes and could see nothing. She had never known it to be so dark here in Jack's bedroom. Very little light shown in from the outside and everything seemed to be bathed in an eerie silence. She slowly reached over to pick up the electric alarm clock with the lighted dial to see what time it was and noticed that the dial didn't glow as it used to. She tried the bedside light and the click of the switch failed to bring light. Her hand next dropped to the telephone receiver and slowly raised it...silence rewarded her efforts instead of the expected dial tone. Now she was wide-awake. Obviously

there was no electricity and no phone service. Her
breathing had slowed to almost nothing, but her heart
was racing faster than she had remembered it doing in
years. She then heard a creak on the two hundred-year-
old stairway that led to the lower level. She hoped
against hope that it was Jack returning home and not
wanting to wake her, but she knew better.

Rose's body tensed and was prepared to move at an
instant's notice. In what light that did come from the
hallway, she saw the figure of a large heavy man standing
in the bedroom doorway. It definitely wasn't Jack. From
where his hand should be, a red glow emerged and she
could see a red dot move across the room and towards
the bed. It didn't take much to recognize a laser beam
from an automatic pistol that was aimed in her direction. The red dot moved up the bed sheet until it
stopped on the sheet over her breasts. Rose suddenly
lifted the bed sheet with both hands and in a move like
a bullfighter, twisted her body violently to the left. A
rude spitting sound erupted from the hand of the form
in the doorway and the red dot on the bed sheet turned
into a hole. A burning sensation suddenly seared her
right breast; she knew she'd been hit by the bullet and
could feel the warm wetness spread down her side. Rose
saw the form duck into the room and move sideways to
the right. She threw off the sheet and dove for the doorway sliding through it cleanly and scrambled down the
stairs. Her naked white body gleamed in the darkness;
in a detached way, she swore she'd never sleep in the
nude again...she'd wear dark clothing to bed. At the
bottom of the stairs, she slipped into the study and
crouched under the large walnut desk. Her breathing

was coming in gasps now and she fought to get it under control and stay as quiet as possible. She held her right breast and pressed it tightly, trying to stem the flow of blood. Looking out from under the desk, Rose could see the outline of Jack's model four-masted man-o'-war on top of the table between the windows. She wished so much that Jack would have been here now.

A reddish glow came from the hallway and she could see the red dot travel down the stairway and shift from side to side finally hitting the wall inside the study. Upstairs, she heard the noise of someone's heavy footstep at the top of the landing, then a screech and a long loud yowling noise followed by someone falling. Silence and then cursing first in Russian and then in English. Despite the pain of the wound on her breast and the coldness of the night, she had to smile to herself and congratulate Sam on tripping up the intruder. That's a damned good cat...Jack would be proud of Sam, she thought to herself.

A narrow, intense beam of white light cut through the darkness of the study, sweeping into the dark corners of the room and finally coming to rest on the large walnut desk in the center of the room. Rose could feel the light land on her leaving her with a helpless feeling of being fully exposed, naked, alone, and helpless. She couldn't see who was behind the light, only the harsh beam and darkness surrounding it.

"Aren't you fetching, though...where's your boy friend?" a gravel voice demanded.

Rose said nothing, trying to hide her nakedness. Under the glare of the light, she looked down at her breast and the open and bloody crease that the bullet had left and closed her eyes. Was this the way it was to end? She had wished for a little more dignified end at least. She wondered what the detectives and patrolmen would say at seeing her naked body crouched under the desk.

"Well?" the disembodied voice demanded again.

"Go to hell, asshole!" she responded, amazed at her own bravado.

"You've been a pain in the ass, sweetheart, I'm going to enjoy this." The red beam from the laser on the pistol caught Rose in the eyes and she closed them against the red glare and said a quick prayer.

Instead of the spitting thud of the silencer, she heard a throaty, gargling gasp and the flashlight crashing to the floor. This was followed by darkness and the sound of a large body falling against the desk over her head. As the body slid to the floor, Rose rolled out of the cavity of the desk and sprinted for the doorway of the study. She scurried up the stairs to the bedroom where she slammed the door shut behind her and turned the key in the lock. "Where the hell are my clothes?" she asked herself searching with her hands around the chair next to the bed. All this and no makeup either. Damn, this sucks. She located her sweat suit and climbed into it all the while evaluating whether she could climb out the window or not. At least she would have clothes on, if not makeup and her hair combed. She felt for her cross trainer shoes under the chair and quickly slid them on. Then she put her ear to the door and listened for some noise downstairs…nothing. She was debating whether or not to open the door when a screech of tires outside made her glance towards the window.

Flashing red lights illuminated the outside and the street below; she rushed for the window. Outside, she could see two cars with flashing red lights on the roofs parked in the middle of the street and three police cars just entering the street, two from the right at the top of the street and one coming up from below. One of the two parked cars was Jack Deiter's Jaguar. She opened the window and yelled out, "Jack, Jack, up here!"

"Rose, stay where you are, I'm coming up!"

"There's a guy downstairs in the study…he's trying to kill me!" she shouted. Rose pulled her head in the window and went to the door of the bedroom. She turned the key and slowly opened the door to hear the front door crash open and several people rush in. Within ten seconds, Deiter had bounded up the stairway and enfolded Rose in his arms. "Thank God, your safe."

As he brought her close to him, he could feel the blood soak through the sweat suit and his sweater. "You're hurt!" he exclaimed.

"It's OK, I think it just creased me," she said and then collapsed in his arms.

When Rose opened her eyes, it was daylight and Jack Deiter was sitting on the bed next to her. She jerked awake and started to get up. "Whoa, take it easy; you're OK, but you've lost some blood. The EMT patched you up," Deiter reassured her.

"What about that guy?" she asked.

"Haponchek's dead. They've already taken him away."

"That was him, then?"

"Yeah, that was him all right."

"How come he didn't come after me again? I thought he'd kill me for sure."

Deiter chuckled, "I guess you can say that Doctor Kilyaikin was responsible for saving your life."

"I don't understand," she responded, shaking her head in exhaustion.

"We found out that Haponchek was here when we couldn't find him in the hotel. There wasn't enough time for us to get all the way here; by the location, we figured he was already inside the house. The NSA sent out the modulated signal from Kilyaikin's list on Haponchek's frequency to the chip imbedded in him. It looks like he just had a stoke." Then he added, "I don't think that there'll be any publicity or official investigation. Just a hotel guest who had a stroke. They'll find him in the hotel room. The cleanup team will take care of that."

Rose closed her eyes again. When she awoke, Deiter was sitting in the easy chair next to the window. He was reading a book and Rose didn't want to disturb him, she just wanted to watch him. How had this wonderful man come back into her life so suddenly and completely? Finally she smiled and said more as a statement then a question, "Don't you have anything more important to do?"

Looking up, he returned her smile and said, "Not at the moment. Everything I have that's important is right in this room," Deiter stood up and walked over to sit on the side of the bed. "Now that you're awake again and I'd imagine a little more rested, I have a couple of questions about last night."

"OK, shoot. On second thought, that's a bad choice of words," she said with a grin.

"I know the EMT was confused on how you got the bullet wound and the bullet didn't go through your sweat suit, and so was I."

"Mr. Deiter, I swore last night that I'll never sleep in the nude again. I ended up completely naked under the desk in your study. Then when I ran out of there, I came back up here and put on my sweat suit and my shoes. I thought I could get out of the house across the roof."

"Haponchek's body had signs of bruises on his head and shoulders as well as his arms and legs...you must have really clobbered him...I'm amazed you still kept all that training."

Rose giggled. "It wasn't me. You've got Sam to thank for that, he's the hero!" She stopped there and tilted her head to one side, looking up at him; then she flashed him a big grin. Someday, she'd tell him what happened, but not today.

CHAPTER THIRTY-ONE

▼

POETIC JUSTICE

Jonathan Banks, Inc.,
Chevy Chase, Maryland
Monday Morning, November 17th 1997

Sean was leaning back in his chair in front of his computer with a package of papers in his hand. He shook his head at what he was reading. "Charlie, I can't believe how much misery those two have caused for people," he remarked in a low voice. Charlie Waggner looked up from her computer screen and over at him and was about to make a flippant remark when the look on Sean's face stopped her and she rose and came over towards him pulling out a chair to sit next to him.

"What?" she asked simply.

"I have the list of at least a dozen people who've been confirmed to have died in the last few months...all of whom were discovered to have had an implant."

"Who were they?"

"Some were single, but most had families. All of them, except for Haponchek, had either dropped out of existence, that is they had different names from the ones on the files, or were known to the FBI or the NSA as defectors. I guess that confirms what the Countess related to your father about Kilyaikin, he was a confirmed Communist, even though he may have earlier had a softer side."

"Did Kilyaikin get the money?"

"It looks like it. Most of the accounts now are under his name. Three are under Haponchek's name," Sean totaled up some figures he had jotted down. "It comes to a total of fourteen accounts, for a total of $35 million."

"What's going to happen to it?"

"I don't know, I don't think that the Agency wants to be connected with it and the FBI doesn't want to get into a position where they have to explain how that kind of money finds its way into the Agency's budget," He turned and looked up at Charlie. "This is only the beginning. We're dealing with less than ten percent of the number of agents...and ten percent of the money. Unless I'm wrong, we're looking at nearly a billion dollars; you can't hide that kind of money even in the government."

"What about the families? Do you think any of them know what went on...or why the deaths?"

"Some, maybe, but my guess is that most of the spouses were completely in the dark."

"I have an idea," she said with an impish grin on her face. Charlie leaned back and after contemplating what she was thinking about, nodded her head.

"I'm not sure I want to know anything about this," Sean returned with a smirk. He looked at her out of the corner of his eyes and then said with a sigh, "OK what's in that pretty head?"

Charlie almost giggled as she laid out her idea. Sean thought it was brilliant and chuckled, "Poetic justice, absolutely poetic justice. But how do we pull it off?"

Charlie tilted her head and then screwed up her mouth at him. "You don't have a criminal mind, Sean Stephenson, how can I expect you to know?"

"And you do?"

"Yes, of course, I'm a woman, aren't I?"

The telephone rang, interrupting their conversation and Sean answered it. "Yes?" After a few moments he replied, "I'll set it up. One–thirty OK?" He paused and then said, "Done."

"What was that all about?" asked Charlie.

Sean grinned and raised his eyebrows, "Jonathan Banks wants a meeting this afternoon. Looks like you'll get a chance to offer your suggestion on the money." Charlie beamed at that.

It was one–forty–five and Sean looked from his watch to the clock above the doorway and shrugged. "This isn't like Jonathan," he remarked to the group around the table. "He's always precisely on time." Following his call that morning, he had contacted Jack Deiter and Rose McGuire to join them. He didn't know what to tell them except that the boss wanted a meeting. He was relieved when the door finally opened and Jonathan Banks escorted in the NSA/CSS Deputy Director, Shirley McHendrie and COL Hank Henderson.

"I'm sorry that we've kept you waiting; there were a few problems we needed to sort out before we could meet," said Banks motioning his guests to seats around the conference table. "We still have some problems that need solutions and I hope you can help us find them."

When everyone had been seated around the table, Banks continued. "You have found and neutralized a killer. That was part of our mission. It did not solve our main problem, however. With the money still out there and still available to whatever Mafia type organization that wants to get it, we still have a threatening situation. These people may be deep agents, but in my judgment, they probably only want to be left alone at this point to raise families and be just plain Americans. To do anything else would mean to risk a lot for no great reason. Our problem is that, although we'll be able to locate and expose all the rest of the deep agents, it's not clear that it would be in the best interest of the Country to do so. We now know who and where they are. The important thing is that there is a great deal of money that is connected with this operation and there are forces that would stop at nothing to get their hands on it." Banks paused. "We need a solution that would keep this whole business under wraps and prevent the wrong elements from getting their hands on the money. That amount of money, estimated to be about $800 million could bankroll the criminal element to the point that it would be an extremely serious threat to this Country's stability and very existence. We can't let that happen."

"Charlie's got an idea," suggested Sean looking over at her and smiling.

"Oh?" returned Banks now looking at Charlie. "As if I'm not surprised. What is it?" he asked. Banks sat down at the table for the first time indicating that he was relinquishing the floor to her.

"I haven't thought it out completely, and some of it may sound foolish," she started tentatively. "The basic plan would be to first of all access the money from the accounts that Kilyaikin transferred into his name. If he could do it so can we..."we" being Jonathan Banks, Inc.; I don't think the accounting process of the government will allow it to go into the general coffers without raising some question. The firm can cover it easily. Next, the families of those Kilyaikin killed would be compensated for in relationship to the amount in the accounts. The details and the amounts can be worked out either on a case-by-case basis or by some other protocol. In return for the settlement, they would remain silent. It could be suggested that this was some sort of insurance policy that the victim had taken out earlier. There would be no reference at all to the business of deep agents." Charlie leaned back in her chair and considered what she would say next and the group allowed her to continue by their silence.

"The rest of the agents can be investigated to see what their willingness might be to arranging for their cooperation in return for a sizable remuneration and continued existence in their cover," Charlie continued. "The remainder of the money, which it appears no agency wants at this time, will remain under the control of Jonathan Banks, Inc. for those assignments which may not be funded or be too sensitive to allow for public funding."

There was silence around the table as everyone sought to find holes in the plan. Finally Banks spoke up, "I think that's a good solution, Charlie, and worthwhile probing further. There is one thing right up front that I think is only right to do." He turned to Sean and said, "Sean, you have been the catalyst who has uncovered the entire project. It would be only fitting that now you know the codes to the account with your name on it, that it should belong to you with no questions asked. I feel the same about the two accounts for Jack Deiter's parents. I think that with a little searching we could come up with the code number for those accounts."

"That won't be necessary, Jonathan," Deiter responded. "I think I have a pretty good idea what they are. One is 071008 and the other is 091705, the birth dates of my parents. I was given this pocket watch by my father just before his stroke; inside was engraved those two sets of numbers. I always thought that he was reminding me of their birthdays, just so I wouldn't forget. Instead, he was giving me a legacy, if I ever found a way of decoding it and finding it."

Jonathan Banks stood up saying, "Let's see what problems we come up with in this plan and I want an organization designed to implement it. I'd like the both of you to stay on, if the FBI will release you," he said gesturing towards Deiter and Rose.

"I think that can be arranged," responded Deiter.

EPILOGUE

Costa del Sol

Spain

Early Sunday morning, January 25th 1998

"It was certainly a much more civilized way of doing the same thing," Rose thought as she sat on the porch overlooking the sandy stretch of beach that separated the house from the endless repetition of waves that crashed and then scampered up the sand. "Why did Kilyaikin think that he had to destroy the evidence by killing all the deep agents? This way was simpler, mutually beneficial and financially a gold mine for almost everybody." She simply couldn't have guessed six months ago that her life would have changed so radically, nor that she would ever be this happy. She stretched out languorously on the chaise lounge beach chair. Her full dark red hair was drawn up in the rear and shone in the midmorning sun. She looked down at her two piece swim suit with critical appraisal. Not too bad, she thought. I'm 50, but I'm in damn good shape, I'm healthy; I'm as independent as I want to be and...I'm sharing in a wealth beyond my wildest dreams. I've got a good twenty–five years left in which I can have the time of my life. She was so lost in her reverie that she failed to see the figure who quietly moved up behind her. The sense of a presence caused her to turn her head and look around.

"You are still a most gorgeous site, my dear," quipped Deiter. "I never cease to be amazed at you."

That was the most important thing that Rose realized she was happy about. She had just married someone who could really make her very happy. She smiled, turned her head back to look at the ocean and put up her right hand for Deiter to take. "Shut up, Jack Deiter the third," she said. "Kiss me and then tell me how much you are captivated by my beauty.. and also what you've been up to."

Deiter moved around the chaise lounge and sat down on the end of it facing her. She lifted her arms and threw them around him; he embraced her and gently kissed her open mouth. After a moment he said "Mmm, time for that later; right now I've got to tell you something." She put on a fake pout and pulled away from him. "You're no fun any more," she teased.

"The papers we found on Haponchek included only the seventy–one deep agents who had defected or disappeared; that you know. It did strike me that Kilyaikin may not have wanted to destroy any loyal agents, only the ones whom he knew had defected or might be dangerous to him or his cause. The amount of money from those listed agents alone would have easily satisfied the needs of a man like Kilyaikin." He paused and then continued, "According to what John Waggner learned from the Countess, Kilyaikin was a dedicated Communist. I'm sure he must have thought that the current regime would finally topple and he would again gain power and continue the fight with the West."

"That makes sense," Rose interjected. "What happens to the ones not on his list?"

"Well, first of all, Kilyaikin would have left them alone until he needed them. But, if Haponchek had known that there existed a list of the rest of the agents, he may have somehow found it and eliminated the loyal ones too.

"And that's why Kilyaikin endured so much torture to protect the larger list of agents; he knew that Haponchek would have gone after them too. Haponchek was totally ruthless and ambitious," Rose added. "I wonder if they'll ever know how much he suffered to save their lives."

Deiter took a sheet of paper from his shirt pocket, unfolded it and looked at it. "I've contacted another ten people on this list, every one of them have been more than eager to cooperate. A million dollars each for their own use seems to be a welcome bit of security to assure their continued safety...and their silence. I'm not sure any of them have thought about the interest that was due them...maybe they just wanted to take the money and run."

"I take it that the interest is safely invested?" Rose inquired.

"You can rest assured of that," Deiter replied smiling.

"Did you see Charlie and Sean yet this morning?"

"They are resting up after their trip and will fly back to Washington in the morning. I understand that their visit with Charlie's father and the Baroness was entirely successful. We figure that the four of us can take shifts working out of Washington. At least for the next few months. We should have most of the contacts made and accounts cleared out by June. I told them that the NSA had provided us with the best electronic equipment possible so that we could work from the firm and not involve the Government in any way in the project."

"What about the microdots and the copies made by the police and NSA?" Rose asked.

"We've received all copies at the firm and they're under safe keeping. The NYPD was glad to get it out of their hands now that their murder-torture case has been solved for them."

He leaned over and kissed Rose and then took her hand, lifting her to her feet. "Let's go back to the house," he said. The couple slowly walked up the pathway and through the garden arm in arm. Life has a funny way of working out...sometimes.